The Ca
Bu...

Michael Whitworth

Cahill Davis Publishing

ISBN 9781739801519 (eBook)

ISBN 9781739801502 (Paperback)

Cahill Davis Publishing Limited

www.cahilldavispublishing.co.uk

For my family

Part One

The story came out on October 29, 2014. It was a Wednesday. The *Kingsley Echo* always came out on a Wednesday. Thomas Mirren was a fraud, or at least that's what the *Echo* said. He hadn't served in the war, and in fact, he hadn't even been in the army. Understandably, this came as something of a surprise to Thomas.

Chapter 1

Thomas and Ian

"Bloody hell, those boxes were heavy this morning."

It was October 22, the day Thomas and Frank were due to start selling poppies. They'd brought the boxes from the Legion to the supermarket in Frank's car. They always used Frank's car now. Thomas didn't drive anymore. Not at his age.

"I'm getting too old for this." Thomas laughed.

"*We're* getting too old for this," corrected Frank. It had been raining earlier, so Frank had decided to wear his heavy winter coat. As usual, Thomas was wearing his blue blazer. Frank never saw that blazer any other time of the year. He'd asked Thomas about it once, but his friend had just shrugged, saying he liked to look smart. Frank had laughed at that; he certainly didn't look smart for the rest of the year.

The supermarket had set up a table for the two men in the entrance area just before the tills but far enough away from the doors that they wouldn't get cold. They'd also brought over a fan heater.

"They do this every year, you know," complained Frank, pointing to the fan heater. "I'm practically melting."

Thomas laughed. "I thought you served in the desert."

Frank shook his head and smiled. "Not in this coat, I didn't."

After a few minutes, Jenny, the store manager, came over to see if they wanted something to drink. She'd had her hair cut but didn't like it, so now she was wearing a large headband. Thomas didn't mention the odd headband even though he wanted to, opting instead to request a whisky.

"I'll see what I can do." She winked and laughed before disappearing, leaving the two men to shuffle their poppy boxes around the table. When she returned, she was carrying a small tray with two cups of tea and a small cake on it. The cake had a candle in the centre with the sugary figure of a soldier next to it, its left side melted by the flame.

"Happy birthday, Thomas," she said, handing him the cake. "How old are you, if I may ask?"

"Very old," he replied. That was as much as she was getting. He thanked her for the cake, and she smiled before going off to check on the tills.

"Mustard gas," whispered Frank, pointing at the figure of the soldier on the cake, but Thomas shook his head.

"Mustard gas produces blisters," he replied. "This looks more like radiation."

"Perhaps we shouldn't eat it then," said Frank, though Thomas could see he was smiling.

"I think we'll be fine."

Very soon, the cake was gone, the injured soldier put out of his misery.

As Thomas wiped crumbs from the table, Frank rifled around in his coat pockets, pulling out a small parcel wrapped in plain paper and a little bigger than a packet of playing cards. "Here," he said. "Jane and I got this for you." He was smiling as he handed over the present, and it was so carefully wrapped that Thomas couldn't help but hesitate before opening it.

"Cocaine?" asked Thomas, slowly untying the silver ribbon that was neatly formed into a bow. Each loop was of equal length, the bow itself precisely in the middle.

"Not far off," said Frank with a smile, watching as Thomas unwrapped the gift before folding the brown paper and placing it into his pocket. It was a packet of cigarettes.

Thomas chuckled. Frank always bought him cigarettes. "The Camels are coming," he said, more to himself than to Frank, turning the box over in his hands and remembering how soft the packet had felt all those years ago. Not like now with its square edges and pointed corners. "You know, more doctors smoke Camels than any other brand. At least, that's what they used to say."

"I know, but I'm not sure that's the case anymore." Frank leaned over and shook Thomas's hand. "Happy birthday, my friend," he said. "Go easy on the Camels, though. I want another ninety years out of you."

The morning went slowly. Frank said it was due to the weather, but Thomas wasn't so sure. It had been like that the last few years, and he wondered if people were starting to forget. Not that he minded really. We forget everything given time. They decided to give it another hour before finishing and heading off to the Legion.

At twelve-thirty, Thomas started to pack up, carefully closing the boxes, making sure not to bend any of the poppies. Frank dealt with the pins and the metal badges. Things had picked up over the last hour, so it hadn't been such a bad shift after all.

"Look at these two," said Frank suddenly, tapping Thomas on the arm and pointing to a couple of teenagers who had just walked in, one male and one female. They went over to the far wall and stood by the chiller cabinet. "Here we go," he whispered as the boy took two bottles of Coke from the display and put them into his pockets. "I knew it," he said, turning to his friend. But Thomas had already gone. "For God's sake, Thomas," he sighed, setting off after him.

By the time Frank caught up with him, Thomas was deep in conversation.

"I bought them," said the boy as Thomas stood there, arms folded with a stern look on his face. "Who the hell are you anyway?"

"It's that old fossil from the poppy stand," said the girl, and Thomas burst out laughing. The boy spread his arms and smiled.

"If you're trying to intimidate me," said Thomas, "it's not going to work." He paused for a moment, and Frank saw that he'd stopped laughing. "I've experienced far worse."

The girl was about to say something when there was a noise nearby, and Thomas turned to find Colin, the store security guard, approaching. Colin was an extremely smart, tall man. He'd worked there for the last five years, and Thomas liked him, with his carefully ironed shirt and neatly pressed trousers.

"Everything alright?" Colin asked no one in particular. He looked at Thomas and Frank, then turned to the teenagers.

"Colonel Sanders here is trying to act hard," said the girl. Thomas noticed the boy had slid the two bottles onto a shelf behind him. "Thinks he's some sort of war hero when he hasn't even got any medals." She pointed to Frank. "Not like grandad there. At least he's got a couple." Frank had three medals which he always wore in the run-up to Remembrance Day. Thomas never wore medals. "Probably got them for folding blankets, though."

The thought of Frank folding blankets tickled Thomas, and he turned to his friend. "Blanket folding, Frank?" he asked as Frank rolled his eyes. Frank had served in Kenya during the Mau Mau Uprising. Not much need for blankets there.

Thomas didn't mention the bottles, and in the end, the two teenagers were asked to leave. The girl, whose name was Shell, and her friend Jonesie were politely told they were no longer welcome at the store. Which was a bit of a problem, as that's where they did most of their shoplifting.

"You're looking at things from the wrong perspective," said Brian to a somewhat downcast Ian. Brian had tried to break it gently, but it hadn't worked. He was now attempting the more direct approach. "You need to write about things that interest people, Ian. Not just things you're interested in."

Ian nodded. He *was* doing that. At least, he thought he was.

"People buy the *Echo* to read about Kingsley. Give them that." Brian paused to let the information sink in. "This is your last chance, Ian. If you can't deliver what I want, I'll find someone who can."

His last chance.

Ian shook his head as he left Brian's office. He wasn't sure when his *first* chance had been.

The phone started ringing as he got back to his desk.

"Hi, love," said the voice at the other end of the line. It was his wife, Debbie. "Can you pick up some bread when you're out this lunchtime? I need some for your sandwiches." Ian smiled to himself. She was always thinking of him. He loved that about her. He decided not to mention the conversation with Brian. He'd work it out, so there was no need to worry her. And she *would* worry.

"Sure," he replied. "I'm going out in a minute, so I'll head over to the supermarket. See you normal time." Debbie blew a kiss down the phone, then hung up.

"Eff you, Brian," muttered Ian, looking around to see if anyone had heard him. He didn't like to swear. "Making me lie to Debbie." He knew it hadn't really been a lie but he told Debbie everything, so it still felt bad. And that was Brian's fault.

The gravel crunched under his feet as he walked the short distance from his office to the supermarket. It looked like it had been raining. Ian had his new shoes on—a brown leather pair Debbie had bought him. She'd said it made him look the part; he didn't really know what she'd meant by that. There were a few specks of mud on one toe, so he stopped by a bench in the small park by the supermarket, taking a paper tissue from his pocket and cleaning off the dirt. As he was about to leave, he noticed two people on the next bench, sharing a cigarette and swearing. The kids always seemed to swear, and he didn't like it. He wouldn't say anything of course. Not every battle was worth fighting. But Ian had never fought *any* battles. He was too afraid of what might happen.

"That old fart's going to pay for that," said Jonesie, taking his phone from his pocket and flicking at the screen. "Who the hell does he think he is?"

Shell took a long drag on her cigarette, then passed it to her friend. "I told you, I bet he's not even been in the army. Making out he's all that when he's just a fraud. Not a single medal. And they all got medals."

Jonesie laughed, an idea forming in his head.

Inside the supermarket, Ian took off his coat and slung it over his arm. It was unusually stuffy, most likely due to a fan heater he noticed in the corner blasting hot air across the entrance area. There were two old men by a table, clearing away some boxes of poppies. He hadn't bought one yet, so he went over and asked if he could have a metal one. One of the old men shook his head, but the other one smiled. He seemed the older of the two, but he looked strong as though he'd been quite something in his day. A little over six feet, he was taller than his friend and had the most amazing blue eyes.

"I'm sorry, son, but we're all packed up for the day," he said, fumbling around in his jacket pockets—a smart blue blazer. Finding nothing, he reached for his lapel and unclipped his own badge. It was small with red lacquer on the front and gold-coloured plating on the back. Handing it to Ian, he said, "Take this. You can pay for it next time you see me." And with that, the two men took their boxes and left.

After getting some bread and picking up his usual bottle of water and a small salad bowl, Ian went to the supermarket cafe. It was an excellent way to kill thirty minutes over lunch with the added bonus that it kept him away from Brian and his constant complaints. All that Brian was interested in was gossip. He ran a newspaper but had no interest in news. Ian wondered what had happened to make him change. By all accounts, he'd been a good journalist in the past; inquisitive and fearless. But not now.

Jenny came over and said hello. She was a friend of Debbie's. He'd known her ever since she'd moved to the area and started working in the supermarket some years ago. She'd met Debbie at a yoga class at the leisure centre. Or was it Pilates? Something like that. Back then, she'd worked the tills, but pretty soon she'd made her way up to assistant manager. Then, when old Mr Jessop had left, she'd taken over. Brian suspected something sinister, of course, and had asked him to find some dirt. For once, he'd refused. Not a good career move in hindsight.

"What's the name of the old guy selling poppies?" he asked Jenny. "The one with blue eyes."

Jenny smiled as though remembering something good. "That'll be Thomas," she replied. "Thomas Mirren. The nicest man you could wish to meet. Why do you ask?"

Ian shrugged. "He gave me his poppy earlier. Said I could pay him later. Can I leave some money with you?"

Jenny thought about it. "Best you give it to him if that's what he wanted," she said. "He'll be here every day for the next week or two."

Ian nodded and thanked her. He'd bring the money the next day.

The remainder of his lunchtime consisted of the side salad and the water. Debbie made him sandwiches every day, but he liked to eat those when he got back to the office. It killed a few extra minutes and made him feel as though he'd had an extended lunch break. He'd tried the mixed salad recently but hadn't like it much: too peppery and not enough tomatoes. Today, he'd opted for the Mediterranean Bowl which was much better.

The two teenagers were still sitting on the wooden bench when he left, still swearing. The boy was laughing hysterically and pointing to his phone. The girl was laughing too, though her laughter sounded cruel. Ian took the long way back to the office, past the swings and round the carved animals so that he wouldn't have to walk past them.

Ian was relieved to find that Brian was in a meeting all afternoon. He leafed through the cuttings on his desk as he ate his sandwiches: snippets of social media mainly, sourced by the press desk. 'Press desk' sounded grand. In reality, it was just Anna and George, the two trainees, who sifted through social media all day, printing out stories which might be of interest. That day, there was nothing.

There were four other journalists in the office but none of them were around. The only people in that afternoon were the administrators and the finance team. There was a lady who did all the HR too but Ian couldn't see her. As a result, it was pretty quiet, and that was how he liked it. It gave him time to think. He tried to concentrate on the papers in front of him: complaints about the council and the terrible state of the roads, but by four-thirty, he'd had enough, so he decided to pack up for the day. All he wanted to do now was go home.

The journey from the office to his house was no more than twenty minutes on a good day, double that if traffic was bad. He'd bought a new car recently, all-electric and with as many gadgets and gizmos as you could possibly want. Brian had called it a waste of money; said it was the Chinese who were destroying the environment, so one person over here made no difference. But, as usual, he'd missed the point. Ian couldn't change what other people did but he could do something himself. *Every journey starts with a single step*, isn't that what they said? Well, Ian's family was a first step.

Besides, Brian always blamed foreigners. Truth and the facts never bothered him.

Because it was still early, he decided to take the long route home. He enjoyed driving his new car, which had cost a small fortune. It was exciting to drive along silently, feeling like James Bond with all the computer readouts flickering on the dashboard in front of him. He didn't know what most of them meant but they looked impressive, all the same. When he asked for some classical music, a lady's voice came out from the speakers:

"Okay, here's a station you might like—classical music for a relaxing bath."

Ian laughed. Fantastic. Odd but fantastic.

As he was passing the Legion Club, he noticed the two poppy sellers from earlier. He thought about stopping to give them the money for the poppy but it was warm in the car and the music was good, so he didn't. He'd give it to them tomorrow.

"Not a bad morning all told," said Frank, taking a sip from his drink. They always went back to the Legion after a morning at the supermarket. They'd stay a couple of hours, then head home. Frank did most of the talking while Thomas listened. "And what about those two we caught shoplifting?"

Thomas shook his head.

Derek from behind the bar leaned over and asked what had happened, and for the next few minutes, Frank regaled him the story of the two teenagers and their pitiful attempt at stealing.

"One of them called Frank a blanket folder," said Thomas, laughing. "So, they were pretty sharp."

"She called Thomas a fossil," added Frank to even up the score.

"Like I said"—Thomas smiled—"pretty sharp."

The three of them were still laughing when the door opened and in walked the Colonel, looking as spritely as ever despite his ninety-plus years.

"Colonel," said Derek and Frank in unison. He nodded and then turned to Thomas and smiled.

"Thomas," he said simply. "Happy birthday." Looking back at Derek, he added, "These drinks are on me."

The Colonel had served in the war at the same time as Thomas, though he had been injured. As a result, he'd returned home early while Thomas had stayed until the end.

"A word if that's okay?" he said to Thomas as he made his way over to his usual chair. Thomas nodded and went to join him. The two of them moved to a small table in the corner where there were several large leather armchairs, and the Colonel sat, indicating to Thomas to join him. The chair's leather felt cold against Thomas's back, making him wince as he pushed firmly against it.

The Colonel stared at him, his concern evident. "Back playing up?"

"A little."

Derek came over, placing two large whiskies in front of the men. The Colonel handed one to Thomas, and raising his glass, he smiled. "To you."

A minute later, Frank arrived. He was carrying three more drinks—two whiskies and a beer—and was struggling with his choice to not use a tray. Thomas got up to help, but Frank shook his head. As they sat there, Frank watched as Thomas rubbed at the back of his shoulders, his long fingers digging in so that he grimaced. It wasn't long before Frank had seen enough.

"Get that sorted, Thomas," urged Frank. "For Christ's sake, it's painful to watch."

"I will," agreed Thomas, though they all knew he wouldn't. Frank and the Colonel had watched him for years, hands working at his shoulders and back, but not once had either of them heard him complain. Thomas had never been the sort to make a fuss.

The three of them chatted for a long time that afternoon, Frank filling the Colonel in on the first day of their poppy sales. Neither he nor Thomas mentioned the two teenagers, and by four-thirty, they were beginning to feel drunk. As they got up to leave, the Colonel asked Thomas what his plans were for the evening.

"More of this." He laughed, finishing off his drink. "Though at home, of course, with Ellen."

The Colonel left first, Frank and Thomas following soon after.

Outside, it was a lovely afternoon, so the two men decided to walk home. Frank left his car at the Legion. It would take him ten minutes to get back to his house, double that to Thomas's. The roads were beginning to get busy as people made their way home from work, and the sun had come out. Not for the first time that day, as a trail of sweat made its way down his back, Frank regretted his choice of coat.

At the end of the road, the two men shook hands.

"See you tomorrow," said Frank.

"For another tough day at the office," Thomas added.

As Thomas walked home, the old terraced houses lining the streets looked cold and deserted, not at all like the house he'd grown up in as a child. He smiled at the memory: the tiny front room with the crackling coal fire, his parents, the meals, the comfort and warmth. Another world altogether, now long gone.

He returned home to his cold house. Turning on the central heating, he went into the bathroom and took off his shirt. His back had been much worse than usual today, and as he looked into the mirror, he traced the latticework of scars with his fingertips. Across his shoulders and down his back, white welts burned angrily, his skin resembling that of melted, scored plastic. It was just a flare-up, he told himself, a small price to pay for what he'd done.

He changed out of the rest of his clothes and put on his suit. He always wore his suit on this day of the year. In the kitchen, he fetched a glass and a bottle. It wasn't every day he turned ninety. And today, it was a double celebration.

Standing in front of the electric fire, fake flames swaying gently, Thomas gazed adoringly at the photograph on the mantlepiece. It showed a young man, strong and handsome, laughing. Next to him was a woman around the same age with brown hair, shoulder-length and wavy, held back at the sides by two clips. She was holding a red rose.

Thomas felt the breath catch in his throat. Just like it did every time he looked at her.

"Happy anniversary, Ellen."

Chapter 2

Nicole and Michel

Nicole Moreau was out of bed at six-thirty. The same time every day. The exact time she had risen every day for eighty years in that same town, that same house. Give or take a few months during the war and a couple of years she wished to forget. She would set the fire, then brew a fresh pot of coffee. No day should start without warmth and coffee. A little later, she'd wake her brother, Michel, the lazy one of the two children, or so her parents had always joked. He could easily stay in bed until half past seven, sometimes later. But not today.

"Is some of that coffee for me?" asked Michel, rubbing his eyes sleepily. His hair was dishevelled, but he was dressed, his old grey suit faded but still smart. Nicole liked him in that suit. He'd ironed a white shirt, and a dark blue tie hung loosely around his neck.

Nicole snapped her fingers. "Top button, please, Brother." Michel saluted, tidying himself up at once. Nicole laughed. "Perfect." She smiled as Michel walked over to embrace her.

"I suppose you were expecting to wake me?"

Nicole shook her head. She never had to wake him on this day of the year.

Handing him a cup of coffee, the two of them went to the table by the window. They stared outside at the warm autumnal morning, the rolling green fields spreading out before them, and in the distance, the small town of Saint Martin.

"They'll be expecting you in town today, Mr Mayor," said Nicole after a while. "As they always do."

Michel laughed, putting down his coffee for fear of spilling it on his suit. "It's ex-Mr Mayor," he said. He looked at the small buildings of Saint Martin across the fields, like tiny black boxes with the old church at the centre, and for a moment Nicole recalled another time. But then Michel looked at her, and he was smiling, that mischievous smile he'd had since they were children.

"Besides," he said, "they know what today is, so they should never have arranged the meeting as they did. I won't go, and they know it."

By mid-morning, they had completed their chores, and it was time to start the preparations. Each year, Michel went into the loft but it was always Nicole who unwrapped the figure. It had been that way for over fifty years.

The nerves were getting to Nicole as midday approached. Michel kept a close eye on her to make sure she was okay. He was nervous too, of course, but he couldn't let Nicole know. It was his job to look after her.

"What time are the others arriving?" he asked, already knowing the answer.

Nicole didn't look up as she fussed about the room, straightening chairs and plumping cushions. "Lunchtime," she replied. "Same time every year." Michel nodded, then helped Nicole move the large table into the centre of the room. Very soon, everything was done.

"You should go and get it now," said Nicole. Michel rubbed his hands on the front of his shirt, then quietly left the room. He looked at his hands in the dim light of the narrow hallway, making sure they were clean. Satisfied, he went upstairs.

The bedroom was large. It had been Michel and Nicole's when they were young, and little had changed save for new wallpaper and a carpet where it had previously been bare boards. Now, it was Michel's. Nicole had moved out many years ago but was soon back, daughter in tow and husband long gone. She had needed her brother's strength, and he had given it without question. But Michel had never left, even when he'd married Jeanne. They'd had a son, Jean-Luc, but then Jeanne was gone too; a short illness followed by a long mourning. So, Nicole had become a mother of two. Michel had needed *her* strength then, and she had given it. Without question.

They called the room next door 'the loft'. It was small, too small for anything practical, and attached to the bedroom by a door. Nicole and Michel had played in there as children, the two of them hiding in the dark and spying through the floorboards at their parents below. They could see everything, but now the floorboards were covered by an old rug. One day, they had seen too much.

Turning on the light, Michel went over to the door and slid back the bolt. The hinges groaned, and a plume of dust escaped like a ghost rushing from the darkness, making Michel cough as he fumbled along the wall for the light switch. As the light flickered on, he stepped inside.

It was the first time he'd been in the loft for exactly a year. And after today, it would be another year before he was in there again. It was empty save for the rug and a large leather chest in the corner. He couldn't remember what was in the chest, but on top of it sat a small wooden box. Their father had made it for them, a strong place in which they could keep their most valuable things. Nowadays, it contained only one item.

Michel carefully took the box and exited the room. He wanted to spend as little time in there as possible. Turning off the light, he bolted the door and quickly left the bedroom. With both hands gently holding the rough wooden box, he made his way down the stairs, wondering to himself what would be worse, falling or dropping the box? His body would mend, albeit slowly at his age, but he could not afford to break what he was carrying. He smiled to himself at the answer. There had never been any doubt.

Nicole was waiting for him when he returned. She had removed everything from the mantlepiece, and on it, she had placed two candles with photographs of the family to either side. There was one of their parents standing together in the field outside the house, smiling and with the town in the background. Another showed Michel and Jeanne on their wedding day, the happiest day of his life. Next to that was a faded picture of Jeanne with Jean-Luc. Jeanne was ill at the time, clearly noticeable in the picture, and had died shortly afterwards. It was the only picture he had of the two of them together. The last picture showed Michel and Nicole. It was taken in 1942, precisely seventy-two years ago. Nicole was wearing a dress and Michel had on shorts and a white shirt with braces. They were holding hands, and they were smiling.

In the middle was an empty space.

Without saying anything, Michel handed the box to Nicole. She stared at it, gently stroking the rough wooden surface. Carefully lifting the lid as though anything more forceful might destroy what was inside, she looked at Michel, and he nodded.

Nicole slowly lifted a tiny figure from the box. The two of them walked together to the fireplace, where Nicole placed it in the space between the two candles. It was a toy. A small figurine made of lead, with chipped paint and a reddish-brown mark on the base.

A camel.

Chapter 3

Ian

Ian was up at eight o'clock. He'd had a couple of drinks the night before which had left him with a headache. Debbie had opened a bottle of wine guessing him in need of it when he'd walked in, and as usual, she'd been right. They'd sat up until late, and by the time they'd gone to bed, a second bottle was well on the way to being finished.

As a rule, Ian always sought Debbie's advice when he had something on his mind. She invariably had the answer. Or at least *an* answer. The previous night had been no different. He had explained the situation at work, listing off Brian's shortcomings with well-rehearsed precision, and Debbie had listened. He was being pushed in a direction that made him uncomfortable, more towards gossip and further away from news. Debbie's advice, as usual, had been straightforward.

"Don't do what you're uncomfortable with, Ian," she'd said. "If you don't like it, you can always find somewhere else. We don't need the money anyway."

But that was the problem: they *did* need the money. There was no escaping that fact.

As he sat at the table that morning, playing with his toast while Debbie tapped away on her phone, he couldn't help but focus on the problem that he didn't want to go to work. And that wasn't like him. Not like him at all.

To take his mind off things, he asked Debbie what she was looking at.

"Facebook," she replied.

"Anything interesting?"

"On Facebook?" She laughed. "No, the usual rubbish." She scrolled down, where she came across a post on the council's page. "There's even someone here trolling an old guy. Something about him being a war fraud." She put down her phone and took a sip of her coffee. "I don't know why I bother looking at it, to be honest."

Ian shrugged. He wasn't sure why anyone looked at social media but they all did. It was a bit like looking at an accident: you knew you shouldn't but you just couldn't help yourself.

At nine o'clock, he left the house.

"What time do you call this?" shouted Brian from his office as Ian walked through the door. He was grinning as he looked at some papers. Before Ian had time to answer, Brian waved him into the office.

"Here you are," he said, handing Ian a sheet of paper. "Don't say I don't do anything for you."

Ian looked at the paper. There was a mark in the corner—grease from one of the pastries on Brian's desk. He groaned inwardly: a Facebook printout.

"It seems we have a military imposter," declared Brian, delighted by the possibility.

"How do you know?" asked Ian.

"I don't," said Brian. "That's what you're going to find out." He picked up the calendar from his desk and pointed to a date. "I need it by Friday if it's going to get into next Wednesday's edition." Ian watched as he skittered around the room like an overexcited child. "This is potential dynamite." Brian laughed. "It's Remembrance Day soon and it's a big one—a hundred years since the start of the First World War. And someone's going around pretending they were in it." He was shaking his head. "Disgraceful."

"I think you mean the Second World War."

Brian waved his hand. "Whatever. Just get me the story."

Before Ian could say anything more, he was shooed unceremoniously from the office.

Ian had only glanced at the printout in Brian's office but he was pretty sure it was the same thing Debbie had mentioned that morning. If Debbie was correct and it was just another person being nasty, it would be cleared up in no time. But where to start?

He was sitting at his desk, pondering what to do, when Amanda, one of the other reporters, came over and glanced at his printout.

"He's got you looking into that, has he?" she said. "I've not seen him so excited since that train crash a few years ago." Ian remembered it well. Nothing much had happened: a train had derailed, and Brian had thought there could be fatalities. When it had turned out there were none, he'd been in a bad mood for days. It would probably go the same way this time.

"I hope he's wrong," said Amanda. "He's such a nice guy."

"Who, Brian?" asked Ian, raising an eyebrow.

Amanda giggled. "No, stupid, the Facebook guy." She looked at Ian, cocking her head as if expecting him to say something. He didn't. "You know who it is, don't you?"

Ian shook his head; he hadn't got that far.

"It's the guy who sells poppies at the supermarket." She sighed. "Well, one of them. His name's Thomas Mirren. Lovely guy." Before she could say anything more, her phone rang. She disappeared, leaving Ian to read the piece of paper more carefully.

Ian knew the story must be false. He'd seen the man many times over the years. He'd even seen him coming out of the Legion yesterday. A quick online search should clear things up, then he could tell Brian and get on with some proper work. Job done.

But he couldn't find Thomas Mirren anywhere. Thinking he must have made a mistake, he went over to Jean, the office manager, who was making a cup of tea in the kitchen. Jean had lived in the town her whole life and knew everyone. She was humming to herself as he approached.

"Hi, Jean. Quick question."

Jean looked up from her tea making and smiled. They'd always got on well, and while she was quiet around most of the people in the office, she often chatted with Ian.

"Do you know the guy who sells poppies in the supermarket?" he asked.

"Which one?" replied Jean, and Ian smiled to himself. Of course, she would know.

"Striking blue eyes."

Jean nodded. "Thomas Mirren. And before you ask, yes, he *did* serve in the army."

"So, you know about that, do you?"

Jean explained to Ian that Thomas Mirren had sold poppies for as long as she could remember, which was a very long time. She hadn't spoken to him—he seemed relatively quiet—but she was confident he'd served in the war.

"World War Two," she added loudly, looking towards Brian's office.

Ian laughed. "Do you know which regiment?"

"No."

"Do you know where he served?"

"No."

"The thing is, Jean, I can't find any record of him online. Bit odd, don't you think?"

"Not really." Jean shrugged. "Just because you can't find something doesn't mean it's not there." Her tea had finished brewing by this stage, so she rinsed the teaspoon and refilled the kettle. She left, leaving Ian to wonder what his next move should be.

Back at his desk, just in case he'd made a mistake, he tried the military records website again. There was no Thomas Mirren. There was Marron, Marino, and Marney but no Mirren. He widened his search to cover the post-war period.

Still nothing. Very odd, he thought. Maybe there was something to it after all.

As Ian was leaving that evening, Brian waved him into his office. He was speaking on the phone, so made Ian wait by his desk. He was grinning broadly. From what Ian could glean, he was talking to someone from one of the nationals, though he couldn't imagine what interest they would have in the *Echo*. After five minutes, Brian put down the phone.

"This could be big. Very big." He walked around the large wooden desk and stood next to Ian. "That was Jacqueline Chambers from the *Chronicle*. They're doing a series on Remembrance Day. I happened to mention we have something in the pipeline, and she seems quite interested. Of course, I didn't give any details. Not yet." He paused. "So?"

"So, what?" asked Ian, much to Brian's irritation.

"The military imposter..."

Ian was still far from comfortable with the whole situation, but he told Brian what he'd found—very little. Brian, of course, seemed delighted.

"I knew it," he said. "Nothing in the records."

"Nothing that I've found," corrected Ian.

"Like I said, nothing in the records." Brian moved back to the other side of the desk, where he busily scribbled something into a small notebook next to his computer. He tore out a page and handed it to Ian. It was a phone number.

"This is my mobile number," he said. "Don't give it to anyone else. I want that story by close of business tomorrow. Give me a call if you have any problems."

That was Ian's cue to leave. It looked like tomorrow was going to be a busy day.

Before heading home, he decided to go to the supermarket. He needed to pick up a couple of things and it wouldn't do any harm to ask the odd question about Thomas Mirren while he was there. It wasn't exactly investigative journalism but at least it gave him something to do; something which Brian approved of anyway. He couldn't care less what the man thought of him but he could do without losing his job. He tried to convince himself he was doing the right thing, but in reality, he knew he wasn't.

It was five-thirty by the time he arrived at the supermarket, and it was already busy with people picking up last minute bits and pieces before heading home. The poppy table was there but there was no sign of Thomas Mirren. Ian imagined he had left and that he'd missed him, and he felt a strange sense of relief.

Picking up a basket, he made his way along the fruit and vegetable aisle, then turned to pick up some detergent. The next aisle housed a vast array of wines from all over the world, although mainly France and Australia. Most of them were too alcoholic—fourteen per cent or more—and it took him several minutes to find one which was both drinkable and within his budget. He and Debbie liked a glass of wine with dinner, but yesterday had been excessive. He promised himself he'd stick to the one glass that night.

"Can I check you're twenty-five, please, sir?" said a voice from behind him as he placed the wine into his basket. He turned to find Jenny, hands on hips, grinning beneath her headband.

"Is the thinning hair proof enough?" he asked with a smile.

"It'll do," she replied, laughing.

Jenny was usually finished by five o'clock, so Ian asked her why she was still at work. It turned out there had been some trouble with a couple of teenagers earlier; known shoplifters who'd tried to get into the store even though they'd recently been banned. Ian shook his head sadly. His daughter, Ellie, was eighteen. He couldn't imagine her doing something like that.

The two of them chatted for a few minutes, and Ian asked Jenny what she knew about Thomas Mirren.

"Why do you want to know?" she asked.

"It's nothing really," he replied. "It's just that after he gave me his poppy yesterday, I was kind of curious. Do you know much about him?"

"Not really. Just that he's nice," she said. "Oh, and that he sells poppies."

"But do you know where he served, or what his regiment was?"

"No," she said flatly. "He doesn't talk about the past, and I can't say I blame him."

It was clear he wasn't going to get any information here, so making his excuses, he said goodbye and headed towards the checkouts.

Just as he was about to join a queue, he noticed Thomas Mirren and his friend entering the store. Thomas Mirren was carrying an old umbrella and laughing at something his friend was saying. The security guard said something to them, and Thomas Mirren's friend smiled and nodded. He was wearing a large grey coat. Thomas Mirren was pulling at the coat and laughing as his friend slapped at his hand. Ian felt a sudden surge of guilt, and all he could think about was getting home. Away from this place, from Thomas Mirren, and from what Brian had asked him to do. He needed to talk to Debbie again.

"Don't do it," advised Ellie as she sat at the kitchen table that evening, the three of them surrounded by empty plates. "It'll just be some idiots messing about."

Debbie agreed. "Even if he is making it up, what harm is he doing anybody? There'll be reasons. He's doing something good selling the poppies, isn't he?"

Debbie had made pasta that evening. Ian had eaten too much, and with his fullness mixing with the glass of wine he was drinking, he could quite easily have fallen asleep. Ellie was involving herself in their mealtime discussion for once, her phone remaining off by her side, where normally she would have been tapping away. It was their opinion that he shouldn't write anything about Thomas Mirren. The reasons were threefold: firstly, it wasn't thoroughly researched save for a few internet searches and the odd bit of gossip; secondly, he was one of the good guys, raising money while most people couldn't be bothered; thirdly, Brian was an arse.

It was hard for Ian to argue against that, especially the third point. However, since he'd been home, he'd already drafted a piece. It was good, and he hadn't mentioned Thomas Mirren by name. Instead, he'd written a balanced article about why people might invent a past life— loneliness, insecurity, wanting to fit in—and whilst he'd included the rumour of a local poppy seller pretending to be a war veteran, he'd been careful not to say who it was. But it was obvious: 'with his blue blazer and gentle manner'.

Sitting at the table in his nice house, drinking his nice wine, he looked at the two people he loved most in the world. And that's when he knew it: there was no question of him losing his job. He couldn't let it happen. He really didn't want to write the story. But he had to.

Chapter 4

Thomas

The poppy sales had been slow that morning, and when Thomas and Frank packed up, they decided it would be nice to head out of town for lunch.

"No point being poor if you can't spend your last few quid on a pint and a sandwich," said Thomas as Frank put on his heavy coat.

Thomas needed to go home first to pick up a few things—hat, scarf, umbrella—things he'd not thought about when he'd set out that morning. Frank offered to give him a lift home, but Thomas declined, saying he wanted to walk. Besides, Frank was such a slow driver that Thomas would be quicker on foot.

Inside his house, Thomas took off his blazer and hung it on the coat peg by the door. Rummaging through the pockets for his wallet, he felt something cool and sharp-edged. It couldn't be his wallet—that would be warm given the number of times he'd used it that morning to buy Frank packets of crisps and bags of sweets. It was amazing he wasn't the size of the Hindenburg. No, it was the packet of Camel cigarettes Frank and Jane had bought him. He smiled to himself as he walked over to a set of wooden drawers by the fire. Opening the bottom drawer, he carefully placed the cigarettes next to the dozen or so other packets that were there, all unopened and all gifts from Frank and Jane. He liked the gifts and what they represented, so he'd never told Frank he'd stopped smoking and Frank had never asked. But he was pretty sure Frank knew, all the same. He'd stopped smoking years ago, the day after Ellen had died. She'd never liked him smoking, so he'd given up. Given up too late. He remembered the day well: it was the first time he'd cried. Not because he was sad but because he was stupid. He should have stopped when she was alive, then started after she had gone.

"Filthy habit," he said, looking at the picture of Ellen on the mantlepiece. "You were right about that too." And she smiled at him, that beautiful smile. He picked up the picture and kissed her.

A car horn sounded. Thomas said goodbye to Ellen and left the house. He locked the front door, checking it was secure. Twice. It was called being careful, although there would probably be other words for it too. As he walked down the short path, he noticed the Colonel in the back of Frank's car—an old Volkswagen—and he waved. The Colonel raised his hand in reply. It wasn't really a wave, thought Thomas, because his hand didn't move. It was more like a photograph of a wave.

Thomas got into the front seat, next to Frank. The seat next to the Colonel housed a large bag, and Thomas could hear bottles chinking as the car set off.

"I see we're prepared then," said Thomas.

The Colonel laughed. "Preparation—the key to victory."

Frank and Thomas looked at each other.

"I thought that was sacrifice?" said Frank.

The Colonel chuckled behind him. "That helps too."

The journey took a long time—around an hour when it should normally have taken forty-five minutes. The Colonel and Thomas took turns teasing Frank about the speed of his driving, the Colonel observing that he would have made a terrible dispatch rider. Thomas reminded him that Frank was a blanket folder, at which point Frank burst out laughing, saying if that were true, they would all have frozen to death. They eventually arrived at a little after two.

Their destination was a pub called The Olde Hall. Thomas had only been there a couple of times before. It was set back from the main road, down a short lane which was in dire need of repair. The numerous potholes had caused Frank to slow almost to a standstill, the car shaking violently from side to side as the Colonel worried about the beer bottles in his bag, afraid they might explode. Thomas smiled to himself; the Colonel had a habit of getting blown up.

The Olde Hall was a grand old building, its blackened stone front reminding Thomas of the buildings he'd encountered as a young man, burned out and on the verge of collapse. Damaged, just like the three of them. It wasn't particularly cold, so Thomas suggested they sit outside, and as the Colonel shrugged, Frank set off in search of food. The Colonel unzipped his bag and pulled out three bottles of beer.

"You know, we're meant to buy the beer from the bar," said Thomas, and the Colonel shook his head.

"We're buying the food, aren't we?" he replied, producing a bottle opener from his jacket pocket. He opened the bottles and handed the first to Thomas.

After Frank returned, they sat together at a wooden table. There were two benches attached, one on either side, and in the centre was a parasol, open despite it being the middle of October. The table was situated near a low wooden fence at the furthest point from the pub, and a few feet away was the start of a field, a sea of deep green rolling out into the distance. At the far side was a village. Thomas recalled again the blackened buildings of his youth, and he pictured a girl, her eyes wide with horror.

And then he heard Frank. "To the loneliest men in the world," he said, raising his bottle.

The Colonel huffed theatrically. "I can think of jollier toasts," he said. "Though few more accurate." The three of them touched bottles, and Thomas smiled. It was true, they *were* lonely, especially Thomas. But they weren't sad. That time had passed.

After several bottles of beer, the Colonel reminded Frank that he was driving. Thomas and Frank looked at each other, surprised. The thought hadn't even occurred to them. As the Colonel reached into his bag, producing three more bottles, Thomas wondered how many he'd brought. Though large, the bag looked far too small for the number of empty bottles now littering the surface of the table.

"We'll get a taxi back," announced the Colonel. "Then, I'll pick up the car for you tomorrow, Frank, if that's okay?"

Frank already had the next bottle pressed to his lips, and he nodded, fumbling in his coat pocket for his car key.

The taxi arrived at four forty-five, and they were back in Kingsley for five-thirty. Thomas and Frank left the Colonel at the Legion, and the two of them headed off to the supermarket. Frank wanted to pick up a bottle of wine, and Thomas had run out of whisky.

On the way in, Frank said hello to Colin, the security guard, who looked like he was ready to pack up for the day. He noticed the fan heater in the corner.

"They've still got that heater on," he moaned. "It's like a greenhouse in here."

Thomas laughed and pulled at Frank's coat while Frank pretended to slap his hand away. It was easier to complain than to take it off. As they made their way over to the alcohol aisle, Thomas noticed the man he'd given his poppy to the previous day. The man looked busy, so he decided not to say anything. He'd catch up with him eventually.

Half an hour later, the two men could be seen disappearing back out the supermarket door, into a rapidly darkening car park. Thomas was carrying the bag, an old Marks & Spencer affair he'd used for years and always carried around in his coat pocket. There was no point getting a new one every time he went shopping, and besides, he reckoned they'd soon be charged for them. He'd said as much to Frank once, and Frank had laughed, not believing a word of it.

The bag contained the two bottles of alcohol as well as a prawn cocktail sandwich for Thomas and a microwaveable meal for Frank. Thomas didn't believe in microwaves; someone had told him microwaves used radiation, and he'd seen the effects of radiation during the war. It wasn't pretty, so he steered well clear. Frank had laughed at that too.

"Fancy popping into The Royal for a pint before home?" asked Frank as they strolled down the street.

Thomas looked thoughtful, as though mentally checking his diary to make sure he wasn't double-booked, then nodded.

Frank rolled his eyes. "Thanks for making time for me in your busy social schedule."

Thomas told him he was welcome, and they both entered the pub.

It was nearly empty inside, and they found a table in the corner, with two small stools pushed underneath. There was an empty pint glass and a packet of crisps on the table, and Frank took them to the bar. While Frank ordered the drinks, Thomas took a tissue out of his pocket and wiped the table, sending small fragments of crisps tumbling to the floor where they joined an old bus ticket and a chocolate bar wrapper.

"The Colonel was on good form today," said Frank, returning when he returned to the table with the drinks. "It's usually a tough time of year for him." He looked at Thomas. "And you too."

Thomas nodded. The Colonel's wife had died twelve years ago, a couple of years before Ellen, though it had been the same time of year for both. Neither man looked forward to October, but at least the Remembrance Day preparations were a distraction. Frank's wife, Jane, had passed away more recently, although he still bought presents from the both of them. Thomas had done the same thing too. For a while, at least. He smiled to himself—*the three lonely men*.

As the pub started to fill up, they decided it was time to go. Finishing their drinks, they left The Royal and headed for home. It was fully dark now, and the shops had all closed. Thomas frowned. It was his least favourite time of the day. Like the town was dying.

"I'll walk with you to your place, Frank," he said. "Then, I'll make my way home from there. I could do with the walk after all we've drank today."

Frank laughed, and the two of them set off along the street, Frank with his hands buried into his coat pockets, Thomas gently swinging his Marks & Spencer bag by his side.

Ten minutes later, they stopped outside a small bungalow surrounded by a neatly mown lawn with short bushes behind a low stone wall. There was a light on in the porch.

"Money no object, I see, Frank," joked Thomas, pointing towards the house.

"I don't like coming home to an empty house," he replied. Thomas knew the feeling very well. He wondered if perhaps he should leave a light on too. Ellen would have laughed at that.

"See you tomorrow," said Thomas, and Frank nodded, fumbling in his pockets for the door key. "Another busy day."

It was eight o'clock by the time Thomas got home. The house was in complete darkness. He turned on the hallway light and made his way into the living room. Turning on the fire, he watched as the fake flames swayed and the filaments crackled into life.

"Bit of a late one today," he said to Ellen. "Frank and the Colonel tried to get me drunk, but as you know, that's not an easy thing to do." He picked up the photograph and kissed Ellen's smiling face before carefully putting it back on the mantlepiece and heading to the kitchen. From the carrier bag, he removed the sandwich and the small bottle of whisky. He placed the sandwich on a plate and the whisky in the cupboard. He'd had enough alcohol for one day, so he made himself a cup of tea instead.

There was a documentary he wanted to watch on the television that evening—something about great railway journeys. Tonight, it was the Trans-Siberian from Moscow to Beijing. Ellen and Thomas had always wanted to make that trip but had never found the time. Then, time had run out. It would be interesting to see what they'd missed.

The programme started at eight-thirty, and Thomas sat in his armchair, sandwich in one hand, cup of tea in the other.

By nine o'clock, he was asleep.

Chapter 5

Nicole and Michel

The family started arriving at lunchtime. First, Jean-Luc with his wife, Claire, and their two daughters, Eva and Belle. The adults hugged while the children rushed past, waving and shouting as they made their way to the back garden. Michel and Nicole smiled to one another and signalled for Jean-Luc and Claire to go into the lounge. Five minutes later came Marie, Nicole's daughter, and her son, Victor.

"Mother," she said, hugging Nicole closely. She smiled and turned to Michel. "Uncle." Victor had already found his way into the back garden.

Although this was an annual event, it was not the only time the whole family got together. Everyone lived in Saint Martin, so they saw each other often. But today was special.

"How are things in the town?" asked Michel as he and Jean-Luc moved from kitchen to lounge, carrying plates and glasses to the large dining table. A tablecloth had been laid and on it sat an assortment of bowls with vegetables and meats, cheeses and pâté.

Jean-Luc shrugged. "Busy," he said, "as always this time of year." He placed a large plate of bread in the centre of the table, though not before stealing away a piece for himself. Michel coughed. "What?" Jean-Luc laughed. "I'm hungry."

It turned out things in Saint Martin were hectic indeed. The Armistice Day celebrations had become increasingly elaborate over recent years, and this one was no exception. It seemed most of the town was involved.

"You know, they were hoping you'd go to the meeting today," said Jean-Luc. "Your opinion is always valued."

Michel snorted. "Not enough to have arranged it for another day."

Over lunch, they talked about the things families always talk about—school, neighbours, petty annoyances, and so on. The children were all doing well at school, though Victor could be working harder. Victor shook his head, and the two girls giggled. Marie explained that her neighbour had just bought a dog and it kept her awake at night. She said she was thinking of poisoning it, and she laughed at the horror on Jean-Luc's face. Of course, she was joking, she said, but at least it would let her sleep. Michel suggested she poison the neighbour instead. Jean-Luc reminded Nicole and Michel how fortunate they were to be living so far from the town, with its bustle and its noise, but Nicole shrugged. She had seen it much worse.

As they were coming to the end of the meal, Victor got up from his chair. He wandered over to the mantelpiece, where he was joined by Eva and Belle. They stood looking at the photographs.

"You were beautiful, Grandma," he said, looking at the old photograph of Nicole and Michel. His mother shook her head.

"*Were?*" Nicole laughed. "But not now?"

"I'm sorry," he said quickly, though he knew Nicole was joking. "You looked so young."

Michel frowned, then looked directly at the three children. "It is the greatest mistake of the young," he said gently, "to assume the old have never lived."

"Your grandparents have seen things I hope the rest of us never have to," said Jean-Luc, and for a moment, a quietness descended upon the room. Eva and Belle looked at the other pictures while Victor picked up the small figurine of the camel. As Michel made to stand, Nicole placed her hand on his arm.

Victor turned to face his grandparents, the camel still in his hand. "Grandma, would you please tell us again the story of the Camel?"

Everyone looked at Nicole.

"The Camel is not a thing," began Nicole, "it is a man." She paused. "Or *was*. No more than a boy. And he is the reason we are all here today." Smiling at Michel, she added, "Not just at this meal but *really* here. Were it not for him, my brother and I would be dead."

The children came back to the table, Victor still carrying the small figure.

"The town was on fire," continued Nicole. "I remember it like yesterday. We were standing in the garden and it was as if every colour in the world had gone away, leaving only oranges and blacks. Two days earlier, Raymond Aubrac, the resistance leader, had been rescued, and the Germans were not happy. They were venting their anger on the local towns, and the noise was terrible. There was so much smoke, like an old film where everything looks unreal. At first, Michel and I didn't know what was happening, but one look at our parents and we knew it was bad. Father was a good man but he was not brave. He stood there and stared as our mother shouted at him, telling him we had to leave. But it was so loud; perhaps he couldn't hear her. The explosions were like huge fireworks, celebrating the beginning of a new era."

"Or the end of an old one," muttered Michel.

"My story, Michel," she admonished him. "Or perhaps you would like to tell it?"

Michel apologised and asked her to continue.

"But where was there to go?" she said. "Really, where? We had lived here all our lives, in the same house, with the same neighbours, and the same friends. Outside of Saint Martin, there was nothing for us. Everything we had was here."

The room was silent now, each person caught up in a story they had heard many times.

"Eventually, our father was roused," continued Nicole. "You didn't ignore Mother for long. He shouted to us to go into the house. Mother turned out the lights, and we sat there, in this very room, staring out across the field, hoping the darkness would protect us. I remember Father took Mother to one side and spoke to her. She started to cry, shaking her head, and holding him as though at any moment he might disappear. And then we waited."

Everyone was looking at Nicole now. She noticed Victor had put down the camel and his father had his arm around his shoulder. Michel stared ahead, reliving that evening through her words.

"I don't know how long we waited that night. It seemed to us children, at least, to be a very long time indeed. I was with Michel, kneeling on the floor, staring out of the window. Our mother and father were behind us. Mother was crying; loud at first but soon small sobs which wouldn't stop. I'd never seen her cry before, and it was that which made me realise how bad things really were. But then, suddenly, the crying stopped. Our parents stood, and Father said something I couldn't hear. They were staring at an object in the distance, but from where Michel and I were kneeling, we couldn't see it. We got up too, and the four of us stood there, Michel and me at the front, Mother and Father behind. Father had his arms around me, and Mother held Michel. I could feel his arms trembling and hear his breathing, loud and afraid. Then, we saw it too.

"At first, it was just a silhouette; a figure emerging from the flames and the smoke, walking towards the house."

Nicole paused and pointed towards a spot in the field.

"But as the figure came closer, I could see it was a man. He had a rifle in one hand and he was carrying another person over his shoulder. My father's arms were shaking uncontrollably by this stage, as though he had seen the Devil itself.

"Then, I felt Father kiss the top of my head, and next he kissed Michel. He hugged my mother last. 'Goodbye, my love,' he said, and then he was gone, out of the door and into the night.

"Mother's arms were around us both now, and we watched as he ran across the garden and out into the field, heading towards the Devil with nothing but a small knife in his hand. He had become a brave man."

"And then what happened, Mother?" asked Marie, though she had heard the story many times before.

"Well, it wasn't the Devil." Nicole smiled. "As Father ran towards him, the man held up his hand. It was a signal for Father to stop. He said something, and my father dropped the knife. I could feel Mother's heart beating against the back of my head as Father pointed towards the house, and the man nodded. The next thing I knew, the lights were on and the two men were walking through the door. There was Father, his eyes wide and his hands trembling. And next to him was an angel."

Everyone had finished eating, so Nicole announced she would finish the story once the table was cleared and desserts had been eaten. There was no point in rushing a good story. Though the children were frustrated, the thought of cake took their minds off their disappointment. Jean-Luc and Marie tidied up the plates while Claire helped Nicole refill the glasses. Michel picked up the camel and went outside for a cigarette.

It was warm in the back garden, and Michel looked out across the field to the spot where he had first seen the man all those years ago. It was such a hard thing to imagine now, and his memories seemed like ghosts. As though they had happened to other people. Actors in a play, written to scare future generations.

"Mind if I join you?" asked Claire. She was wearing a large winter coat, and in her hand was an unopened packet of cigarettes. Michel offered her one of his own, which she accepted, putting her own packet back into her pocket. There was a gentle breeze coming in off the field, and Claire pulled the collar of her coat close around her neck as Michel lit a cigarette and passed it to her.

"This is a hard day for you, Michel, isn't it?" she said after a while.

"Not really," he replied with a sigh. "But it is hard for Nicole. You see, Claire, I'm not a brave man. A bit like my father in that respect. I saw very little that night because I hid my eyes. But Nicole refused to look away. And it has haunted her ever since."

Claire touched his shoulder reassuringly. And for the next few minutes, they stood in silence, staring out across the field as their cigarettes burned away.

Everyone was once again sitting at the table. Michel tapped a knife against his glass, calling for silence. Nicole looked at him crossly, the way one would at a mischievous child. She was not comfortable at being so obviously the centre of attention. Noticing, Michel looked away, and Nicole quietly cleared her throat.

"As I was saying," she said softly, slowly looking around the table to make sure everyone was ready, "it was not the Devil." She looked at the children and smiled. "Quite a relief, I can tell you."

Eva and Belle giggled.

"The two men were soldiers, British soldiers, and the one who had been carried was badly injured. I don't know how old he was because there was a lot of blood covering his face, but the other man, the one who had carried him, was young. Maybe twenty. I looked at this man who had walked from a burning town, carrying his friend on his shoulder, and he smiled at me as though he had done nothing special. And though I was scared, I smiled too because he made me feel safe.

"The injured man had been placed against the wall, and I could see blood on his jacket. He was very pale. He was talking to Father and his friend while Mother went to the kitchen to fetch water and some towels. When she returned, the first man wet the towels and pushed them beneath the bleeding man's coat. He grimaced but didn't complain. Then, my parents and the two men talked quickly, as though there wasn't much time. Their French was quite good, and my parents spoke English well."

Nicole stopped and took a sip from her wine.

"Suddenly, the injured man introduced himself, as though we were somehow meeting at a party. His name was Adam, and he apologised for ruining our towels. It was so ridiculous that my mother and father started to laugh. And it was a beautiful sound. Our parents introduced themselves, and after that, they were quiet for a while. Then, Mother turned to the other man and asked him his name."

Chapter 6

Ian and Ellie

On Friday morning, Ian went straight to Brian's office. He handed him the article he'd just printed from his laptop and then went to make a cup of coffee. Fifteen minutes later, Brian called him back to the office. He did not look impressed.

"This looks like a piece on mental health issues," he said as Ian stood across the desk from him. "I thought we were looking into the military imposter, not why people are lonely." He looked calm, but Ian could tell he wasn't. "You've got something about the guy, at least, but you don't even mention his name."

"I didn't think it was fair to use his name," replied Ian.

"It's not fair to pretend to be a war hero either, is it?" snapped Brian. "What's his name anyway?"

Ian could see where this was heading. "Thomas Mirren," he replied. "But we don't know for certain that he wasn't in the army."

"Did you find him in the military records?" barked Brian, and Ian shook his head. "So, he wasn't in the army then, was he?" Brian re-read the story as Ian stood there, unsure if he was required to stay or go.

After a few minutes, Brian looked up from the sheet of paper. "It's salvageable," he announced, shooing Ian out of the door.

When Ian got back to his desk, he just sat there. He had a bad feeling about what had just happened. Salvageable. The word filled him with dread. Surely Brian wouldn't re-write his piece? No, even Brian wouldn't stoop that low. Nonetheless, he wished he hadn't mentioned Thomas Mirren by name.

"Where do you want to eat?" asked Ian.

He made a point of meeting Ellie, who was studying at the local college, for lunch once a week. It was Ian's favourite day. They could chat, and he could forget about work. He would ask her questions and she would answer, not like at home where she seemed to have her phone permanently in her hand. On these occasions, it would be on the table instead— within view, of course, but at least away from her fingers.

He unbuttoned his coat. It was warm today, so he'd decided to wear his lighter coat. Not the padded monstrosity he wore most days during the colder months. Debbie and Ellie always teased him when he wore that coat, calling him Scott of the Antarctic. He'd shake his head, acting annoyed, but he secretly enjoyed it. It was good to be noticed.

"La Rocca?" replied Ellie. Given a choice, she always opted for La Rocca. Ian didn't mind; he liked Italian food, especially the penne carbonara served at La Rocca. Quick, filling, and cheap, it ticked all the boxes. Ellie would go for the arrabiata; he was sure of that.

He smiled as Ellie linked her arm through his, and they strolled along the narrow street, heading away from his office and towards the park. She was like a mini Debbie—beautiful and thoughtful. Though she was as tall as her mother now, she would always be his baby girl.

They walked in silence as they passed the new council building on their left, then turned up the short path flanked by old stone cottages and abandoned shops. Ian had always liked those cottages, with their weather-beaten fronts and deep-set windows. If he'd been single, they were precisely the kind of house he would have bought, set back from the bustle of the streets but close enough to be convenient for work. But they were also small and he wasn't single, so he would never have one. No, he'd stick to his big new-build, with its central heating and walls so thin that he could hear the arguments of his neighbours.

At the end of the path, they came out into the park. It was more a small expanse of grass than a park with its few trees and benches but that's what everyone called it. The early morning rain had left the ground damp, and short pieces of grass stuck to their shoes as they walked. A few metres away on one of the benches, a couple of teenagers were talking, eating fast food, and dropping their empty boxes onto the ground next to them. Ian shook his head sadly, glancing at the bin less than six feet away. Ellie cursed.

"Just ignore them," said Ian, but Ellie was too much like her mother for that.

"Put your rubbish in the bin," she said angrily as they walked past. Ian recognised them as the two teenagers he'd seen a couple of days ago laughing and swearing.

The girl swore at them. Predictable. But then, to Ian's surprise, the boy picked up the boxes and took them to the bin.

"Happy?" he said to Ellie as he walked back to the bench. Ellie didn't say anything but as they carried on across the grass, Ian could see she was smiling.

It didn't take them long to reach La Rocca from the park, and very soon they were seated.

La Rocca was a pleasant enough restaurant. It had been there for as long as Ian could remember, and he and Debbie had spent many an enjoyable evening there before Ellie was born. After her arrival, evenings out became something of a rarity until they stopped going out altogether. They drank and cooked at home now, which wasn't quite the same.

"I was proud of you back there, Ellie," said Ian after a quick glance at the menu. "I always find it easier to say nothing."

Ellie smiled. "I know them, so it wasn't a big deal."

"How do you know them?"

"They both went to my college but they soon dropped out."

"What do they do now?" he asked.

"Slag people off online, from what I've heard," Ellie replied. "They'll post something, then ten minutes later they'll have forgotten all about it."

When Ian asked why they would do that, Ellie shrugged. "Anger? Communication? I don't know," she said. "They think the world's out to get them."

Ian couldn't begin to understand, and that made him feel old. To change the topic, he asked Ellie what she wanted to eat, and when she said arrabiata, he laughed out loud.

"Penne carbonara?" she asked with a grin, and Ian nodded. "Touché."

Over the course of the meal, it became apparent to Ellie that something was on her father's mind. He had never been one to keep things from her or her mother, so she asked him what was wrong. Ian looked at her but didn't reply.

"Well, you can keep quiet all lunchtime if that helps, or you can tell me what's wrong." The corners of her mouth curled into a grin. "You know you're going to tell me sooner or later anyway."

They both knew that was the truth. Ian sighed before reluctantly explaining to Ellie what had taken place with Brian that morning, what he had written, and what Brian had said.

"Salvageable, eh?" said Ellie, rolling the word around in her mouth. "That doesn't sound good."

Ian had a pretty good idea what Brian intended to do, but he still hoped to be wrong.

Their food arrived with a small basket of bread rolls, and for a moment at least, they were distracted from the conversation. Ian spent the next couple of minutes cutting the bread rolls in half, then applying so much butter to each piece that Ellie pulled a face and told him to stop. Inevitably, the conversation turned back to the story.

"I didn't mention the man by name in the article," said Ian, "but I told Brian who it was. I feel stuck between trying to do the right thing and not wanting to lose my job."

Ellie looked at him closely. "So, is there a chance you could lose your job then?" To Ian's surprise, she didn't look overly concerned at the prospect.

"Maybe. I'm not sure. Anyway, what I'm trying to say is that I may not have done the right thing." He paused, biting the inside of his bottom lip. "In fact, I'm pretty sure I haven't."

"We don't always get things right, Dad," she said. "*You* don't always get things right. But that's okay because when you do, you're pretty great." There wasn't much Ian could say to that, so he reached across the table and squeezed her hand.

"Thank you," he said, and he really meant it. "It's a shit job anyway."

Ellie wasn't accustomed to hearing her father swear and was caught between a gasp and a laugh, the result of which was a fine spray of arrabiata sauce spattering onto the tablecloth in front of her. She looked so shocked at the crimson stain, like specks of blood, that Ian laughed and nearly did the same. Ellie quickly poured some water onto the stain while Ian wiped it with his napkin.

"There," he said. "No one will notice."

"Except anyone who can see," replied Ellie, moving the basket of bread to cover it.

The waiter came over and asked them if everything was okay.

"Everything's perfect, thank you," Ellie answered.

At one o'clock, Ian said goodbye to Ellie. He watched her as she walked away, her long auburn hair tied back, a brightly-coloured backpack slung casually over one shoulder. She was a young woman now, dispensing wisdom in the same easy manner as her mother, and he wondered just when she had become so grown up. As she turned the corner, she waved to him.

"Take the roads back, not the industrial estate," Ian shouted.

She smiled but he was sure she hadn't heard him. Then, she disappeared.

He had come to a couple of decisions over lunch: the first was easy—he just had to see Thomas Mirren; the second would be more challenging.

Inside the supermarket, he looked for Thomas Mirren and his friend. At first, he couldn't see them. The usual spot for their table was now empty and in its place was a yellow sign warning of a slippery floor. As a result, he turned to leave, but as he was doing so, he noticed another table further away, near the cafe. There they were. One of them was wearing a blue blazer, while the other was wrapped in a massive winter coat. It looked like they were ready to leave, so Ian hurried over.

"Thank you," said Thomas Mirren as Ian handed him a ten pound note. "I'm afraid we don't have any change." He rummaged around in his pockets to try to find some.

Ian shook his head. "Call it interest for not paying you on time," he said with a smile.

"That's a very high rate of interest." Thomas laughed and turned to Frank. "You're the numbers man, Frank," he said. "What rate of interest would that be?"

Frank thought about it for a moment, then grinned. "A lot."

Thomas nodded, then turned back to Ian. "He's a mathematical prodigy, our Frank." He told Ian he would give him the change the next time they met.

Ian shook Thomas's hand and left the supermarket. He didn't doubt Thomas's words about the change for one minute.

Walking back across the park, Ian was in an excellent mood. His lunch with Ellie had been great and he had paid his debt to Thomas Mirren. He'd meant to ask the old man about his time in the army, but when the opportunity had arisen, he'd decided against it. It was silly really—he was a journalist after all—but for some reason, he wasn't comfortable asking. As though it was an intrusion.

He decided to take a detour before returning to the office, to pick something up for Debbie. He'd be late back to work and Brian would be angry, but he didn't care. Not caring about what Brian thought was a nice feeling.

The shopping precinct was always busy and the shops were invariably full. Not the best shops but they served their purpose, providing a wide range of goods so that Ian rarely had to travel far to get what he needed. There were a lot of phone shops, and if you liked coffee and cheaply priced birthday cards, it was the ideal place. There had been an independent record shop at the far end, but that had closed down a few years ago, replaced by a large HMV. The HMV had closed recently too. It was now a confectioner, selling cakes and a dazzling array of sweets. It was to there that Ian headed, and ten minutes later, he was in possession of a large box of chocolates, made by a company he'd never heard of but with a foreign name which made them sound exotic.

"Would you like a bag?" asked the lady behind the counter. Ian shook his head, reaching out with his credit card. "Card machine's broken," apologised the lady, forcing him to hand over the remainder of his cash. He'd have to go to the bank now, as he didn't like to be without at least some money in his wallet. Fortunately, there was a bank next to his office. That was another thing the town centre had plenty of.

By the time Ian made it back to the office, he'd been out for an hour and a half. Jean raised an eyebrow at him as he walked through the door, tutting playfully.

"Brian wouldn't be happy," she said, tapping her watch theatrically.

"That's fine," replied Ian, "I need to speak to him anyway."

"Not today. He's out for the afternoon. Won't be back until Monday."

Usually, this would have been good news for Ian, but today he'd finally decided to stick up for himself. He needed to make sure Thomas Mirren wasn't named in his story.

"What's he up to?"

"Not sure." Jean shrugged. "But he was quite excited. I think he's meeting someone from the *Chronicle*."

Ellie was going to be late for her lecture. She'd been late to the same one last week too. As she saw it, she had two options: firstly, she could take the usual route up Knox Road, along Winstanley and then round the sports centre; or secondly, across the industrial estate. The first way, she would definitely be late. But her dad didn't like her going across the industrial estate and she didn't like to make him worried.

Just then, her phone pinged, and a message appeared on the screen. It was from Lucy.

"You'd better hurry up or Dr Banner is going to eat you alive!" The message was followed by several emojis of an angry face.

It wasn't good to make Dr Banner angry.

So, it was decided. At the top of the road, rather than turning right onto Knox Road, she continued straight into the industrial estate.

In the past, it had been an impressive place with a steady stream of lorries passing through the large, wrought-iron gates. The stream was now no more than a trickle, one an hour, if that. All sorts of buildings had lined the main road, from steelworks to bootmakers, carpenters' workshops and even a small paper mill. At the end of the road were cavernous warehouses, and these were now the only buildings still in use, the others standing derelict like tired husks in bombed-out cities. Halfway to the warehouses was a short path at the end of which was the college and Dr Banner's fiery temper.

As Ellie walked along, she heard a noise behind her. She turned to see a large yellow truck thundering up the road. It hooted its horn as it passed, and Ellie coughed at the cloud of dust thrown up from its tyres. She huffed and brushed herself off. At least there shouldn't be another one for a while. Taking her earphones from her bag, she placed one bud in each ear and turned on her music. Another message pinged, and she laughed: three smiling faces with a picture of a woman running.

She was nearly at the path now, her fingers tapping away at her phone. She would be at college in two minutes. Then, she stepped into the road.

The driver of the green truck was using his phone too. He didn't feel the impact or hear a thing as Ellie flew through the air and landed back onto the pavement. Two trucks in the same hour—what were the chances of that?

The sun was bright as Ellie looked up from her position by the road. She couldn't move or feel anything. She wondered where she was. Her phone pinged, and she groaned. And then everything went black.

Chapter 7

Thomas

Thomas Mirren was running late. He'd returned home after the supermarket but had arranged to meet Frank and the Colonel at the Legion. He wasn't bothered about being late but he didn't want to miss out on the first round, as it was Frank's. As he saw it, he had two options: firstly, around Brier Drive, then up Cyprus Road and past the cricket ground; or secondly, past the college and through the old industrial estate. He'd be damned if he was going to miss Frank's round, so he set off towards the college.

It must have been time for afternoon lectures to start—students everywhere, darting through doorways and tapping away on their phones. Thomas didn't have a phone. He had one at home, of course, Ellen had insisted on it, but he couldn't see much point in carrying one around. He didn't like talking to people at the best of times, so why make it easier for them?

The path from the college to the industrial estate was long and overgrown. Perhaps that was why so few people used it.

Or maybe it was overgrown *because* so few people used it. Either way, Thomas used it a lot. Walking through the industrial estate, with its broken buildings and cracked pavements, he was reminded of Italy and France back in the day. It made him feel oddly nostalgic, even though he'd spent much of his life trying to forget those times.

As he emerged from the path, he heard a pinging sound. He looked around to see who was there. He couldn't see anyone. Then, he heard the sound again. A short distance away, he saw a phone lying on the ground. Next to it was a young girl.

He walked over to the girl, and the phone pinged again, its screen lighting up to reveal a smiling face. Picking up the phone, the words *Enter Pin Number* flashed up on the screen.

Standing next to the girl, he couldn't help but notice how dusty she was, as though she'd been rolling around in sand. He took a handkerchief from his pocket, unfolded it, then wiped it across her face, feeling her soft breath against his hand. Well, at least she wasn't dead. That was a start.

A short distance away was a brightly coloured backpack, battered and torn and revealing a few books and a pencil case. Thomas picked up one of the books and looked at the cover. *Ellie Rogers, U6A.* Next to the name was a crude drawing of a smiling face—two black dots and an upturned mouth.

"So, Ellie Rogers," he said as he knelt beside her, "are you able to talk?" The girl let out a small groan and opened her eyes. He waited, silence stretching out between them, and he wondered if perhaps she was in shock. "Okay then," he continued, "I'll do the talking."

Wiping his hands on the handkerchief, he placed his right hand against her forehead. He wasn't sure why but he'd seen it done in a film when he was a boy.

"You've got yourself into a spot of bother, Ellie," he said, "but everything will be fine. I'm not sure anyone's coming along any time soon, so we need to get you to the college." He looked at the college buildings in the distance, grey and unwelcoming, and he estimated them to be several hundred metres away. "I don't have a phone, I'm afraid," he said apologetically, "so, it looks like I'm going to have to carry you." The girl stared up at him, then rolled onto her side and vomited.

After wiping clean her mouth and making sure she wasn't choking, Thomas stood and went to collect her bag. It was still useable. Putting the phone inside, he added the books and the pencil case. When he got back to the girl, she was shaking, so he sat her up and took off his blazer. Placing it over her shoulders, he continued to talk to her. It was good to keep talking, not only for the girl but for him too. It had been a long time since he'd carried anyone. He wasn't even sure if he could.

"Well, I won't know unless I try," he muttered quietly to himself.

Placing the straps of the backpack across one shoulder, he slowly bent down to the girl. With one arm under her shoulders and the other behind her legs, he gently lifted her off the ground.

"There, that wasn't so bad, was it?" he said as he turned and headed off towards the path.

Ellie could hear the man's voice, gentle and calming, but she couldn't see him. She knew her eyes were open because she could see light; but there was no detail, nothing to show her who the man was or why he was talking to her. And she remembered being sick. But she didn't feel ill. Strange. And why was her body hurting so much? She was going to be late for her lecture, and Dr Banner would be livid.

Daniel was sitting behind his desk in reception. Lectures were finishing in about twenty minutes, so if he were going to have time for a cigarette, he'd have to go soon. Putting on his jacket, he took one final look at the video monitors. Pictures flickered from shadowy hallways to deserted staircases like an old video game in which you had to survive a night in a haunted house. He checked his pockets for the cigarettes, then made his way over to the large table in the centre of the foyer. He'd spent the last hour unboxing the Open Day brochures and getting them exactly how he wanted them on the desk. With one final adjustment so that they were positioned precisely, he smiled to himself and turned to leave.

Then, he stopped. There was something coming towards the college. At first, it was just a shape; a figure emerging from the path that ran from the industrial estate. But as the figure came closer, he could see it was a man. He had a backpack across his shoulder and was carrying someone in his arms. As the man got closer, Daniel could see he looked old, so he rushed to the door to help him. But the man continued, walking past him, and gently laying the young girl on the desk in the middle of the foyer as Open Day brochures tumbled to the floor.

"This one needs medical assistance," said the old man simply, and it was like a command. "I imagine she's been hit by a truck or at least some form of vehicle."

Daniel rushed over to the table. When he got there, he gasped. It was Ellie Rogers, U6A. She was covered in dust and clearly injured, with grazes to her face and her right arm bent unnaturally at her side. She reminded Daniel of a discarded doll, and it was all he could do not to look away. Around her shoulders was a blue blazer, an enamel poppy pinned to the lapel. It was too big for her and made her look like a child. Fumbling in his pocket, he located his phone. It was next to his cigarettes.

"Thank you so much for helping her," said Daniel as he turned to face the old man. "Can I take your name?"

But there was no one there, just a torn backpack leaning against the wall.

"Christ, Thomas!" Frank laughed as Thomas walked through the door of the Legion. "Have you suddenly become a chionophile?" Thomas stood there, confused. "Someone or something who doesn't feel the cold," explained Frank. He'd been reading his 'Word of the Day' calendar again.

"Blazer?" The Colonel smiled.

Thomas grunted. "It's got a tear in it," he lied. "Must have caught it on something yesterday."

The Colonel looked at him suspiciously as Frank handed over a drink. "Didn't want you to miss out on the round."

Thomas grinned. "The thought hadn't crossed my mind."

The three of them were meeting that day to discuss the forthcoming Remembrance Day parade. Being the senior officer in the town, the Colonel always arranged it. He would march at the front, chest weighed down by medals, as dozens of ex-soldiers followed. Thomas always walked next to him; the Colonel insisted on it. But Thomas never wore his medals.

Frank was adamant he should carry the wreath this year, informing his two friends that it had been a long time since he'd last had that honour.

"I thought Frank carried it last year," said Thomas to the Colonel, and the Colonel nodded.

"Oh no, you bloody well don't," said Frank. "That was Peters. And you know it."

Thomas looked across at Frank, eyebrows raised in puzzlement. "Peters hasn't got any arms, Frank."

"Legs, Thomas," he said. "He doesn't have any legs."

The Colonel was chuckling into his beer as Thomas tried his best not to laugh. "Well, I've got no problem with you carrying it then," he said at last. "If you think those spindly, blanket-folding arms can lift it."

Frank stuck up two fingers, and the three of them laughed together.

There were over two weeks until the big day, and there was still a lot to organise. In general, Thomas left those sorts of things to Frank and the Colonel; he didn't much like details and arrangements. Of course, he would never miss the day itself. It was too important—a time to remember all the things he wanted to forget.

"Let me know if you want me to do anything," he said.

"Don't you remember what happened the last time you *helped*, Thomas?" Frank guffawed. Thomas did remember, of course. The previous year, he'd been responsible for sourcing post-parade food, none of which had turned up. It was another thing he tried hard to forget. The Colonel placed a hand on his shoulder, gently squeezing it as he smiled benignly.

"There are many things you're good at, Thomas. *Very* good. But administration isn't one of them."

Well, at least he'd offered.

For the next hour, Frank and the Colonel discussed the details of the parade—what time they would meet, where they would start from, and so on. They rambled on, and Thomas wondered why they bothered; it was the same time and place every year. The same people, the same wreath provider, same photographer, same everything. But it seemed to make them happy.

At three o'clock, they left the Legion. It had started to rain, and small drops of water dripped from the metal sign above the door. The Colonel pulled them inside and asked them to wait. He'd forgotten to pick something up. A few moments later, he returned carrying a blue raincoat which he handed to Thomas. It was too small, and Thomas's arms poked out several inches from the end of the sleeves.

"Arms like a bloody gorilla," said Frank, watching Thomas zip up the coat and straighten the collar. He was just about to step out into the road when Thomas grabbed him and quickly pulled him back onto the pavement. A small white car sped silently past.

It was fortunate for Frank that Thomas had such long arms.

Chapter 8

Nicole and Michel

1943

Nicole's mother was staring at the man, but he didn't reply. So, she asked him again.

"What is your name, sir?"

"They call me the Camel," he replied simply. Nicole Moreau watched as he pressed the towels against his friend's wound.

She crawled over to her parents and looked at the man. "That's a funny name," she said. "Why do they call you the Camel?"

He reached into his breast pocket and pulled out a packet of cigarettes. "Perhaps because of these," he said, showing her the picture of a camel emblazoned on the front of the packet.

He reached into his other breast pocket and pulled out a small toy. "Or perhaps because of this." It was a small figurine made of lead with rough, chipped paint: a camel. A small drop of blood fell onto the base from a cut on his hand. He apologised and held it out towards her. "Please take it," he said, handing her the figure. "I've had it for years, but I'm not sure I'll need it where I'm going."

"Where are you going?" asked Nicole. She was met with silence.

As Nicole turned the camel over in her hands, inspecting it from every angle in the dim light, Adam shifted and cleared his throat.

"You shouldn't believe a word he says." He laughed. "The real reason we call him the Camel is because he never stops. No matter what you do to him or how badly hurt he is, he never stops." He sighed and closed his eyes. "Oh, and he's stubborn. *Very* stubborn."

Nicole thought he'd fallen asleep, but the Camel reached over to him and placed his right hand onto his forehead, pressing down gently until his friend's eyes opened. He then stood and went to the table to fetch more water, and when he came back, he was smiling. He placed a bowl of water next to Nicole's mother and then turned to face her.

"You can call me Thomas Haven, if you prefer," he said.

A few minutes later, there was an explosion in the village, and the Camel moved over to the window. "I expect they'll be here within the hour," he said, glancing at his watch. It was a quarter past eight. Looking at Nicole and Michel's parents, he asked if there was anywhere in the house for the family to hide. Nicole's father pointed to a small hole in the corner of the ceiling.

"There is a small room next to the bedroom, above that hole. We can pull a wardrobe across the door so no one will find us if we're quiet. But it is not big."

"Don't worry," said the Camel, "I'll be staying down here."

"Me too," said the other man. "I'll be more help down here."

The Camel laughed. "Remember the last time you *helped* me, Adam?" he said. "I ended up carrying you up that bloody hill." He turned to Nicole's father. "Make sure everyone's quiet. And make sure when this is all over, you get Adam out of here safely. He's going to be an important man one day."

He explained to everyone that he'd have to make the house look as though it had been abandoned, and as they made their way up the stairs, he set about breaking furniture and overturning tables. He smashed some windows and tore at the curtains. When he had finished, he went up the stairs too and pulled a large wardrobe across the door to the small room.

"If this goes better than I'm expecting," he said through the wardrobe, "I'll return one day to say hello. In better times."

He returned to the main room and lit a cigarette.

Then, he waited.

At around nine o'clock, the first wave arrived. The Camel finished his cigarette and threw it onto the floor before picking up his rifle and leaving the house. In the small room above, Adam held a finger to his lips as Nicole pushed her eye against the small hole in the floor to see what was happening. She could see the centre of the room but little else: smashed furniture and a smouldering cigarette.

Suddenly, there were several loud bangs. And then, just as quickly, it was quiet again. Moments later, the door opened, and she heard footsteps. Nicole had been holding her breath, scared to make a sound. She exhaled loudly as the Camel walked into the centre of the room. He looked up and smiled.

"Four down, plenty more to go," he said, sitting on the floor. "Oh, and only two more bullets."

Adam cursed from the corner of the room. "Bloody madman."

It wasn't long before the next lot arrived. Once again, the Camel stood. He picked up his rifle and then looked to the ceiling.

"Don't forget to be quiet," he said. "No matter what you see or hear, don't make a sound. They mustn't find you." He took one last look around the room. "And make sure Adam is okay." And with that, he was gone.

A little later, there were two shots followed by a great deal of shouting. Something broke and then the door opened. Soon, Nicole heard footsteps, more than before, and then she saw the men. There were seven of them in total—the Camel and six others. The other men did not look happy.

For the next few minutes, the men punched and kicked the Camel and hit him with their rifles, trying to gain information. They asked where the owners of the house were and what a British soldier was doing there. At first, they spoke in German, then French, and finally in English. But he said nothing. Several men were sent to search the house. Nicole could hear them in the bedroom next door, opening drawers and laughing as they smashed and stole everything they could find. The wardrobe door next to their tiny room opened, and she held her breath, her eyes tightly shut as tears streamed down her face.

And then they were gone.

Downstairs, the soldiers talked urgently among themselves. Their commander, a tall man with dark hair and broad shoulders, kept asking the Camel what a British soldier was doing in Saint Martin. He seemed to have lost interest in who might be in the house, perhaps because the search had revealed nothing. But he was fixated on the Camel. At first, his questioning was calm, very much in keeping with his pristine appearance, the clean uniform, and brightly polished boots. But as the silence continued, he became more and more agitated until finally he struck the Camel with his pistol. Blood sprayed onto the commander's jacket, and he roared with disgust. At that point, he signalled to one of the soldiers out of sight for Nicole who was still hiding in her tiny room. He was handed a short leather whip coiled around itself and fastened with a metal clip. The commander made another signal, and two soldiers took hold of the Camel and forced him onto one of the dining room chairs. They sat him backwards, tying him so that his shoulders and back faced the commander with his eyes facing the wall. Then, they tore off his shirt.

After the first few hits, Nicole felt like vomiting. The sound of whip on flesh, the trails of blood, and the stoic silence of the young English soldier was almost too much for her to bear. She held her hand to her mouth as she gazed through the small hole in the floor. The Camel, his back and shoulders streaming with blood, still refused to speak. Staring straight ahead as blow after blow landed, he seemed on the verge of fainting when suddenly his piercing blue eyes lifted and met Nicole's. He smiled. And then he was gone.

The last thing she saw of the Camel was his bloodied body being dragged towards the door. Someone spat at the chair, and there was the sound of furniture breaking.

Then, finally, there was silence.

Nicole and Michel, 2014

Nicole didn't say anything for a while. Michel put his arm around her shoulder.

"The Camel is dead," she said simply. "I have long hoped he would come back to say hello, as he said, but I know that will not happen. But, because of him, I have this man." She kissed Michel on the cheek. Then, she looked around the room, her eyes resting on each person in turn. "And all of you here."

It was the same story each year, and they could recite it by heart. But it was good to hear and something they would always do. It was the least they owed the man who had saved their family.

Later that afternoon, Michel was once again standing at the back of the house, cigarette in hand, staring into the distance. And once again, Claire joined him.

"He would be in his nineties now," said Michel after a while. He wanted to say more but he didn't have the strength.

"Perhaps he *is* in his nineties," said Claire. "Have you considered that?"

"We all did," he said. "My parents and us two children. But Nicole was the only one to see him, and though she has never described what she saw in detail, she assures us he couldn't have survived." He sighed sadly. "No matter how much we want it to be so."

Michel was mentally and physically tired. Although it was a day he enjoyed—the whole family being together always made him happy—it was also a hard day for him and Nicole. Not only did he think about that day with the Camel, but it also reminded him of his parents and the hole their passing had left. They had survived the war and remained at the house, but the sense of debt had weighed heavily on them both. It had been hard for them to owe so much yet be unable to repay it. It was his parents who had set aside this day each year, but it had always been Nicole who told the story.

"What happened to Adam?" asked Claire, finishing her cigarette.

"I don't know," replied Michel. "He was hurt, and he stayed with us for several days. Then, one day, he told us he was okay to walk and it was time for him to leave. He thanked us, said goodbye, and left. And that was the last we saw of him. When my parents had asked him where he would go, he'd told them about someone in the town who could help him get home. We didn't ask who, and he didn't tell us. I suppose it was safer that way. I don't think he was really over what had happened to his friend."

"I don't think he's the only one to feel that way," said Claire, looking at Nicole through the window.

It was going to be another beautiful evening. It was six-thirty and the sun had started its slow descent through the sky behind Saint Martin. This had always been Michel's favourite part of the day, at least as an adult. There was a peacefulness and a sense of satisfaction that another day had passed safely. He was happy, his family was happy, and that was all that mattered.

"Are you coming inside?" Claire asked.

Michel nodded. They were getting ready to go home, and he could see Victor through the window, yawning in the big armchair by the fire. Eva and Belle were chasing each other around the room, and Nicole was laughing as Jean-Luc tried in vain to calm them down. Marie was moving the last of the dishes from the table, and it struck Michel once again how much she resembled Nicole at her age. Even her mannerisms were the same—the clipped laugh and the roll of the eyes. The apple had not fallen far from the tree, he thought to himself. It was good that she wasn't like her father.

By eight o'clock, Nicole and Michel were once again alone. It had taken some time to tidy the house but it was finally done. Sitting by the fire, they drank coffee and ate leftovers from lunch.

"I often wonder what happened to Adam," said Michel, thinking back to his conversation with Claire.

Nicole shrugged. It was a war, after all. He could have died, or he could still be alive. It was not something she concerned herself with. He had spoken very little in the days following the death of the Camel, and through no fault of his own, had acted as a reminder to her of what she had witnessed through the floorboards. It was a relief to her when he'd finally left. But she hoped it had worked out well for him. That was what the Camel had wanted, so it was what she wanted too.

"I imagine he's fine," she said as she stared into the fire. "For him, the war was over. At least the fighting. He is perhaps now sitting like us, drinking coffee, and wondering where all the years have gone." She paused for a moment. "Well, I hope so anyway."

It was dark outside and quiet. Every so often, a dog would bark in the woods or a gust of wind would rattle the kitchen windows. Inside, there were two sounds: the crackling of the fire and the loud slurps as Michel drank his coffee. Long ago, the slurping had irritated her, but over the years, Nicole had given up scolding him until it became a comfort—a familiar irritation, and one that she missed when he was not there.

She looked at the mantlepiece and smiled at the photographs lined up once again in a neat row, electric lamp light shining off the glass. She could see Michel's reflection in one with his coffee cup pressed to his lips, preparing for another slurp, and she laughed.

"Would you like to exchange that coffee for a glass of wine?" she asked.

Michel's whole face seemed to smile. "That sounds like an excellent idea, Sister, but please allow me to fetch it." He put down his coffee, and Nicole chuckled to herself as he headed out of the room and along the corridor to the small pantry where they kept their wine. They had several expensive bottles but many more of lesser quality, and she wondered which one he would bring.

Five minutes later, he was back, shuffling into the room with two glasses and a bottle of their finest red.

"Pushing the boat out, aren't you?" She laughed as Michel shook his head.

"Only the best on this day," he said, opening the bottle and pouring two large glasses. Nicole nodded silently, both smiling as they raised their glasses.

As they drank their wine and toasted absent friends, Michel pointed to the figurine of the camel, now standing once more between the photographs above the fire.

"Should I take it back to the loft?" he asked. "It's about that time."

Nicole shook her head. "Not just yet. I'd like to keep it down here for a while, if that's okay with you." Michel didn't like going into the loft, so he was happy for the camel to remain where it was.

"I'm not sure why," said Nicole as she leaned back in her chair and took a sip of her wine, "but this time feels different."

Chapter 9

Ian

Ian's phone rang again. He'd purposely not answered the previous calls from Debbie, as he needed to finish his email to Brian. She would understand once he explained. It hadn't occurred to him that something may be wrong, but as his phone started up again, he suddenly felt uneasy. Debbie wouldn't ring so many times, so saving the email to draft, he reached for his phone.

"Sorry I didn't answer before," he started, "but I've been working on—"

"Ian!" shouted Debbie down the phone, alarm bells immediately ringing in Ian's head. "Come to the hospital." Debbie sounded distraught, and as Ian started to ask what was wrong, she cut him off again. "It's Ellie."

The line went dead, and with it came a surge of emotions: fear and confusion, but above all, dread. Debbie hadn't given any detail; he didn't even know if Ellie was alive. Without thinking, Ian was on his feet and putting on his coat. He'd never heard Debbie so alarmed, and it was that, more than what she hadn't said, that made him realise how serious things were.

His mind was racing as he left the building. Rushing through the door, he wondered if he should tell someone he had to leave. But his legs kept on running, and a moment later, he was outside and halfway across the car park. He wondered what could have happened to Ellie. He'd only left her an hour or two ago, so surely not much. But Debbie's voice...

Arriving at his car, he jumped in and closed his eyes. A deep breath followed by several more. He needed to calm himself down. He'd be no use to anyone if he turned up in a state. Trying to think logically, he replayed their meeting— he'd last seen Ellie at just gone one o'clock, and it was now around three. She'd walked to college and would have been there ever since. So, by way of deduction, she must have hurt herself at college. A fall, perhaps; nothing more. The trip to the hospital must have been a precaution.

He was feeling much better as he finally set off, driving a little faster than usual but nothing excessive. Turning the radio on, he selected one of the relaxing playlists, flicking through the tracks until he came across one he liked: "Pie Jesu" by Sarah Brightman. Christ, that woman had a beautiful voice. Wasn't she a dancer too? He was so preoccupied that when he looked up, he'd almost run over an old man by the side of the road. It was one of the poppy sellers, and he noticed Thomas Mirren behind him, still with a hold on his coat after hauling him unceremoniously onto the pavement. There was another man there too, and that one was laughing. He'd have to remember to apologise the next time he saw them.

The journey to the hospital took about half an hour. The place itself was outside of the town, the old hospital in Kingsley having closed a few years ago to make way for new housing. There had been a chorus of complaints at the time, and Ian had joined them, but as usual, no one had listened. So, now there were more people in Kingsley and one less hospital.

A sudden downpour of rain, no sooner started than it had finished, had left the tarmac leading up to the hospital smooth and black. The sun reflected off the pristine surface, and Ian had to look away for a moment as small lights blinked at the back of his eyes. Surprisingly, he found a parking space almost immediately, and after purchasing a ticket, made his way to the main reception.

There was something about hospitals that always made him uncomfortable. It wasn't the patients lying on their beds, surrounded by screens, nor the long sterile corridors, with their whitewashed walls and randomly discarded wheelchairs. It was more what a hospital represented: a glimpse into the future when it could be him on a bed with a drip hanging from his arm while doctors and nurses chatted about their lunches and their plans for the weekend.

Shaking the thought from his head, he approached a glass screen behind which sat a very bored-looking man with thick spectacles and a bald head. He looked up from a pile of papers and smiled at Ian.

"Hello, sir. What can I do for you today?" His voice was deep and rich, and it sounded wrong coming from the person in front of him.

"Ellie Rogers," he said quietly. "Is she here?"

"Rogers," said the man, tapping his pen against the papers as he scanned the list on his desk. "Ellie Rogers." It seemed to take forever, but eventually he nodded, then looked up. "Ward six. Down the corridor and left at the end. It's the third on the right."

Ian thanked him, and as he turned to leave, he heard the man tapping on the glass with his pen. He pointed to a bottle of hand gel attached to a nearby wall, and Ian nodded, applying a large dollop to each hand. The man smiled, then put down his pen and returned to his papers.

Halfway down the long corridor, the hand gel was starting to dry. At first, it had felt greasy, and Ian had wanted to wash his hands. But soon it was gone and his hands felt smooth and dry.

Left at the bottom of the corridor, then third on the right. As he turned the corner, the corridors became busy. Nurses in light blue uniforms moved smoothly between rooms, pushing wheelchairs and carrying charts. None of them looked up, and Ian wondered how they avoided bumping into each other. Some form of radar, he thought, then smiled at the idea, absurd as it was. As he passed a large room with six beds, three on either side, he stopped for a moment and watched as a large man leaned unsteadily on a male nurse. The nurse was lithe and sinewy and seemed to take the larger man's weight as if it were no burden at all. As they moved towards the toilet, the nurse chatting away to the other man, Ian wondered how someone could do that job and how caring such a person must be.

As he reached a room with 'Ward 6' written on a plastic sign by the door, Ian slowed his pace. He was suddenly nervous about what he would find. Looking at the sign, about twelve inches across, he could see the word 'Ward' was printed, but the number six had been written by hand, as though the room was not always the same number. It seemed odd, and he wondered why that might be.

And then he saw Debbie.

Standing next to a bed by the window, she was looking directly at him, her head to one side and her mouth slightly open. He could see straight away that she had been crying. The bed next to her was empty.

Ian pushed through the door to the ward and raced to her side.

"They've taken her away," Debbie said quietly as Ian held her. It seemed unreal, like it was happening to somebody else. Why had they done that? She'd only fallen over.

They stood there like that for a long time as Debbie sobbed and Ian hugged her. Finally, she pulled away and signalled for him to sit. He realised he hadn't said a word since he'd arrived; she needed more from him than that.

"What happened?" asked Ian, and Debbie joined him on the bed.

She told him all she knew: it appeared Ellie had been hit by a car, or at least some type of vehicle. She'd been taken to the college, and they'd telephoned for an ambulance. The college had telephoned her, and she'd come straight to the hospital. When she'd arrived at the hospital, Ellie had already been taken away. Now, they had to wait.

"Yes, but how bad is it?" Ian asked, starting to panic.

"I don't know," replied Debbie. "We just have to wait."

And so, they waited. Neither of them said much as they sat there together on the empty bed. Then, finally, around ten minutes later, a nurse came over. She was wearing a dark blue uniform and her hair was tied neatly into a short ponytail. In her breast pocket were several pens and hanging down was a small watch. She looked so young. Ian realised what she was about to tell them could very well change his life, and he suddenly felt sick.

But then she smiled and he knew everything was alright. Debbie looked at him with such obvious relief that he felt like crying. So many emotions; it was almost too much to handle.

"She'll be here soon," said the nurse. "She's fine, don't worry. The doctor will explain everything." And then she left.

"Are you okay?" Debbie asked. He nodded. As he was about to ask Debbie the same question, he was interrupted by the arrival of the doctor—Dr Sally Jones, according to her name badge. He squeezed Debbie's hand, bracing himself for what Dr Jones was about to say.

"So," said Dr Jones, "Ellie is doing well." Ian exhaled loudly, making Debbie smile. "From the look of her injuries, I would guess she's been involved in a traffic accident, though we're only going off information provided by

Kingsley College. We received a call from them at around half past one, and she arrived here sometime after that." She looked at Debbie. "I assume the college must have called you?"

"That's right," Debbie replied.

"She has sustained fractures to her right arm and collarbone, and we've fixed those, but she'll be in plaster for several weeks. There was some moderate internal bleeding, which was more concerning, but we've introduced clotting stimulants which will deal with that. It looks like there's also some concussion, but it's quite mild, so nothing to worry about. We'll keep her in overnight just to make sure." Dr Jones took a breath before continuing. "The fact she was found and looked after so soon after the accident means she'll make a full recovery."

"And if she hadn't been found so soon?" asked Debbie, her face as pale as the sheets on which they sat.

"Then, we'd likely be having a very different conversation," replied Dr Jones, and it was clear what she meant. She promptly added, "But someone's quick thinking removed the need for *that*."

"Whose exactly?" said Ian.

Dr Jones shrugged. "I have no idea. Perhaps the college can help you with that."

When Ellie arrived in the ward, she was still unconscious. The nurse explained she was on strong pain medication and it would be some time before she came to. They could stay with her but not for too long, as the doctors would soon be doing their afternoon rounds.

Once Ian was assured Ellie was okay and having thought about things for a while, his mind turned to the role of the college. It was frustrating that Debbie and he knew so little about what had happened. So, it was decided that he should go to the college himself to find out more, as well as to thank them. Debbie wanted to stay at the hospital. There was a small room just off the main ward where relatives could wait, so she relocated there. Ian kissed her and told her he'd be back soon before walking to his car.

The drive back to Kingsley was a great deal smoother than his earlier journey. The sun was out, and it was warm enough in the car that he could turn down the heating. Outside, a patchwork of green fields gently undulated like a vast carpet surrounding the town, dotted here and there by large farmhouses and small clumps of trees. Debbie had always wanted to live in the countryside, but he had always been afraid of the isolation.

Soon, he was turning off the narrow country roads and was back on the main streets of Kingsley, lined with old shops and whitewashed houses. He turned onto Smithy Lane, then headed down Middleton Road. At last, he arrived at the college. It was gone five o'clock by this stage and he hoped there would be someone he could talk to. He didn't expect the students to be there, but surely there would still be some staff.

Inside the main entrance hall, he spotted two people talking to each other. One was a middle-aged man in a black hooded top which made him look a little like a burglar. Next to him was a young woman, perhaps in her thirties. She wore a blue suit and square glasses like those worn by newsreaders. She had long black hair hanging loose at her shoulders, and when she saw Ian coming through the door, she smiled. The man next to her looked up. He was wearing a name badge on his burglar top—Daniel Aveneo. The woman was wearing a badge too—Rebecca Method. In the middle of the foyer was a table, brochures strewn untidily across its surface, and Ian thought how disorganised it looked. It didn't give a good impression of the college.

"Hello," said Ian, walking over to Daniel and Rebecca. "I'm Ian Rogers." They looked at him calmly as if they had been expecting his arrival.

"Mr Rogers," said Rebecca, reaching out and shaking his hand. It was a firm handshake. "How is Ellie?"

"She's remarkably well, all considering," he replied. "Broken bones but she'll be okay." He could see the relief on their faces.

"Thank God." Daniel let out a long breath, shaking his head. "She didn't look too good earlier." He looked oddly embarrassed.

"That's what I wanted to talk to someone about," said Ian.

Rebecca nodded to Daniel. "Daniel was here when Ellie was brought in," she said. "Let's go to my office, and he can tell you what happened."

The three of them went out of the foyer and through a large set of double doors. Ian looked into one of the classrooms as he passed. A small group of students were sitting around a table. They were chatting away—it didn't look like much work was getting done—and it reminded him of his own college days.

Rebecca's office could be best described as 'functional'. There was a large desk with a computer monitor and, behind it, a blue fabric chair. Away from the desk was a circular table with a pile of papers in the centre, surrounded by several metal chairs. There were no pictures, and on the far wall was a whiteboard covered in handwriting so illegible it was impossible to read. He wondered if perhaps they were mathematical symbols.

Rebecca, Daniel, and Ian sat at the table. Ian liked Rebecca for that—Brian always insisted on sitting at his desk to emphasise his seniority.

Daniel cleared his throat. "Well, it was me who rang for an ambulance. But that's about as much as I can take credit for."

"Thank you," interjected Ian. "I just want to say that before you start. You may well have saved Ellie's life with your quick thinking." His emotions were welling up again.

Daniel blushed. "No, you misunderstand. All I did was call for an ambulance." He paused for a moment. "The old guy did all the work."

Confused, Ian looked back and forth between Daniel and Rebecca as if he might find clarification in doing so. He asked Daniel what he meant, and while Rebecca looked on as though she were watching a television programme, Daniel recounted the events of the afternoon.

When Daniel was finished, the three of them sat in silence. Ian remembered the untidy table in the foyer, and he pictured Ellie's broken body sprawled on top of it. It was almost too much to bear. Rebecca was staring proudly at Daniel. Even though he had 'just phoned an ambulance', he had played an important role, and Rebecca knew it. So did Ian, who thanked him again, and Daniel looked embarrassed for a third time.

"So," said Ian as Daniel squirmed uncomfortably in his seat, "who was the old man who saved her?"

Daniel shrugged. "I have no idea. One minute, I'm getting ready to go out for a cigarette..."—he glanced sheepishly at Rebecca— "and the next thing I see is poor Ellie being carried up the path from the industrial estate. When he brought her in, I thought she was dead." He looked at Ian and apologised. "Or not very well, at least," he added. "I don't know how he managed to carry her all that way—it's got to be half a mile—but he did. So, if anyone saved Ellie, it was him."

Ian sat in his car, outside the college, the engine still off as he rested his forehead against the steering wheel in thought. Despite everything Daniel had told him, it still wasn't clear what had happened to Ellie, and given that there was no CCTV at the college entrance—a grave oversight, given what had happened—it probably never would be. But one thing was true: Ellie had nearly died and someone had saved her. The old man had helped her when she'd needed it most and then he had disappeared.

Thomas Mirren suddenly crossed his mind. Brian had said he was a fraud; someone who claimed to be a hero but was far from it. Yet, here was a *real* hero.

Taking his laptop from his bag, he turned it on.

Chapter 10

Thomas

Thomas Mirren woke early that Saturday morning. Early for him anyway. It was around nine o'clock. He'd always laughed when people suggested his generation were early risers. He'd never been that; far from it. Nine o'clock was early enough.

His plans for the weekend were simple—do very little. He had some shopping to do but no poppy selling. He was always clear on that point. The weekends had been special to Ellen and him, and that wasn't going to change even though she was gone.

The first thing he did after getting up was take a wash. For most people, it was a basic act, but it was still a luxury to him; someone who had spent years fighting through mud and dirt. One to be enjoyed and to be thankful for. He would shave for the same reason. Not an electric razor but a proper one. One with blades which cut the hair with clean strokes, swift and precise. Not a small lawnmower, ripping at his face.

He stood facing the mirror, water dripping from his chin, and he wondered if he had always looked like this. The same face stared back at him, the same smile, the same bright blue eyes. But now there were lines. So many lines. It was no longer the smooth landscape of his youth, the taut skin, pale and smooth, stretched tight. Now, his face told the story of his life: the laughter and the heartbreak, the hardship and the joy. They were all there, written in each line and each groove, his face a testament to a life well-lived, chapter by chapter. He smiled to himself. Where would the last chapter be written?

Next, he had to deal with his back. At first, the scars and the constant attention they needed in case they became inflamed had been a chore. He had often skipped his routine of ointments and balms. But with each new infection, he had become diligent, and he had learned once again to take care of himself. Because at first, he hadn't cared. He had seen and done so many terrible things that the patchwork of scars seemed unimportant—a reminder of a time he wished to forget. But then Ellen had arrived and everything had changed. She'd taught him to care again. And she'd needed him, just as he had needed her. Without her, he would have been lost. As he was now.

He finished his breakfast at ten—a small bowl of cereal and a banana. The banana was black-skinned, the best type, sweet and soft. The type most people thought were off. By ten-thirty, he was dressed and ready to leave the house. He no longer had his blue blazer, so he opened the cupboard by the front door and took out a light, woollen coat with large pockets and a brown leather collar. It was old, though still smart, and he'd never liked it. But Ellen had bought it for him, so he cherished it. He found an old toffee in one of the pockets, still fresh in its black and white striped paper. Probably still okay to eat, but he took it to the kitchen and dropped it in the bin anyway. Not worth the risk, he thought to himself, then laughed out loud. He had taken so many risks over the years.

Locking the front door, he gave the handle a couple of firm tugs, then set off down the path, hands in pockets, with a small rucksack on his back. It was a beautiful morning, if a little cold, but it was the kind of sky that always heralded a warm afternoon. That was what the rucksack was for. Small but big enough to hold his coat. He noticed he'd left the bedroom curtains closed and thought about turning back. But in the end, he couldn't be bothered.

"What will the neighbours think, Ellen?" he chuckled to himself as he headed off down the road.

The country park was about three miles from his house, a place the two of them had visited often in the past. When Ellen was alive, they had always walked there from the house, so Thomas had kept the habit going. It would take him forty-five minutes, or nearer to an hour if he decided to dawdle. But dawdling wasn't something Thomas did very well. So, it would take forty-five minutes.

At the end of the road, the industrial estate rose high above the trees. It made him think about Ellie Rogers, and he hoped she was okay. Maybe he would telephone the hospital later; but then again, perhaps not.

As he walked down the main road, the number twenty-three bus approached, half full as usual, with the word

'Hospital' in orange lights on the front. It would pass by the park too. Thomas carried on walking. He'd have to run to get the bus, which was undignified for a man of his age.

Approaching the turn-off to the park, he noticed a small white car coming towards him. As it got closer, he recognised the driver as the man he'd given his poppy to earlier that week. He was talking to a woman in the passenger seat and seemed very animated. The good kind when you're happy and excited. It was an odd car, thought Thomas, it made no noise.

At the junction, he pulled his sleeve over his hand and pressed the button at the pedestrian crossing. God knows how many people had pressed that button and no doubt some of them never washed properly. He thought about the time a couple of days ago at the supermarket when he'd been to the toilet and someone had come out of one of the cubicles, then left without washing his hands. He'd told Frank about it, and Frank had been forced to hold him back when they'd later seen the man squeezing fresh baguettes with those very same hands. Disgusting.

After the crossing, it was another mile or so to the park. That was the nicer part of the walk, taking place on quiet country lanes and grassy footpaths. In the past, he'd hold hands with Ellen as they walked, arms swinging like lovestruck teenagers. Ellen would mimic Thomas's strides, the two of them marching along, left, right, left, right, like a couple of oddly matched soldiers, giggling at jokes only they understood. Even now, Thomas could remember her laughter.

"Crazy woman," he said to himself, smiling, as he turned and passed through a small wooden gate to the park. The gate closed quietly behind him.

The park itself was a very grand affair, though rarely busy. That was one of the things Thomas liked about it— somewhere to think without life's interruptions. At its centre, on top of a steep grassy hill, was a large memorial building that had been built in the early twentieth century by a wealthy industrialist in memory of his wife. He had later bequeathed the entire area to the people of the town, and the park had been named after him: Roberts Park.

The view from the top of the memorial was spectacular, taking in much of the town and the surrounding area. Thomas had never been a great fan of heights, so had been to the top just once at the insistence of Ellen. She had teased him for the entire climb—around one hundred and fifty feet of stone staircase—and when they had come back down, she had kissed him and told him how proud she was. Before adding that it was strange for someone who'd jumped out of aeroplanes to be afraid of heights. She had never asked him to do it again.

The real reason for their visits, however, was not the views, nor the vertiginous climbs. Not even the beautiful lakes and lush manicured gardens. No, the real prize was the Butterfly House. The best coffee and cake in the area.

Situated next to the memorial, the Butterfly House was a huge glass building, divided unequally into two parts. The main area was given over to a beautiful collection of butterflies, thousands of them, fluttering around in slender trees and bright foliage. Ellen had loved those butterflies and could have watched them all day if it hadn't been for Thomas. He'd sit next to her and smile, trying his best to look impressed, but she'd known he was only doing it for her. And she'd loved him for that. Thomas, for his part, had never really seen the point of butterflies. But they reminded him of Ellen, beautiful and distracting, and for that, at least, he was thankful.

The second part of the building served as a cafe. Though smaller than the other section, it was equally impressive, at least to Thomas. Mainly because of the cakes. He used to devour one after another while Ellen laughed, making the other patrons stare at him. Which would make her laugh even more. She'd tell him to slow down and say they couldn't afford so many cakes, but Thomas would only smile. He'd eaten rats and insects during the war, so a few cakes were the least he deserved. And it was difficult to argue with that.

By the time he arrived at the Butterfly House, it was quarter past eleven. As far as Thomas knew, the cafe only employed two members of staff: there was a boy, probably a teenager, and a girl in her twenties. He liked them both, and the way they talked to him made him laugh. They spoke slowly and pointed a lot, as if he might have difficulty understanding, and they watched over him like hawks, as though at any moment he might topple over and die. He was probably in better shape than both of them. Definitely the boy anyway.

It was beginning to get warm and the cafe was hot. Time for Thomas to take off his coat. No sooner had he started than the girl was behind him, helping him to remove it.

"Thank you," he said. "It can be a bit difficult at my age." The girl smiled at him, and he had to stop himself from laughing. She looked at him in that way young people often looked at the old—as if they've always been old and never had a life before that moment. She asked him if he wanted her to bring over a menu, and he thanked her but declined.

The boy took over once he was at the till. Thomas announced that he would like a cake and some coffee, and the boy pointed to each cake in turn, slowly enunciating their names so that Thomas's feeble mind could understand. He chose the carrot cake, and once his coffee was ready, he paid and left, shuffling out of the door as slowly as he could manage.

In winter, he would usually eat inside the cafe, but today it was like a greenhouse, so he opted for one of the benches outside, in front of the memorial, and with an excellent view over the town. From where he sat, the town looked just as it had done for decades. The odd detail was different—new houses here and there—but essentially, it was unchanged. People come and go, he thought, but at least the town stayed the same.

This had been Ellen's favourite bench. She'd said as much to him one day, and they'd both burst out laughing at the absurdity of having a favourite bench, but he understood what she meant.

Once, when he was serving in Italy with Adam, they'd been walking through a town when somebody had been shot on a bench a few feet away from them. The bullet had gone straight through the man's head, and he had toppled over so that it looked like he was sleeping. Thomas remembered clearly how peaceful the man had looked as people ran shouting and screaming all around. He'd gone back to that town many years later with Ellen and had found the bench. A young boy was standing on it, selling postcards, and it was as though the other man had never existed.

The cake was small; he finished it in three bites. He thought about going back for another but it was so hot inside the cafe that he decided against it. Leaning back against the cool metal of the bench, he looked around the park. There were very few people but it would get busy soon, so it was time to set off. He didn't really like people, if he was honest.

Finishing his coffee, he took his cup and plate inside and handed them to the boy, then headed down the hill, towards the exit. On the way, he passed a small bandstand with several people exercising inside. One muscular man was encouraging four others to do twenty press-ups. Three of them seemed fine, but one of them, a balding man probably in his thirties, was puffing and panting, and Thomas knew he'd fail. He stood watching, and sure enough, after eleven, the bald man collapsed onto his stomach. He waved apologetically to the muscleman, who clapped as though they had just completed a marathon.

As Thomas passed through the gate and exited the park, a bus was coming along the road. The narrow lane was barely wide enough for the bus, and it trundled along at little more than walking pace. Without thinking, he held out his hand, and the bus stopped.

"Hospital, please," said Thomas, showing the driver his pass.

The driver nodded. "Would you like me to let you know once we've arrived?"

"No, thank you," Thomas replied. "I've been there many times."

The driver waited until he was sitting down and then slowly set off.

Thomas was not a whimsical man but over the years he'd done many things without thinking and often for no good reason. Today was no different. He hadn't planned on going to the hospital, his hand had just shot out, almost of its own accord. Nevertheless, now he was going, he decided it was a good thing to do.

It was half past twelve, and the journey would take thirty minutes. Thomas stared out the window, across the fields, their boundaries marked by stone walls and thick hedges. Like a colossal chessboard in shades of green. He wondered what the fields were used for: there were no animals and no buildings. Perhaps crops, or maybe nothing. Not everything had to have a use.

Ten minutes into the journey, they arrived at the junction he'd crossed earlier that day. There was a small group of children at the crossing, and he smiled as they waited for the signal to change even though the road wasn't busy. The light turned to red, the bus stopped, and a moment later, the children were gone.

Kingsley was not a pretty town. He'd always thought as much, but that had never really bothered him. Sure, it had some nice parts, but in general it had little to set it apart from most other towns. And that was fine. There was a comfort in conformity.

As morning turned into afternoon, local people poured onto the streets and everywhere became busy. All around, people chatted and planned their days, keen to enjoy the sunshine before it inevitably disappeared. Small cafes had placed chairs and tables on the wide pavements, and groups of young adults sat laughing, enjoying their expensive coffees and minuscule pastries. Thomas shook his head. Why eat next to a road when there was a beautiful park nearby?

He got off the bus one stop early. He always did that. Ellen had spent a short time in the hospital before she'd died, and he liked to prepare himself. Getting off the bus at the hospital seemed too sudden. He would approach at his own pace, on his own terms. At least for now. One day, he would be delivered there, but not yet.

"Can I help you, sir?" asked a matronly looking woman at the main desk. She looked old, very old, although no doubt much younger than him. She had long hair cascading past her shoulders and down the front of her blouse. Old people usually had much shorter hair, thought Thomas, and he decided he liked her, sitting there as she was, sticking two fingers up at convention.

"I'm looking for Ellie Rogers," said Thomas, and the woman looked down at a sheet of paper in front of her. She ran her fingers down a long list of names before finally stopping near the bottom.

"Ward six," she said. "Down the corridor and left at the end. Third on the right."

"Well, at least she's alive," said Thomas, more to himself than to anyone else.

"I certainly hope so," said the woman, and she smiled as though she'd said something funny. "We aim to keep as many people alive as possible."

"Admirable," observed Thomas as he set off down the corridor.

As he approached the main wards, it became busy with nurses and doctors rushing from bed to bed. Thomas felt like he was in the way and was just about to turn back when he heard a voice from behind him.

"Are you here to see someone?" The woman was wearing a long white coat, and Thomas wasn't sure if she was a doctor or a porter. He assumed doctor based on the stethoscope and the name badge—Doctor Jones.

"Ellie Rogers," said Thomas. "Ward six."

"Yes," said Doctor Jones. "She's one of mine. She's asleep right now but you can go in if you like."

Thomas was surprised she hadn't asked who he was. Nonagenarians were not known for causing trouble, but she still should have asked, all the same.

"It's fine," he said. "I don't want to disturb her. Thank you, Doctor."

And so, without even going into the room, Thomas turned back. She was okay, and that was what mattered. The bus back wouldn't be for another twenty minutes, so he headed off in search of a sandwich.

That evening, sitting in his armchair and staring at the fire, Thomas suddenly realised he barely remembered what Ellie Rogers looked like. It had all been such a mess. He'd hardly looked at her as he'd carried her to the college and placed her on the table. He chuckled at the idea of him in the ward, unable to recognise the person he had come to see.

"Another lucky escape, Ellen," he said to the photograph on the mantlepiece, and Ellen smiled back at him.

Just then, he remembered the bald man panting away in the bandstand. He stood and unbuttoned his shirt. Placing it on the back of his chair, he looked into the old mirror above the fire. Three ceramic butterflies clung to the wall above it, bought many years ago by Ellen from a zoo in London. He looked at the scars criss-crossing his shoulders, and he sighed.

"I've got old, Ellen," he whispered. "When did that happen?"

He lay on the floor and raised his hands to his shoulders. Twenty press-ups later, he stood and smiled.

"Life in the old dog yet," he said.

And indeed, there was.

Chapter 11

Thomas

1948

August 20, 1948 was a date Thomas would never forget. It was a Friday and it was the first time he saw her. The woman who was to change his life.

It had been nearly three years since the war in Europe ended, and Thomas had stayed in the army until he was sure everything was over—he didn't trust politicians. But sure enough, nothing had happened, so after two more years, he decided it was time to get a proper job. His mother had never considered killing people to be a proper job even though Thomas had proved himself good at it, and on her deathbed, she had advised him to look for a job which involved numbers. But Thomas had never been good with numbers.

"You pick things up very quickly, Thomas," his mother had said, and Thomas had promised her he would try. "You can't spend your whole life killing people." Which was probably true.

When Thomas had been called in for an interview at the local bank, his mother had beamed with pride. Then, she'd died. But at least she'd died happy.

"You don't have a huge amount of experience, Thomas," said Brian Healer, the bank manager, at the end of the interview. "In fact, none. At least not in banking." He interlocked his fingers on the desk, his lips curving into a smile. "But you come highly recommended, so I'm sure you'll be fine."

Thomas had no idea who had recommended him, and he didn't ask. If the person had wanted him to know, they would have told him.

It had been an odd interview, thought Thomas. If you could call it an interview. They'd mostly just chatted. There'd been a brief overview of the bank and what the various jobs entailed, which all sounded pretty straightforward, and then they'd discussed Thomas. Mr Healer did not look like a military man, and he'd been very interested in Thomas's time in the war. Of course, Thomas had kept his answers vague. If Mr Healer really knew what he'd done, he would probably have thought twice about hiring him. And he was running low on money. Thomas had quickly learned that civilians had a very romantic idea about war—no one was killed and there were lots of heroic deeds. Thoughts of blood and dirt, screams and mutilation—the reality—these were things they didn't wish to know. But it wasn't Thomas's job to educate, so he'd given Mr Healer what he wanted and saved the truth for himself.

He was living in London and was renting a room in a large house in Archway with three others, a young couple and another man. Thomas lived on the top floor. On the ground floor was a kitchen, and on the floor directly below Thomas were two other rooms. He didn't speak to the couple much and they didn't really talk to him. They were out most of the time, but when they did bump into each other, they seemed pleasant enough.

The single man was a different story. His name was Clarence, and it turned out that he too had served in the military, though in more of a support role than Thomas. He was in his late twenties and now did something involving sales, though it wasn't clear exactly what Clarence sold. He had bombarded Thomas with questions almost as soon as they'd met, and Thomas had been happy to answer, though not the questions about the war. But when he had finally given in and mentioned his regiment, Clarence had stared at him, mouth open like a puzzled dog.

"I heard you lot were all dead," he'd said, his head cocked to one side.

"Not all of us. We're quite stubborn."

Clarence had shaken Thomas's hand for an uncomfortably long time, and when he'd finally stopped, Thomas knew that he had found a friend. Since his return home, such people had been in short supply.

It turned out Clarence was a bit of a celebrity in the area. He could get his hands on just about anything for a price, and that made him popular. But Thomas didn't ask for things.

"I'm going to the Palace tonight," said Clarence that Friday morning as they sat in the kitchen, drinking tea and smoking cigarettes. The Palace was the local dance hall. "Fancy coming along?"

Thomas thought about it, then shook his head.

"If you help me move some boxes, I'll pay you," added Clarence, and Thomas laughed. It was no wonder Clarence looked so out of shape; he never did any of the hard work himself.

An hour later, they were back in the kitchen, plumes of smoke rising into the air once more. Clarence reached into a bag and pulled out a carton of Camel cigarettes. He pushed them over to Thomas.

"You're paying me in cigarettes?" asked Thomas, and this time it was Clarence's turn to laugh.

"No, Thomas," he said. "Those are on me. *This* is for you."

He then held out a one pound note, green and dirty, with creases from one end to the other. But a one pound note nevertheless.

"No," Thomas said flatly. "Thank you anyway." It was half a week's wage, and he wouldn't accept it for an hour's work. "One pound for carrying a few boxes?"

"It's not just for the boxes, Thomas," said Clarence, pressing the note into Thomas's hand. Standing up, he walked over to the door, pausing for a moment as he turned back to face his friend. "You'd better get ready for that interview," he said, then disappeared up the stairs.

Thomas was still smiling to himself later that day, standing in his vest and trousers in the kitchen. Earlier that morning, he'd had no money and no prospects. Now, he had a job, a pound note in his pocket, and he was going out for the evening. Things were looking up.

He'd checked over his suit and was in the process of ironing a shirt. The electric iron was still a source of amazement to him, removing creases like magic, and so much easier than the old steam iron his mother had pushed around when he was a child. In no time, everything was done, so he made himself a cup of coffee before sitting down for a cigarette to ponder the evening ahead. It had been a long time since he'd been to a dance, and he was acutely aware that his clothes were unfashionable.

"Good for a bank," he said to himself. "Perhaps not so good for a dance." But they were all he had. And he couldn't just turn up in casual trousers and a shirt. He picked up the clothes hanger from the table and slotted it into his shirt, and after finishing his coffee, he set off to his room to get ready.

The room itself was pleasant, much better than he was accustomed to. He'd thought finding a job would be easy, but as the weeks had passed, he'd realised the room was more expensive than he could afford. But now he did have a job, so it wasn't a problem.

"I work in a bank," he said out loud, and he smiled. It was not a statement he had ever envisaged saying. So, he said it again: "I work in a bank." His mother would have been delighted.

In the corner, underneath the window, was a single bed. When he'd first moved in, the mattress had been on a metal frame, but he preferred to sleep on the floor, so had moved the frame into the storage building behind the house. It had two white sheets—one cotton, the other thick wool—and one pillow. He'd never worried about the cold, so two sheets were enough. Other people may have found it strange, but no one ever came to his room, so it didn't matter. He wondered if anyone *would* ever come to his room.

In another corner of the room was a small settee, plain purple and a little worn. It looked just about big enough for two people, though it had never been put to the test. Above it was a small photograph of his mother, faded and in an old wooden frame. There were no photographs of his father.

Then, there was a wardrobe, big and much too roomy for the amount of clothes he owned, and next to it was a small table with a wireless and bible. The bible had been there when he'd moved in, and he was afraid to move it in case it brought him bad luck. Thomas didn't believe in God but the bible stayed, just to be safe.

On the floor was a large rug, a strange mishmash of browns and yellows. Unlike the furnishings in the rest of the room, it was made of a modern material, the name of which Thomas couldn't pronounce. It was unnatural to the touch, and he didn't like it much.

Finally, there was the mirror which was screwed so tightly to the wall next to the door that it couldn't be removed. Thomas didn't like his reflection, the thick lines on his back an unwelcome memory of things done to him and things he had done. He'd thought about covering it, and one day he would, but today, at least, it had its use.

He stood in front of the mirror and played with his tie. A necktie could be done up in many ways, but Thomas knew only one—the four-in-hand knot, also known as the simple or schoolboy knot. It was the easiest to tie.

He locked his door and put the key into his suit jacket pocket. On his way down the stairs, he passed the young couple, and they smiled, so he said hello and wished them a pleasant evening. The front door was unlocked, and outside the early evening sun was beginning to set. He checked the time on his watch. It had been given to him by Adam several years earlier and though a little battered, it was one of his most precious possessions. It was eight o'clock, and he was going to be late.

At the end of the road, the 609 bus into the city was just about to leave. Thomas watched as the last person got on, then the conductor rang the bell and the bus slowly pulled away. The next one wasn't for fifteen minutes, so he started to run, finally reaching it as it turned the corner onto Holloway Road. The conductor shook his head and reached for the ticket machine as Thomas jumped onto the platform at the back of the bus. It would cost Thomas one penny.

The journey was short, taking between ten and fifteen minutes depending on traffic, despite what the timetable might say. He found a seat next to a proud looking businessman who had a thick moustache and small, round spectacles. The fat of his neck spilled over his tightly fastened collar, and Thomas noticed his tie had a Windsor knot. It looked much nicer than his own. He was surprised to see the man's shoes were dirty. Thomas's, by contrast, were clean and well-polished. You could always judge a man by his shoes.

As the bus arrived at the stop for the Palace, Thomas jumped off, thanking the conductor. The conductor smiled and touched the peak of his cap. He was still smiling as the bus pulled away.

Thomas found himself standing behind a long queue of people, mostly couples, chatting away and linking arms, waiting to get inside. He didn't realise it at the time but that evening was to change his life.

When he finally got inside, he placed the entrance ticket into his jacket pocket. A wall of heat greeted him, smoke filling the air, and there was so much sound that he found it hard to think. As crowds of people danced around him in their sharp suits and floral dresses, he searched for Clarence. It wasn't until he was beginning his second circuit of the room that he felt a hand on his shoulder and heard a familiar voice shouting in his ear.

"You're late," Clarence yelled. "Come up here. I've got us a table." He took Thomas's arm and pulled him through the crowd, up the stairs to a balcony overlooking the dancefloor. The balcony was huge, completely encircling the dancefloor below, and at each of the thirty or so large tables, groups of men and women laughed and smoked and spilled their drinks. At the far side of the room, a woman in a blue skirt was dancing on a table as a group of men dressed in army uniforms clapped and cheered. To their right, someone was passed out on the floor.

It was much quieter up here, and Thomas was taken to a table next to a wooden balustrade overlooking the dancefloor. He was introduced to several people, smartly dressed in their fashionable clothes, and when they asked him what he did, he told them he worked in a bank. Clarence smiled, which made Thomas laugh, and the two of them went over to watch the dancing.

"I'm not really one for dancing, Thomas," said Clarence. "Are you?"

Thomas shook his head. He'd tried once or twice, mainly in front of the mirror, to the sound of the wireless in his room, but it had not gone well. "Two left feet," he replied.

Dancing was not a problem for the people below as they twisted and twirled, jiving in time to the music. Thomas watched as they moved, seamlessly dissecting the dancefloor in their yellows and blues, khakis and greens. They looked so happy, and it was hard to imagine that a few years earlier it had been reds and oranges; blood and fire.

Directly beneath the balcony, by the side of the dancefloor, were dozens of boxes. Thomas asked Clarence what they were for, and he shrugged.

"Decorations, I think," said Clarence. "You know, flags and such. There's a do here tomorrow. War stuff, I think. They mustn't have had time to move them yet."

In the middle of the dancefloor was a young woman in a red dress, laughing and smiling as she danced. With her was another woman with long blonde hair and a green dress fastened tightly at the waist. But Thomas only saw the woman in red. He watched her as she danced, her long brown hair, tied up at the sides, swaying as she moved. And how she moved! Thomas was mesmerised, and it wasn't until he felt a hand tapping him on the shoulder that he realised Clarence was talking to him.

"I'd forget about that one if I were you." He laughed. "Never seen her leave with anyone, and there's many that have tried. What do you think of her friend? The one in green."

Thomas looked at her. "Very pretty," he said. Clarence seemed happy with his response. Taking out a cigarette, Thomas glanced back at the dancefloor, but the woman in the red dress had gone.

Back at the table, Clarence asked Thomas what he wanted to drink. Thomas asked for a beer, and Clarence said he could have a cocktail if he preferred—a Green Dragon perhaps, or a Gin Rickey. Thomas shook his head and smiled. He couldn't picture himself in his suit, sipping a Gin Rickey, whatever that was.

They chatted for a while, and one of the women at the table asked Thomas what he did at the bank. When Thomas replied that he hadn't started yet, she giggled and told him he had something to look forward to then. She placed her hand on his arm, but when he politely moved it, she turned back to the man she'd been talking to beforehand. Clarence nudged him and grinned, then attempted a wink. It made his face look odd.

A little later, as they were starting another glass of beer, a group of people came up the stairs and headed in the direction of the table. Among them was the blonde woman in the green dress. She came up to Clarence and sat on his lap.

"Thomas Mirren," he said, "may I introduce you to Mary McClure?" Mary smiled at Thomas, and it was as though her whole face lit up.

"It's my pleasure, Thomas," she said. "Clarence has told me a lot about you."

"All bad," announced Clarence, raising his glass.

"That's all there is," replied Thomas, and the three of them clinked glasses. Thomas noticed Mary had a cocktail. It was the colour of bile.

Seeing him looking at the drink, Mary giggled. "Between the Sheets," she said, turning to kiss Clarence's cheek.

"Lovely." Thomas laughed as Clarence blushed.

At that moment, several men walked past, a few in army uniforms, one sailor. They were laughing and shoving each other playfully. Mary was looking past them as though she were looking for something and the men were in the way. Then, she smiled.

"There you are," she said. "I thought I'd lost you."

Thomas turned to see who she was talking to, and as he looked up, his heart thumped in his chest. The woman in the red dress.

"Thomas Mirren," Clarence said, pausing dramatically. "Ellen Ward."

Ellen laughed. "Hello, Thomas," she said as he stood. "Clarence has told me a lot about you."

In later years, Thomas would say the days before he met Ellen had been like walking in shadows. After he met her, he walked in the sun. And as he stood before her that evening in his unfashionable suit and polished shoes, everything became that little bit brighter for Thomas Mirren. He looked at her, she looked back, and for a while, she said nothing. And then she smiled.

"I work in a bank," said Thomas as Clarence disappeared with Mary for another round of drinks.

"That would explain the suit," teased Ellen, her red lips curling into a broad smile. Her long hair shone in the light, and he could see his reflection in her eyes.

Thomas laughed. "It's all I have, I'm afraid," he said.

They chatted for a while before Thomas asked Ellen what line of work she was in.

"She works in the War Office," said Mary, returning to the table with Clarence, who was carrying a large tray full of drinks. Picking up her cocktail, she grinned at Thomas and nodded towards Ellen. He pretended not to notice. Ellen reached over to the tray, her hand hovering over a cocktail. Then, she picked up a beer, and Mary laughed.

"It's not a bad job," said Ellen, taking a long drink from her glass. "Besides, you used to be in the army, didn't you, Thomas?"

Thomas wondered how she knew, as he hadn't told her. Looking over at Clarence and Mary, he could see they were giggling.

"For a while," he replied. "But that was a long time ago."

Ellen's eyes were focused on Thomas. "Do you like to dance?"

He shook his head and laughed. "I'm actually a very poor dancer."

"Well, I'm a good teacher," Ellen announced, raising an eyebrow.

"And I'm unfortunately a terrible student," Thomas replied, smiling awkwardly.

As Thomas was talking to Ellen, a man dressed in an army uniform and clearly drunk walked straight up to Clarence. Thomas recognised him as one of the men who'd been clapping the woman dancing on the table. The man raised his voice at Clarence which soon turned to shouting. Clarence, for his part, tried his best to calm the situation, talking as softly as possible given the loud music.

Mary looked nervously across the table, catching Thomas's eye. He stood up, Ellen's hand immediately on his arm, gently trying to pull him back to his chair. He hesitated at her touch. But where most people run from trouble, Thomas had always rushed happily towards it. And this time was no different. So, as the man's shouting became louder, Thomas walked around the table. And Ellen followed.

"Sit down, office boy," shouted the soldier as the tall man in the banker's suit and shiny shoes approached.

"I don't start until next week," said Thomas, taking off his jacket. Ellen moved up alongside him, and the soldier turned to face Thomas, a grin on his face as he balled his hands into two great fists.

"Don't you dare," yelled Ellen, and the soldier laughed.

"Need your strumpet to protect you, do you?" he asked Thomas. Up to this point, Thomas had been smiling, but now he wasn't.

So, Thomas hit him, and that was the last time anyone insulted Ellen in front of him. Picking the soldier up off the floor, Thomas lifted him over his head. And as Clarence smiled and the rest of the people gawped, Thomas walked to the edge of the balcony and threw him over the side.

"Don't worry," said Thomas as everyone stared at him. "There are some boxes down there."

"No, Thomas," said Ellen with a smile. "They moved them earlier."

Chapter 12

Ian

Dr Jones headed towards Ian and Debbie as they exited the ward at ten-thirty, ready for the doctors to do their rounds.

"How's the patient?" said Dr Jones as she approached.

Debbie smiled. "I think that's something I should be asking you, isn't it?" she replied.

Ian was relieved to hear Dr Jones laugh. So, things couldn't be too bad, could they?

"She's fine," said Dr Jones. Her expression took on a more professional air as she perused her notes. "The bleeding has definitely stopped, and we've completed another scan. She should be fine to go home in a day or so."

Debbie's grin was one of such relief that Ian put his arm around her shoulders and kissed her.

Outside in the car park, Debbie cried. She was usually strong, but she'd worried so much since the accident that it was little wonder she was going to break slightly at some point. Ian held her tightly until she was finished, then thanked her for being so resilient. If it hadn't been for her, he didn't know how he would have coped.

The car park was unusually quiet that morning. On most days, especially early in the morning, it was almost impossible to find a space, people having to use the shopping centre half a mile down the road. But that morning, they'd found a space right away. Debbie had said it was a good omen. She'd been right.

They were soon in the car, driving down the main road. Ian was telling Debbie his plans for what they should do once Ellie was back home.

"We should have a party," he announced excitedly. "Maybe invite some of her friends around."

Debbie laughed. "I haven't seen you so animated in a long time." She was probably right. It had taken something so potentially horrendous to make Ian realise just how lucky he was.

Just then, he noticed Thomas Mirren walking along the road towards the junction to the park. For some reason, the old man annoyed him, sauntering along without a care in the world. A pale shadow of the real heroes out there, like the man who'd saved his Ellie. At that moment, he didn't care so much about the story he'd written. It was unimportant. What mattered now was his new piece; the one about the man who'd saved his daughter. *That* was important, and he was going to make damn sure everybody knew about it.

As they passed Thomas Mirren, Ian outlined his plans to Debbie.

For her part, Debbie thought a story about the accident was an excellent idea, though she was not comfortable with Ellie being named. The focus should be on the person who'd saved her, she said. She was also adamant that the poppy seller shouldn't be mentioned in the other story, despite Brian's insistence. Nobody knew enough about him, and there was likely a perfectly reasonable explanation for things. And even if he was in the wrong, it wasn't right to focus on him. The story was about loneliness. Deep down, Ian knew she was right. But with all that had happened, the email to Brian asking him to remove all mention of Mr Mirren was still in his drafts. It was too late. He told Debbie as much, and she glared at him. It was a look of such disappointment that he didn't know what to say. So, he said nothing.

The remainder of the drive took place in frosty silence.

Debbie was never able to stay mad for long, so by the time they were home and Ian had made them a coffee, they were fine again. They decided to have an early lunch, then go out for the afternoon before going back to the hospital. Ian took his coffee to the back garden while Debbie phoned her parents to provide an update. They had already left three messages on the answerphone that morning.

It was warm outside, and the relative chill at the start of the morning had all but disappeared. Ian opened one of the chairs they'd bought during the summer and sat with his coffee, staring into the distance. They'd had the option to buy chairs with small tables attached for drinks and such, but the extra fifty pounds had seemed extravagant to Ian at the time. He wished he'd paid it now.

Their garden wasn't large; probably no more than twenty feet in each direction. The tall surrounding fence provided enough privacy that no one could see in despite the fact they lived in a new development with dozens of houses crammed into a small space. It wasn't their first house but it was the first that Ian considered a proper home. The two they'd lived in beforehand, after they were married, had been rented, and whilst they were nice enough, they were small. With Ellie's arrival, they'd needed more space, and so, bursting with happiness at the prospect of parenthood, they had bought this place, impressively large and with an equally large mortgage. Just another of the debts Ian and Debbie struggled to service. Like the car. That had been bought after Ian got a pay rise, which should probably have been used to reduce their debts rather than increase them.

But none of that mattered now. Ellie was coming home, and no amount of money could compare to that.

As he was about to go back into the house, he heard giggling from the other side of his fence. It sounded like the Smith children, Kelly and Luke. He looked to where the noise was coming from, and Luke's head suddenly appeared above the fence, followed by the familiar sound of trampoline springs. The next moment, he was gone and it was Kelly's turn to appear. Then Luke, then Kelly, with a metronomic frequency Ian found comforting. He remembered the old trampoline his parents had bought him as a birthday present one year and the number of times he'd bounced onto the concrete yard or into the flowerbeds. As the last of his mother's tulips had disappeared, his parents had decided to sell it, replacing it with a football and a new pair of boots. It was a poor swap and he'd never liked football as a result.

After a few minutes, the rhythm of the bouncing changed, and suddenly he heard a cry and the sound of breaking pots. Kelly's head appeared, but Luke's didn't. Ian took this as his cue to leave. Throwing the dregs of his coffee onto the lawn, he pushed the chair against the wall and went into the house. Mrs Smith was going to be furious.

Ian's study was not really a study, it was a box room. But there were no boxes and there was a computer, so to Ian's mind, that made it a study. The room itself was eight feet by five, with a window at one end and a door at the other. When they had first moved in, they'd thought about putting a bed in there for guests, but when they'd tried it out, it had taken so long to remove the bed that they'd given up on the idea. So, it had become a study. Even though it was a box room.

Along one wall, to the left of the window, was a small desk with a laptop and a blue leather-bound notebook. The desk itself took up most of the wall. Next to it was a filing cabinet where Ian kept his paperwork. There was a high-backed black leather chair at the desk with wheels which slid around on the bare laminate flooring. Above the desk was a long row of photographs: two of Ellie, several of the family, and one of Ian in his twenties, clean-shaven and with long hair—the way he preferred to remember himself. On the other wall was a picture of his school class and one of his parents. Neither of these were visible when sitting at the desk.

Turning on his laptop, he moved it to the side and reached for his notebook. The book was A4, and he had divided each page into two vertical columns using a pen and ruler which were also on the desk. Turning to a new page, at the top of the left-hand column, he wrote, 'What we know'. In the other column, he wrote, 'What we don't know'. Every page was filled out in the same way.

'What we know is a drop; what we don't know is an ocean.'

It was a quote by Isaac Newton, one he'd heard many years ago, and it was the basis for most of his work. He would not write an article where the unknowns outnumbered the knowns. That was his rule, and he adhered to it without exception. At least until recently.

New page: 'Thomas Mirren'. Left-hand column: 'No military history'. Right-hand column: 'Work? Family? Birthplace?' The list was long. Ian knew nothing about Thomas Mirren, and he should never have written the article. He knew that now.

Sighing, he stood and moved to the window. Outside was the spot in the garden where Ellie's swing had once been. They had gotten rid of it several years ago when she'd stopped using it, but the concrete circles were still there where Ian had secured the four legs. They reminded him of Ellie, and he smiled. It may be too late for Thomas Mirren, but at least he could do justice to the man who had saved her.

Back at the desk, he looked at the next page in the notebook: 'Hero'. For the sake of the story, the only thing he didn't know was the man's identity. But that was the point. He knew what he'd done, when he had done it, and where it had happened. He knew who was involved, and he knew the outcome. In short, he knew everything except who the man was. But it was enough.

Putting the notepad to one side, he turned to his laptop and began typing. Once his ideas were clear, Ian had never found it difficult to write an article. He had started to draft something on the day of the accident, so now it was easy, and over the course of the next hour, he produced something he knew Brian would want. All he had to do was make it seem like it was Brian's idea, and he knew exactly how to do that.

Afternoon visiting hours at the hospital were from two o'clock to four o'clock. Having an hour to spare, they decided to visit the park on the way. Debbie liked the Butterfly House, especially the cakes, and Ian liked the coffee, so it was an ideal stop-off point. Much better than the smoky coffee shops along the streets further on. As they were leaving, Ian noticed that Debbie was carrying a blanket in her arms.

"What's the blanket for?" he asked.

"In case Ellie can come home with us."

When Ian kissed her, he could see tears in her eyes. He asked her if they were happy or sad tears, and he could see she was disappointed that he didn't know. But he really didn't know. Yet he knew that he should.

After ten minutes of driving, they pulled into the park. The car park was at the bottom of the hill, a short walk from the memorial, near to the pedestrian exit and the bus stop. They'd bought an annual pass, so they headed straight up the hill towards the cafe, bypassing the ticket machines and the notices warning of wheel clamping for non-payment.

As they passed the bandstand, they noticed a group of people exercising. There were three women and a man, and in front of them stood a tall instructor in a black vest who was shouting encouragement even though he looked a little bored. For some reason, he seemed annoyed. He reminded Ian of Brian, though with more muscles and less redness in the face.

"No cake for them." Debbie laughed once they were out of earshot as she reached out to take hold of Ian's hand.

At the cafe, it was the usual two people serving—the pretty girl and the fat boy. It was no surprise to Ian that the boy always served the cakes, but when he'd joked about it one day with Debbie, she had told him off and said how polite the boy was, unlike Ian. He didn't say it again but he still thought it.

Debbie ordered the carrot cake and a glass of water. Ian opted for coffee. They decided to sit outside, as Ian found the butterflies in the next room off-putting. Every now and then, one of them would hit the glass window: a quiet thud before flying away as though nothing had happened.

There were several benches in front of the memorial. None of them were taken, so Ian and Debbie sat on the nearest one. They spent several minutes in silence as Debbie nibbled at her cake and Ian slurped his coffee until suddenly Debbie asked Ian if he'd finished the article about Ellie's accident. He told her he had, and they agreed to look over it when they got back home.

Ian's coffee was giving him heartburn, so he didn't finish it. As they walked back down the hill to the car, Ian rubbed at his chest while Debbie made soothing noises even though he could tell she found it funny. She'd always thought him a bit of a hypochondriac.

By the time they arrived at the hospital, he was feeling better.

"Kind of ironic, don't you think," said Debbie as they got out of the car. "If you're going to get ill, a hospital isn't a bad place to be."

They weren't sure how long they'd be there, so just to be on the safe side, Ian paid five pounds for the car park ticket —three to four hours.

"Imagine if someone's in hospital for weeks," said Ian as they walked along the path to the hospital door. "It would cost a fortune."

It was a new person at the customer service desk that day, a youngish man with gelled hair and a pair of fashionable glasses. He was very good-looking, except he had an enormous spot on the side of his nose. Ian wondered why he didn't just pop it, as it had become the focus on an otherwise flawless face. When they set off towards the wards, he asked Debbie if the spot had put her off. She smiled and replied that she hadn't noticed it, but Ian knew she was lying.

The corridors between each of the wards were as busy as ever, and Ian found himself constantly apologising to one person or another as he stumbled along. Towards the end of one particularly busy corridor, he spotted Dr Jones.

"We meet again," said Ian, walking up to her.

Dr Jones looked up from her clipboard. "Does that surprise you, Mr Rogers? Given that I work here." Ian wasn't sure if she was joking or not, but he could hear Debbie giggling behind him.

"Are you here to pick Ellie up?" she asked, catching both Ian and Debbie off guard.

"Can we?" asked Debbie quickly. "I mean, I didn't think she'd be ready to leave so soon."

Dr Jones explained that aside from the broken arm and collarbone, Ellie was now fine. There was no reason to keep her in. She needed to come back in six weeks to have the cast taken off, and she would need a sling for that time too. But apart from that, there was nothing more to be done.

"Make sure she keeps the sling on," said Dr Jones. "And although I think the concussion is mild, keep an eye on her. Any drowsiness, dizziness, or double vision, come back straight away."

Ian and Debbie nodded.

Inside the ward, Ellie was sitting on the edge of her bed. She was wearing faded jeans and a white shirt which Debbie had brought in for her the day before. On the bed next to her was her brightly coloured backpack, battered and beaten and with a large tear along the top. Ian couldn't bear to look at it.

"I'm so sorry," said Ellie as they entered the room. Debbie hugged her as the tears flowed.

When they left the hospital that evening, no one remembered the clothes Ellie had been wearing on the day of the accident, sitting inside a small white cupboard next to the hospital bed: a pair of ripped jeans and a light grey hooded top. They had been neatly folded and placed into a white plastic bag.

On top of the bag was a blue blazer.

Chapter 13

Nicole and Michel

It was cold that Monday morning as Michel Moreau walked out of the house. He felt tired, having done no exercise all weekend, save for running around after the children and eating too much. A thin frost covered the fields, and though barely noticeable, it was the first one of the year. An hour of sunshine and it would be gone, but it was a sign of the cold weather to come.

Behind the house, just past the back door, was an old shed in which Michel kept his bicycles. He'd cycled a great deal in his youth, and after his body had become tired, he'd taken to building his bikes, then stripping them, then building them up once again. An unending circle of destruction and restoration. At any one time, there would be several bicycles at one stage or another of conception.

His racing bike was leaning against the far wall of the shed, fresh tape on the handlebars, brakes and gears thoroughly tested. Michel smiled to himself. This was to be the inaugural journey, into town and back—about three miles in total.

"My finest creation," he said as he pushed the bike through the door and out into the mid-morning light. There was no milometer on the bike, simplicity was the key. It really didn't matter how far he went.

He laid the bike flat on the grass, then stretched down to touch his toes, or at least his lower shins, feeling the muscles in his shoulders and down the back of his legs complaining the lower he went. They complained more nowadays, but he refused to listen. Then, zipping up his jacket, he slipped his left foot into the toe clip and climbed aboard. Both feet could just about touch the ground, and at the lowest point of the pedal, his knees bent slightly. Perfect. He had done an excellent job.

And with that, he was off, slowly at first as he made his way along the short garden path to the gate and onto the road. As the road spread out before him, his legs turned the pedals faster until he was at cruising speed, comfortable yet still requiring effort.

The bike had ten gears, a single chainring at the front and a ten-sprocket cassette at the rear, though in reality, he only ever used one gear—number six. The tyres were full, pumped to near bursting, so that he glided across the concrete, smooth like velvet. With the wind rushing through his hair, he started his descent into town, and as he accelerated, he began to laugh. What greater feeling could there be than this? The moaning of the wind and the smoothness of the road, the exhilaration and the freedom. It was always the same.

But soon the road levelled, and the passing trees began to slow down, catching their breaths after the rush of the race. Michel, too, caught his breath, and he unzipped his jacket, feeling the sweat on his shirt despite the cold. He had overdone it a little. He'd have to be careful with this bike— she was a wild one.

He pushed the bike for the rest of the journey, through the streets of the town, where there were cars and children and all sorts of distractions. The unpredictability made him uncomfortable. As he walked along the pavement, people waved at him and said hello. He was a former mayor, after all. Alain Berger came up to him, with his thick white hair and bushy beard. Alain was a good man, and his father had been the local tailor.

"Mr Mayor," he said, "you're looking well." He complimented Michel on his bike as Michel beamed proudly. "And I'm delighted to see that you wear proper cycling gear," added Alain. Michel's trousers were loose and cut off below the knee. "Not like those fools who ride around in their underwear," he said. "It's downright indecent!"

Michel nodded in agreement, then smiled and said goodbye.

A little further along the street was Madame Bisset, who had owned a clothes shop during the war. These days, she was quite insane, and she tutted at him as he walked past.

"Those clothes will never do!" she said. "Come to my shop later, and we will dress you in something far better."

Michel thanked her, and for a moment, he felt strangely self-conscious.

At last, he arrived at his destination—Maison Mercier. The owner, Robert Mercier, advertised his shop as a market even though it was really no more than a small store. Robert didn't like Michel, and Michel cared little for Robert. When Michel had been made mayor, Robert had thought it should have been him. Refusing to consider Michel the better candidate, he'd convinced himself that something underhand had taken place. But the truth was that nobody liked Robert. He boasted that his father was a war hero when in fact he'd hidden in his cellar. Just like the rest of the town. Michel didn't care, of course, but the townsfolk were less forgiving. Michel understood the terror. Most people would hide away in such circumstances. Most people.

At the back of the shop, next to old adult magazines and out-of-date tins of fruit, was a small display of newspapers. Over the years, Michel had asked Robert, via Nicole, to keep a copy of a newspaper from England. He'd also asked for it not to be the *Chronicle*, which to Michel was no more than a gossip magazine. As a result, Robert only stocked the *Chronicle*.

To be fair to Robert, the papers were always recent, two days old at most. He picked up a copy and checked the date —one day old—then shuddered at the title, "Bonking Britain".

Robert didn't say anything to him as he paid, and Michel did the same. He knew it was petty, but they'd been ignoring each other for so long now that it was almost a game. As if the first person to speak would be the loser.

He didn't buy the local paper. Nicole always got that.

Outside, it was beginning to warm up, and Michel fanned his face with the newspaper.

"Bonking Britain," said a familiar voice from behind him. He turned to find Nicole standing there, her grin almost as wide as her face. "You just can't help yourself, can you?" she said, chuckling.

Michel smiled. "Don't you start. It's hard enough having to put up with that misery." He poked his thumb in the direction of the shop.

"When are you two going to grow up?" Nicole shook her head in mock indignation.

"Never." Michel laughed. "Or maybe when he talks first."

Arm in arm, the two of them walked along the street. Michel handed the newspaper to Nicole so that he could better control his bicycle. Nicole was carrying a large shopping bag, and poking out of the top was a copy of the local newspaper, *La Voix de Saint Martin*. Real stories there, thought Michel—no 'bonking' in this town.

By the post office, at the end of the long hill to Michel and Nicole's house, was Anne-Marie's cafe. It was called The Morning Cafe, the name based on the first letters of her name—AM—and her love for the English language. She had studied in London many years ago, and when she'd returned to Saint Martin, she had opened the cafe with her new husband, Peter Wright. Peter was English, though he spoke with a strange accent.

A small bell announced their arrival, and moments later, Anne-Marie appeared from the kitchen. She waved and pointed to a table by the window with two wooden chairs and a blue and white tablecloth. As Michel and Nicole sat, Anne-Marie disappeared back into the kitchen.

The other customers, two couples, nodded politely to the new arrivals, and as Nicole nodded back, Michel sniffed the air.

"Cake, Michel," said Nicole, noticing his twitching nose.

"Ah," replied Michel, "but what type of cake?"

It was Nicole's turn to wrinkle her nose. "Carrot," she answered.

Michel laughed. "Amazing. Your nose is inhuman." Before he could say anything more, Anne-Marie was standing next to him.

"Bonking Britain," she said with a smile, looking at the newspaper now lying flat on the table.

"Not you too," groaned Michel.

The three of them had been friends for years, ever since Anne-Marie had returned from London. They saw very little of Peter, who was a keen cyclist and spent much of the day on the roads. In the past, he had invited Michel to join him, but Michel had always declined. Peter wore very close-fitting cycling shorts, and it made Michel uncomfortable.

Just as they were ordering, Peter came through the front door with a bag full of groceries and a handful of letters. He walked straight over to Anne-Marie and kissed her on the cheek. He was wearing jeans and a thick black jumper, and it was the first time Michel had seen him in normal clothes. The jeans hung loosely off his hips.

Noticing the newspaper, Peter laughed. "Bonking Britain?"

Michel couldn't be bothered to defend himself again, so he said nothing.

"Mercier still peddling that rubbish, is he?" continued Peter. "I'll have a word with him. See if he can get something a little more..." He paused, searching for the right word. "Newspaper-like."

Nicole thanked him, and he disappeared, closely followed by Anne-Marie.

Five minutes later, Michel was drinking coffee while Nicole ate carrot cake. That would be their lunch. One of the couples got up to leave, and after paying their bill, they thanked Anne-Marie and headed out into the sunshine, turning right out of the door, and disappearing towards the centre of town. That left one other couple—a young man in corduroy trousers and a blue cardigan and a woman of similar age in black jeans, a hooded top, and with short dark hair. For the whole time Michel and Nicole had been in the cafe, they'd not said a single word to each other, preferring to tap away at their phones and giggle to themselves as though no one else was around. Michel felt their relationship seemed dull but as they too left the cafe, they put their arms around each other and laughed as though they were the happiest people in the world.

The large cafe window was like a giant television screen, split down the middle and showing two different programmes. Two worlds colliding. The Morning Cafe was at the very edge of town, and the right-hand screen showed a row of houses, a telephone box, and cleanly brushed pavements. People strolled, chatting and holding hands. The left-hand side showed countryside and a steep hill beyond which lay rolling fields and a blue autumnal sky. It was to this side that Michel was drawn, away from the town and towards his home with its old wooden fireplace and its secret room. Despite having been mayor, he'd never felt comfortable around large numbers of people, and he preferred to spend his time at home. But Nicole liked the town with its bustle and its crowds.

"It has a website," said Anne-Marie, pointing to Michel's copy of the *Chronicle* as he stood, waiting to pay. "Not much better than the paper, but there's more on it."

"I'm sure Michel is very familiar with the website." Nicole laughed, and Michel snorted.

"You can use the computer here if you need one," said Anne-Marie, and the two women smiled to each other.

"I'm not a caveman," replied Michel, "of course I have a computer." Like his bicycles, he had built his own computer. It wasn't difficult, a bit like a jigsaw puzzle with each piece fitting into place. And though it was old and probably considered obsolete, it still served its purpose.

Nicole was not a fast walker. She preferred to do things at her own pace, so she told Michel to cycle on ahead. He shook his head, making her smile, and together they walked up the hill, Nicole with her bag and Michel with his bike. He loved Nicole, not just because she was his sister but also because she was his friend. She was strong, she was good company, and she cared. The world needed more Nicoles.

Chapter 14

Thomas

Monday flew by for Thomas, and before he knew it, he was eating his breakfast on Tuesday. Sometimes, the days went by so quickly that all he seemed to do was eat breakfast. No sooner had he finished one than it was time to eat another.

Frank had called him that morning to say he wouldn't be selling poppies, as he wasn't feeling well. He didn't sound good, and Thomas wondered if it was a bug or a hangover. They hadn't gone for a drink the day before and Frank only went drinking with Thomas, so he guessed it was a bug. Today, he'd be with the Colonel instead, which was good apart from the fact the Colonel always took over. Which is what colonels do.

He had an hour before he was due at the supermarket, so he made himself a coffee and went to sit outside. It was a chilly morning. In his thick woolly jumper, Thomas made his way to the wooden bench by the hedge. Ellen had bought the bench when they had first moved to the house, and they'd spent many happy years sitting there, drinking coffee, and staring at the trees by the tall wall opposite. He wondered how many times he had sat there with Ellen, his arm around her shoulders as she told him about her day and asked him about his. Thousands, most likely. But now he sat alone.

Directly opposite was a scene he knew by heart: to the right was the house and to the left was an old outbuilding now used to store boxes. Between the two, and separating his garden from Mrs Roy's next door, was a line of trees, short and of varying types. There was a fir tree and a birch and at the far left was an apple tree with fruit too bitter to eat. There were other trees too, several metres tall, but Thomas didn't know what type they were. And it struck him then that although he had stared at those trees innumerable times, he had no idea how many there were. So, he closed his eyes and counted.

"Eight," he said, slowly opening his eyes. Then, he laughed. There were nine.

He sat there for a while longer, staring at the nine trees while he finished his coffee, and then finally he went back to the house. The Colonel would be waiting for him.

By the front door, Thomas reached for his blue blazer and sighed as he remembered he no longer had it. He wondered if he would ever see that jacket again. By all accounts, it was going to be a warm day, so it didn't matter. His jumper would do. As he did every day, he said goodbye to Ellen, and a moment later, he was locking the door, followed by several firm tugs of the handle to make sure it was secure. The Colonel was standing at the bottom of the path, hands rummaging in his pockets while he waited for Thomas to finish assaulting the door.

"You can get arrested for that," said Thomas as he approached the Colonel.

"Only in Russia," replied his friend, producing a sweet from his pocket and offering it to Thomas.

"No, thank you," said Thomas. "I'm watching my figure."

The Colonel laughed.

As a rule, whenever Thomas and the Colonel went anywhere, they would walk. Within reason. Frank preferred to go everywhere by car. Perhaps that was why he was ill so often—not enough exercise.

"I took the liberty of arranging for the boxes to be sent ahead of us," said the Colonel as they turned the corner and walked along Longlands Lane.

"Of course you did," observed Thomas with a smile, and the Colonel smiled back, well aware of the meaning.

Organisation had never been Thomas's strong point and never would be. Other people were good at that. He had his own strengths.

As they walked down the road, Thomas noted that the Colonel was walking with a limp.

"You're limping. When did that happen?"

"About the same time you lost your blue blazer," replied the Colonel, and Thomas could see he was smiling again. Thomas shrugged. That was not a conversation he wanted to get into.

"I've got some new shoes," continued the Colonel. Thomas looked down at the Colonel's brown brogues. That would account for the loud crunching noise.

"Don't wear them then," advised Thomas. "Life's too short for uncomfortable shoes."

The Colonel shook his head. "They cost me a fortune."

With the Colonel's limp, it took them longer than usual to reach the park. It was already quite busy, mainly families with small children, but here and there were a few teenagers gathered, talking in loud voices, and smoking cigarettes. On one of the wooden benches, Thomas recognised the two kids he'd caught shoplifting the previous week, and he prepared himself for some abuse as he walked past. But to his surprise, they looked straight through him as though they had no idea who he was. He was amazed at how quickly they could forget.

Once they reached the supermarket and settled at their table, he mentioned it to the Colonel as the two of them were drinking tea and eating cake.

"We've done worse, Thomas, back in the day." And he was right. Far worse. "Anyway," the Colonel added, pointing to the cake, "I thought you were watching your figure."

Thomas laughed. "Only with things that have been in your trouser pocket."

Just then, Jenny came over to see if they had everything they needed. She was wearing casual clothes rather than her company uniform but she still wore the headband. She explained that she was on a half-day and would be leaving at lunchtime. When she asked where Frank was, Thomas told her he had a hangover.

"He has a stomach bug," explained the Colonel, glaring at Thomas. Jenny replied that it was best he wasn't in then, what with all the food nearby. As she left, the Colonel turned to Thomas and grinned. "Actually, I think he got it from the food here," he said.

Thomas had been eyeing a pork pie at the meat counter earlier, but it didn't seem such a good idea anymore.

It was a slow morning for sales. By early afternoon, they decided to call it a day. Neither of the men had eaten much, aside from the cake, and the Colonel asked Thomas if he had any plans for lunch.

"I was going to get one of the pies from here," said Thomas, "but what with Frank and all, I might not bother."

The Colonel suggested they get some lunch at the Legion, but when Thomas declared a craving for fish and chips, they decided upon that instead. The boxes and takings were stored in Jenny's office, which made Thomas wonder why he always lugged them to the Legion when he was with Frank. The Colonel made a comment, something along the lines of poor communication, but Thomas wasn't listening. And then they set off.

If there was one thing Kingsley wasn't short of, it was takeaway shops. Chinese, Indian, fish and chips—whatever you fancied, they had it. Charity shops, phone shops, and nail bars were commonplace too. And tattoo parlours.

But the jewel in the crown, at least for Thomas, was Peter's Plaice, the fish and chip shop at the end of his road. The owner, a middle-aged man with long white hair, sat on a stool by the till while his wife did all the work. He made jokes, which were rarely funny, and would ask for five million pounds instead of five. But the food was terrific.

Ten minutes and ten million pounds later, Thomas and the Colonel were strolling along the road towards Thomas's house. The two of them had chosen large fish and small chips. The Colonel had haddock; Thomas had cod. When the Colonel announced that Thomas should have chosen haddock too, as cod stocks were at dangerously low levels, Thomas asked which scientific journal had told him that. The Colonel replied that it was the *Telegraph*.

"Two things. Firstly, the *Telegraph* is not a scientific journal; and secondly, you only read the *Guardian*." Thomas laughed.

"Correct on both counts," admitted the Colonel. "But that doesn't alter the truth. The genocide of cod, or gaduside if you prefer, is a well-documented fact."

"Gaduside isn't a real word," said Thomas.

"Correct again," the Colonel said, smiling, by which time they had arrived at Thomas's house.

It didn't take the two men long to demolish their food. Years of war had taught them to eat quickly. After clearing the plates and folding the tablecloth, Thomas made some coffee, and they went to sit outside.

The bench was too small for the two of them, so Thomas fetched a deckchair from the outbuilding. It was wooden and stripy and reclined a little too far back, making it look like the Colonel was about to topple over.

A few minutes later, having finished their drinks, Thomas asked the Colonel to close his eyes, which he did without hesitation.

"How many trees do you think there are by the fence?" he asked.

"Eight," the Colonel said, then opened his eyes.

"That's what I thought," said Thomas, "but there are actually nine."

The Colonel shook his head. "The one in the middle doesn't count," he protested. "It's more like a stick with leaves."

"But when does a stick become a tree?" asked Thomas with a smile.

"I have no idea," replied the Colonel. "I specialise in fish, not trees."

The Colonel stayed for most of the day, and by five o'clock, it was beginning to get dark. They had swapped the coffee for whisky, and the Colonel was standing by the fireplace, looking at the photographs.

"How old was Ellen in this?" he asked, lifting the picture of Thomas and Ellen.

"Twenty-six," replied Thomas. "And I was twenty-five."

"Scandalous." The Colonel laughed. "And who's this handsome brute?" He picked up the small picture next to it. It showed Thomas and Ellen standing next to another couple. The man had light coloured hair and was smartly dressed in an army uniform. The woman was looking at him as though he had just made a joke. Thomas and Ellen were laughing, as they always were.

"Some idiot who kept getting himself blown up," replied Thomas as he looked at his watch.

"The same person who gave you that, I suppose," said the Colonel, and Thomas nodded.

"How old was Barbara in the photo?" he asked, and the Colonel smiled.

"Twenty-six," he replied. "A fine age."

"A toast," said Thomas, and the two men raised their glasses. "To Ellen and Barbara."

"Ellen and Barbara," repeated the Colonel, staring at his wife. And for a moment, he was young again.

For the rest of the evening, they watched the television. At eleven o'clock, the Colonel got up to leave. As he reached for the bottle of whisky to take it back to the kitchen, Thomas shook his head.

"I'll have a drink with Ellen," he said, placing his hand on the Colonel's arm.

"Well, tell her you can only have one more. You're working tomorrow." He put on his coat and walked to the door. Thomas joined him, and together they walked down the path to the road, the Colonel's new shoes crunching on the gravel. His limp had gone. Thomas's sleeves were rolled up, and the Colonel pointed to the watch dangling loosely on his wrist.

"What time is it, Thomas?" he asked.

"I don't know, Adam," he said. "This watch hasn't worked for years."

The Colonel laughed. "Why do you think I gave it to you?"

Chapter 15

Thomas

1948

Thomas didn't see Ellen after the dance. Following the incident with the soldier, Clarence had decided it was a good time to leave. People don't take kindly to being thrown over balconies. Thomas had planned to go back that Friday, but when a message arrived from Adam, his plans had to change.

His first week at the bank had gone well. Nothing was too complicated, and he was very soon up to speed with most of what was required of him. The other people seemed nice, and though the work was a little dull, the week passed quickly. Before he knew it, it was Friday again.

At the end of Thomas's shift that day, Mr Healer strode over from his office to catch him on his way out of the building—a rare departure from his large oak-walled office—and handed Thomas a note. Thomas recognised Adam's handwriting immediately.

"A good man that," Brian Healer said, waiting while Thomas read the note. "A good friend of my son too." Thomas started to understand where his 'recommendation' to the bank might have come from, and he smiled. Adam, always arranging things.

"Thank you, Mr Healer." Re-reading it, he frowned. "Where's the Officers' Club?"

"Not far from here," Mr Healer answered, his eyebrows raised in surprise, as though everyone should know where the Officers' Club was located. "Down Overton Road, on the corner of Garstang Street."

He patted Thomas on the shoulder. "You must have done something pretty special to get invited there." Then, he went back to his office, leaving Thomas to wonder what Adam could want at such short notice. He'd arranged a meal for that evening.

Over the course of the week, Thomas had helped Clarence with one or two odd jobs, the proceeds of which he'd used to purchase a new shirt and trousers. He now stood in his room, staring at himself in the mirror. He was smartly dressed—no longer the drab office worker of one week ago. He chuckled to himself at the transformation. The shirt, light blue and with wide collars, had itched his back at first, so he'd washed it several times and now it was fine. The trousers were dark brown and loose and complemented his brown leather shoes perfectly. And while he'd never really been bothered about his appearance, he didn't want to embarrass Adam.

He thought of his mother and how proud she would be with the life he was now leading, far away from danger and with friends and a job. A job that involved numbers. He wished she could see him, and though not a religious man, he glanced upwards and smiled.

Clarence had been around earlier and had loaned him a jacket. Jackets were 'all the rage' at the moment, whatever that meant, and Thomas had thanked him. It was light brown and made of soft wool. It was odd that it fitted him so well though, given how much larger he was than Clarence. Better not to ask where it had come from, he thought to himself.

Outside the door to his room, he paused and listened. The house was empty and quiet. He locked his door and gave the handle several strong tugs, then checked his watch. Six-thirty. He was due to meet Adam at seven. There was plenty of time, so he decided to walk. Going downstairs, he checked his appearance in the hall mirror one last time, then left the house.

At the end of Marlborough Street, he turned right onto Holloway Road and walked west for five minutes before reaching Highgate Hill and the Archway tube station. It was always busy around that area, especially on a Friday evening, and Thomas had to be careful as he walked along the busy pavements. A short distance down Junction Road, he turned right and headed towards Waterlow Park and the cemetery. Soon, the crowds thinned, until at last, he was alone. He preferred it that way.

As the day had worn on, it had become cold, and Thomas pushed his hands deep into the pockets of his jacket. In one of the pockets, he discovered a tie, and he smiled: Clarence had thought of everything. The tie was bright yellow. Thomas chuckled. He'd look like a peacock with the yellow tie and pale blue shirt. He could picture Clarence now, laughing to himself as he placed the tie into the pocket. With luck, he wouldn't have to wear it.

But in this matter at least, luck was not on Thomas's side that evening.

"I'm sorry, sir," said the small man sitting behind the reception desk at the Officers' Club, "but you have to wear a tie. We can provide one if you don't have one with you."

Thomas laughed. "No, thank you, but that's okay," he said. "I have one with me." And before long, he had Clarence's tie around his neck. To his credit, the man behind the desk said nothing, his demeanour professional despite the palette of bright colours. Thomas was directed through a pair of large oak doors. The major and his guests were waiting.

It was only when he caught sight of Adam sitting at a table against the back wall in full military attire that the importance of the occasion struck him. Adam had finally got his promotion, and Thomas was delighted for him.

"Major," he said with a smile as Adam stood to greet him. They shook hands, and it appeared to Thomas that Adam was blushing. "I'm really pleased for you, my friend."

Adam's eyes moved to Thomas's tie, and he burst out laughing, which made Thomas laugh too.

"What are you two laughing about?" said a voice from behind Thomas, and he turned to find Barbara there, a smile so bright she lit up the room. Seeing Thomas's tie, her smile grew broader so that her whole face seemed to be smiling. "Oh," she gasped. "That's quite a tie, Thomas!"

Barbara was wearing a blue floral dress, open at the collar, her hair tied back at the sides. She walked over to Adam, and the two of them sat at the table, backs to the wall and facing the door. Thomas sat opposite. Another place had been set next to him, and he was about to ask who it was for but stopped as Barbara waved to someone behind him.

"Here she is," she said. "Late again."

Thomas turned. For the second time in one week, he was unable to breathe. Walking across the room in wide, flowing trousers and a light blue blouse was Ellen. Beautiful, like a movie star. She noticed Barbara and waved, then seeing Thomas, she smiled as she came over and sat next to him.

Adam made the introductions before adding: "Though I believe you two know each other already."

"How do you know that?" asked Thomas, with a confused frown.

"The balcony at the dance," Barbara answered. "Ellen and I work together, and when she told me about what happened, I had a pretty good idea who the man might be."

Adam laughed. "She's been badgering us all week to set up a date."

"I have not," denied Ellen, though with little conviction. She turned to Thomas and smiled. "Well, maybe a little."

A date. Thomas had never been on a date before. Not a proper one at least. He quite liked the idea.

"It's nice you've come dressed alike," teased Barbara, pointing at their blue shirts. "All you need now is a nice tie, Ellen."

"I'm going to kill Clarence the next time I see him," said Thomas.

As it turned out, Adam had been promoted that week, the meal being a celebration, though he spent most of the time extolling Thomas's virtues as though he were some kind of saint. Which, in truth, he was not. Far from it, in fact. No one walks entirely in the light, and Thomas had spent many years with one foot firmly in the shadows.

When the meal came to an end, Adam and Barbara took a taxi home. Thomas offered to walk Ellen back to her house in Kentish Town, about twenty minutes away. It was the first time they had been alone, and they strolled along the road, shoulders touching. By nature, he was a quiet man, and Ellen was quite the opposite, talking the whole way back as Thomas listened, trying his best to remember every detail of what she said.

They stopped in front of her house, and as they stood there in the shadows of the tall terraced houses, with their dark doors and curtained windows, Thomas wondered if he should kiss her. He didn't know if it was appropriate on a first date, and he decided it wasn't.

"Thank you for a lovely evening," he said, immediately wishing he hadn't. It sounded too polite. Almost like a lie. He wanted to say something witty or romantic or cool. Anything but polite. But his throat was suddenly dry, and that was all he had.

Then, Ellen smiled, a smile so radiant it lit up the whole street. She leaned close to him, and it no longer mattered what he said. So, he kissed her. And it was exactly the right thing to do.

During the war years, people became accustomed to snatching happiness wherever they could find it. As a result, things played out quickly. Over the next two weeks, Thomas and Ellen had three dates, and by the end of the third, Ellen knew pretty much everything there was to know about him. Everything he was prepared to tell, at least. People said he was a good man, but scratch beneath the surface of any good man and there is a terrible violence.

The first date was a visit to the zoo. It was Ellen's idea, and though Thomas didn't like zoos, with their cages and stone floors, he went along willingly. The rough steel brought back memories of times not so long ago when he had experienced captivity from both sides of the bars. Ellen found a butterfly house and was transfixed, marvelling at the creatures flitting here and there, a myriad of colours and sizes. She bought three ceramic butterflies from the shop next door and then they went for a cup of tea. Finding a wooden bench, the two of them sat together, talking of inconsequential things. At six o'clock, he walked Ellen home. And he kissed her again.

When they met the second time, six days later, he took Ellen to a restaurant—Rules, in Covent Garden. They ate quails' eggs and crab salad. Thomas didn't like the food. Ellen said it was delicious but he could tell she felt the same. It was, however, very expensive, so Thomas had to live off tinned food and bread for the rest of the week.

On the third date, they spent the whole day in the park. It was warm and busy, but to Thomas's mind, they were the only people there. He sat, and Ellen lay with her head on his legs. He didn't move, even when it became uncomfortable. That was the first day Thomas opened up to Ellen about the war. She asked him questions, and he answered them as honestly as he could. She was the first person he had told, and she would be the last. And when she announced that he was a good man, he smiled sadly. To some people, he was good; to others, he was a monster.

Late in the afternoon, Ellen bought ice creams, and as they left the park, the ice creams melted and ran down their fingers. It made Ellen laugh, and Thomas realised then that he was laughing too. Really laughing. It had been a long time since that had happened.

This time, unlike their last two dates, Ellen walked back to Thomas's flat. He invited her in, and when she said yes, he felt his heart beating against his chest. Inside the flat, he turned on the wireless and poured two drinks.

"You don't go in for decoration much, do you, Thomas?" Ellen said, laughing. Apart from the picture of Thomas's mother, the walls were completely bare.

"I never thought I'd be staying that long," he replied, looking around the room. He'd not realised how empty the flat felt until now.

A slow song came on the wireless, and Ellen took hold of Thomas's hand.

"Now, for your first dance lesson," she said as she gently pulled Thomas towards the rug in the centre of the floor. Ellen put her arms around his waist and her head rested against his chest.

"What do I do now?" asked Thomas, waiting for instruction.

"You're doing just fine," she replied.

They stayed that way until the music changed and then they moved over to the sofa. Just as Thomas had thought, it was barely big enough for two people. Drinks in hand, they talked about things Thomas had never discussed before—music, books, family. Ellen asked about his parents, and he pointed to the small photograph on the wall.

"My mother," Thomas said softly. "There are none of my father." He looked away. "Not a good man."

Ellen nodded. She looked closely at the picture, seeing much of Thomas in the woman's face—the cheekbones, the eyes, the curve of the chin. At the bottom of the photograph, there were two words written in black ink—Anne Haven.

"Did your mother not take your father's name?" asked Ellen.

"Yes, she did," replied Thomas. "I was Thomas Haven until just after the war. Then, I changed to my mother's maiden name, Mirren." He smiled at the thought. "*That* was one demon I could exorcise."

That evening, Thomas walked Ellen back to her house. It was just gone midnight by the time he got back to his flat. With Ellen gone, it felt empty. He had left her at her door, and now he was alone.

He would never leave her again.

Chapter 16

Ian

Ian got to the office early on Monday. He wanted to be there for when Brian arrived. Despite his faults, of which there were many, no one could deny that Brian was a hard worker. He was always first in and usually the one turning off the lights at the end of the day. As Ian walked through the door that morning, Brian looked up and waved, signalling him to his office.

"I'm sorry to hear about Ellie," he said.

"Erm, right," Ian stuttered, not quite knowing what to say. "She's at home now, at least."

"That's good," said Brian. Ian recognised his face but the caring words seemed wrong. What had this man done with Brian? "You got a good piece out of it though," he added.

Ah, there he was.

"That's what I wanted to talk to you about," said Ian. The sales pitch was ready, but clearing his throat to speak, Brian cut him off.

"Reluctant hero." Brian moved his hands in the air like someone outlining a rainbow.

"I beg your pardon?" said Ian.

"A reluctant hero," repeated Brian. "That's going to be our take on it." And for the next few minutes, Brian outlined the story, where it would be positioned, and what would go alongside it. And to be fair, it was pretty much what Ian had thought.

Ian's original piece, the one about Thomas Mirren—though he would remain unnamed—would go on the left. On the right would be the new article.

"The perfect juxtaposition," declared Brian.

Ian hadn't seen him so excited for a long time. The fake and the real hero, side by side, like two sides of a coin.

"Front page?" asked Ian tentatively. He was starting to get carried away too, picturing the stories, both by him, adorning the front page of the *Echo*. Debbie would be so proud.

"Page five," replied Brian flatly, and Ian sighed.

Five was still good.

As he left the office later that morning to buy himself a coffee and to bask in his good fortune, he wondered how Brian would manage to fit the new story in at such short notice. Hadn't Friday been the deadline?

Inside the supermarket, a familiar sight greeted him—two old men sitting at a table, chatting away as they sold their poppies. Thomas Mirren wasn't wearing his blue blazer for once. The other man was holding his stomach as though he was nauseous. Walking straight over, Ian took out his wallet.

"I'll take two of those, please," he said, pointing to the metal poppies. Even though Debbie and Ellie had already bought their poppies, it seemed like the right thing to do, given that he'd received his own poppy in such unusual circumstances. Handing over the money, a measly thirty pieces of silver, the act went some way to assuaging his guilt.

"Starting a collection?" said Thomas's friend.

Ian shook his head. "It's nice to buy them properly this time."

Thomas Mirren smiled. Ian felt sorry for him, but in truth, he was beyond that now. He was getting two stories. On page five. Besides, the other man—the 'reluctant hero'— that was who really mattered.

With his debts cleared, Ian went to look for a nice bottle of wine. He was in the mood to celebrate. There were two aisles at the supermarket dedicated solely to alcohol: one for beers and spirits; the other for wine. The left-hand side housed the whites, which he rarely drank; the right contained the reds, sorted by country and in price order, with the most expensive at the top. He rarely looked beyond the middle shelf, as the prices at the top made him dizzy. But today he aimed higher. Over ten pounds seemed a lot to pay for something that would make him feel ill the next day but that was where he looked. He walked past the Italians—their rich Barolos and light-bodied Valpolicellas had never agreed with him; he dismissed the Spanish—too oaky; and finally, he arrived at the French. Many years ago, someone had told him the best wines came from France, and though he knew it wasn't true, a part of him still believed it. It was the same reason he bought Japanese televisions.

Even at that price, the choice was bewildering, so he did what he always did—he went with the label. The one he chose had a picture of a chateau and all the writing was in French. So, it had to be good. Also, it was thirteen per cent proof, while the others were fourteen. At least that would be kinder to his head.

As he walked to the checkout, he realised he was whistling.

On the drive home from work that evening, he played his favourite playlist, made up of songs from his youth, each one evoking a particular memory: "The Sign" by Ace of Base—his local pub at university; "Disco 2000" by Pulp—millennium eve party; and "Ashes to Ashes" by David Bowie—just because it was a great song.

He sang along too when he could remember the words.

It had been a busy afternoon. The busiest he'd known for a long time. And he'd enjoyed it. Much of the time had been spent with Brian as the two of them edited Ian's articles to fit their allocated space. It was clear that the first article was far too long, so Brian had decided to trim. The second story was just about right. By four o'clock, Brian had declared he was happy, so he'd pressed the button on his computer, and the stories were sent. Ian had asked if he could see the final version of his first piece.

"You'll see it on Wednesday," he'd said with a smile.

Reaching home, he parked his car in the driveway and sat motionless for a few minutes, letting the playlist finish. As he left the car, he picked up the Chinese takeaway from the passenger seat that he'd bought on the way back. Debbie would be delighted.

"Are we celebrating something?" Debbie laughed as he walked through the door, waving the food bags in the air. "Or is it that you don't fancy doing the cooking tonight?"

It was a bit of both if Ian was honest.

"Just a bit of good news," he replied, and though he was looking forward to telling Debbie and Ellie, it could wait until dinner. "I'm going to get a shower," he added. It had been a long day, and he felt dirty.

Upstairs in the bedroom, he took off his jacket. Laying it on the bed, he looked at the red poppy Thomas Mirren had given him, still fixed to the lapel, its red enamelled petals shining in the lamplight. He thought again about what he had done. He hoped he'd done the right thing. More than that, he hoped Brian had done the right thing. He had two stories in the paper the next day, and despite everything, his excitement and his pride, he couldn't escape the feeling that it was all a bit of a mess. And he *did* feel dirty. It would take more than a bit of soap to change that.

At the table that evening, as they tucked into the food, Ian found he'd lost much of his excitement.

"Well, what's the news then?" Debbie asked.

He told her, and even Ellie looked up from her food. He explained the meeting with Brian, the decision on the stories, and the fact they would both be in the paper, side by side, on the same page. As he spoke, at least some of the excitement returned but it wasn't the same.

"So, why do you look as though you've just been caught doing something you shouldn't?" asked Ellie when he'd finished.

"I don't know," he replied. And it was true, he didn't know. But it was how he felt, no matter how much he tried to feel otherwise. "I can't escape the feeling that maybe I've done something wrong, that's all," he said.

The second story was fine. In fact, it was more than fine: it was one of his best. But the other?

"You didn't mention him by name, did you?" asked Ellie suddenly. "Thomas Mirren."

"No," replied Ian. "But Brian knows his name. And you know what Brian's like." The three of them looked at each other. "My intention was to write about loneliness." He sighed. He knew it sounded like an excuse.

"And that's a good intention, Ian." Debbie reached out and squeezed his hand.

But Ellie wasn't convinced. "Bad things often come from good intentions," she declared.

Which really didn't help.

They finished the bottle of wine and then opened another. Even Ellie had a glass.

At ten o'clock, Debbie went to bed. Red wine always made her feel tired. For Ian, it was the opposite; he always felt tired the next day. Ellie still hadn't finished her one glass of wine, and Ian smiled to himself. Teenagers seemed to be drinking less these days, at least most of them. At her age, he was falling out of pubs most days, and he wondered where she got her good sense from. Probably Debbie, he thought, then laughed to himself as he remembered his wife unsteadily climbing the stairs earlier.

"It's good to see you laugh," said Ellie, looking at him in that way only a loving daughter can.

"It's an ironic laugh," replied Ian.

"A laugh, nonetheless," countered Ellie, picking up Debbie's empty glass and taking it to the sink.

It felt stuffy inside the house, and the smell of takeaway food was making Ian queasy, so he picked up the wine bottle and emptied the last few drops into his glass. Then, he went outside.

Sitting in his wooden armchair, he looked up at the sky. It was a clear night, and he could see Orion, the hunter, who had angered a goddess and was killed by his friend. It was the only constellation he could remember. It was peaceful, almost silent outside, save for the occasional breeze and Ian's breathing. Inside, he could hear glasses clinking as Ellie filled the dishwasher, and then it went quiet, and she came out to join him. Pulling up a chair, the two of them stared out over the garden fence and off into the distance, at Orion, betrayed by the gods.

"It's strange," said Ellie after a while, "we look forward to something for so long, and when it finally arrives, we're disappointed."

It was precisely how Ian felt. A few hours ago, he was singing in his car. Now, things felt like a mess—a mess born out of fear. Fear for his job. Fear for his family. Just fear. He'd always been afraid.

"I'm not sure why I wrote the stories really," said Ian. "Even the second one. I didn't research Thomas Mirren enough. And the other one..." He looked at Ellie. "Your one. Well, I wrote that through emotion."

"And neither feel right?" asked Ellie, though it wasn't really a question.

"No," said Ian.

Ellie turned to her father and smiled. "Maybe they're just two people trying to do the right thing. No song and dance, and no fanfare. Just doing what they think is right, quietly, and in their own way."

She was right, of course. Again. Thomas Mirren hadn't claimed heroics, as far as Ian knew anyway, and the other man had just disappeared. Not everyone wants attention.

He heard rather than saw Ellie leave. It was late, and he'd finished his wine.

"Goodnight, Ellie," he said.

But she was already gone.

Part Two

The story came out on October 29, 2014. It was a Wednesday.
The *Kingsley Echo* always came out on a Wednesday.

Ian was horrified.

Ellie was disappointed.

The Colonel was furious.

And Thomas Mirren laughed.

Chapter 17

Thomas

Thomas was eating a bowl of cereal when the newspaper arrived. His shoulders had been aching during the night, so he'd slept badly. And when he had slept, he'd dreamed of violence and shouting and of towns on fire. It hadn't been a good night.

He rubbed his shoulders as he made his way over to the front door. The *Echo* lay there apologetically, folded over on itself as though wishing to hide what was inside. There were a couple of letters too, brown envelopes hinting at circulars and offers of free insurance. He picked up the letters and dropped them into the recycling basket he kept by the door, where they joined numerous other brown envelopes, all unopened. No one interesting wrote to him, but that was fine.

The *Echo* felt light today, not its usual bulky self, fattened by adverts and stories of the latest footballing defeat. Not much happening, Thomas thought to himself as he made his way to the kitchen. A cup of coffee and a few minutes in the garden before Frank was due.

Outside, sitting in front of his nine trees, Thomas opened the paper, flicking through the pages with well-rehearsed efficiency. The first three pages focused upon the new housing development being built down by the railway station. Construction was behind schedule, and costs were spiralling.

"Could have written that story before they even started," said Thomas. And he was probably right.

But it was a story on page five which caught his attention. Or rather two stories, side by side under the one headline: "Heroes of Kingsley (?)". The brackets looked odd. On the right was an article about a man who had saved a local girl; on the left, a piece about someone masquerading as a war hero. It was obvious who the second man was. He read the whole page. He thought they were good stories. Despite the brackets.

Then, he folded the paper and finished his coffee. Frank would be arriving soon.

Frank was waiting at the bottom of the garden path. He had a copy of the *Echo* in his hand, and the expression on his face hinted at barely controlled rage. It was like he'd swallowed a grenade, and it was about to explode.

"Have you read this crap?" he hissed as Thomas approached. He looked to be shaking.

"I know," said Thomas with a shrug. "The new houses are nowhere near finished."

Frank stared at Thomas, looking like a politician who'd been asked a difficult question. Then, he started to laugh.

"You don't care, do you?" he said.

"No. And so neither should you." He pointed to the newspaper. "Next week's chip wrapper, isn't that what they say?"

Frank shook his head, but Thomas could see he was smiling. "They don't use newspapers for that anymore, Thomas."

"They do at Peter's Plaice," Thomas replied. And there was not much Frank could say to that.

The Volkswagen was nowhere in sight, and for a moment, Thomas wondered if Frank was on a fitness drive. Then, as they turned the corner, he saw it, parked by the old telephone box, and he sighed.

"Baby steps," laughed Frank, seeing the expression on Thomas's face. "It's a good hundred yards from here to your house."

"You'll be running a marathon next," said Thomas as they got into the car.

Driving along, Frank wittered on about the newspaper story, though Thomas wasn't really listening. He was looking out of the window, watching the streets pass by. The same streets he had walked along with Ellen thousands of times before, and for some reason, he found he was missing her much more than usual today. It was like a pain in his stomach, tight and piercing, and he embraced it, as though she was somehow there with him in Frank's Volkswagen, with Frank prattling away in the driver's seat.

"The Colonel's going to be livid, you know," announced Frank, and then Ellen was gone. Thomas looked down at his hands and sighed.

"The Colonel's always livid about something," said Thomas even though he knew it wasn't true. But Frank laughed anyway.

They drove for another few minutes, and then Frank stopped the car, parking it by the post office. It was about a hundred yards from the supermarket.

"Christ, Frank," Thomas said, smiling. "You don't want to overdo it!"

"I know," replied Frank. "It's going to cost me a fortune when my clothes start falling off me." That was an image Thomas didn't want to think about.

It was ten o'clock, and the supermarket was empty. Colin, the security guard, was doing his rounds, checking things which didn't need to be checked, and fidgeting with his tie. He did that a lot. A nervous habit, according to Frank. Thomas had no strong opinion either way. Seeing the two of them, Colin waved, and again, it was one of those waves where the hand didn't move. All very odd.

It wasn't long before tea and cake arrived. Jenny smiled and pulled up a chair, sitting opposite the two men as though she was being interviewed. Thomas thanked her for the cake, but Frank declined his piece, stating proudly that he was watching his figure. The saintly look on his face made Thomas want to laugh, as if he should be canonised for declining a slice of Victoria sponge.

They sat in silence for a few moments, then Jenny leaned over the table and looked directly at Thomas.

"No one believes a word of that story, you know," she said. The look of concern on her face made Thomas want to say something reassuring, but he didn't know what. He thought about commenting on the new houses, like he'd done with Frank earlier, but decided against it.

"It's fine," he said.

"No, it's not," replied Jenny. "I'm going to kill Ian when I see him."

Frank asked who this Ian was that Jenny was so keen to kill, and when she told them, Thomas almost choked on his cake. It was the man he'd given his poppy to, the one who'd nearly ran over Frank in his silent car. Jenny then explained that the other story involved Ian's daughter—she'd been in an accident, and a complete stranger had saved her. This time, Thomas did choke on his cake.

"Are you okay?" asked Frank as he repeatedly slapped Thomas on the back.

"Went down the wrong way," wheezed Thomas when he was finally able to breathe. "What a way to go," he said at last. "Years in the army and I'm finally beaten by a slice of cake." He looked towards the newspaper display. "Or not, if you believe what they're saying."

"Which nobody does," said Frank.

But Thomas wasn't so sure.

The morning went slowly, with very few people coming to their table. Frank had declared a boycott on all newspapers, much to Thomas's annoyance. Colin waved a few times, when he wasn't fumbling with his tie, and by the time one o'clock came around, the two of them decided to call it a day. Someone else would come in to do the afternoon shift, and hopefully they'd have more luck. Frank asked Thomas if he wanted a lift to the Legion, but Thomas wanted to go somewhere else, somewhere he hadn't been for two days, and a place he very much wanted to visit now. He agreed to meet up with Frank at the Legion later, and with that they left.

Fifteen minutes later, they arrived at the cemetery. Frank asked Thomas if he wanted him to wait, but Thomas shook his head.

"I'll walk back," he said. "Should only take me half an hour or so."

As Frank disappeared down the road, Thomas found himself standing by one of the three entrances to the cemetery, each marked by a rusted old gate and a council sign warning of unstable gravestones. Thomas wondered just how unsafe they could be, given the hundreds of years many of them had stood; grizzled sentinels, battered but still upright. All except Doris Singleton's which was flat on its back. Much like Doris herself.

The gate groaned as Thomas pushed against it, scattering small mounds of gravel and revealing the bleached concrete beneath. Even though it was a warm day, the metal felt cold against his hand, and he gripped it tightly, feeling his muscles tense as a chill ran through his fingers. The gate moved, and Thomas entered.

A path ran through the centre of the graveyard, lined with wooden benches, pitted with moss, and barely usable. But at the far end was one bench that was always so clean that it still looked new. Thomas made sure of that—Ellen was very fussy about her benches.

As he approached their bench, he noticed Peter Aldridge placing flowers at his father's grave. Thomas had known his father, Craig. Craig Aldridge had been an idiot. Not the worst kind of idiot, the type who would throw a brick through your window, but the kind who would threaten to but then wouldn't go through with it because they were weak. Unlike Thomas, who was strong, so the idiots had never bothered him. He was an idiot-free zone. Peter nodded to Thomas, and Thomas smiled. Peter was not an idiot.

By the bench, the delicate scent of lavender filled the air. Lavender attracted butterflies, so Thomas had covered the area around the bench with it. Even so late in the year, after the warm summer and mild October, the smell was noticeable, and several butterflies flitted through the air nearby.

Thomas sat on the bench. A few feet away, the gravestone stared at him, all polished granite and gold lettering, standing proudly. Precisely upright, and firmly rooted. No danger of this one falling over. As long as Thomas was alive, he'd make sure of that.

"Sorry I didn't come yesterday, Ellen," he said, looking at the numbers carved deeply into the black slab— "1923–1993". She'd been gone over twenty years. And he'd been hurting every day of it.

"I got into the newspaper today," he continued. "Twice, in fact. Just the local rag, but it's a start."

At the far end of the path, Peter Aldridge was leaving. He smiled to Thomas and nodded. There was another person there too, but it wasn't someone he recognised. A middle-aged woman dressed in a yellow skirt and light blue cardigan. She was carrying roses. Red ones, like the one on his old school badge. He'd always liked red roses.

Thomas sat for a long time in silence, staring at Ellen's grave and remembering her. Her voice, light and happy. And her smile, the kind of smile that told him everything was going to be okay. But it wasn't okay. Not really.

A butterfly landed on the top of the gravestone. It was still for a moment, then flew away. Like his Ellen, beautiful and delicate, but leaving too soon. His butterfly.

"You're probably going to hear some things about me, Ellen," he said at last. "Bad things for the most part. But a lot of it isn't true." He paused and sighed. "Some of it may be though."

The butterfly was back now, whirling in the air before landing once more.

"Anyway, I just thought I'd let you know."

Thomas sat on the bench, chatting to Ellen for nearly an hour. He told her about his morning and how he'd drunk coffee in the garden, on their bench. In front of nine trees, when he'd always thought there were eight.

As he left, the woman in the blue cardigan was still there, staring into the distance. He wondered if he should say something. But he didn't. People don't go to graveyards for a conversation. He nodded to her and smiled as he passed, and she smiled back. It was a sad kind of smile, he thought, but that wasn't surprising, given where they were.

It was getting late. He'd promised Frank that he would go to the Legion, and he always kept his promises. Nearly always.

The road back from the cemetery was, for the most part, a narrow lane with no pavement and with thick hedges on either side. He could hear birds, but that aside, it was quiet. No people and no cars.

By the time he reached the end of the lane, he'd been walking for twenty minutes, and he'd built up a sweat, so he wafted his face with his hands. Which, of course, did nothing. He was wearing his light woollen coat, the one he didn't like but loved because it was from Ellen, and it was surprisingly warm. Carefully unbuttoning it, he smiled as the cool air wafted in, across his chest and down his arms.

And then he realised he was happy—that's what happened when you spent time with Ellen.

Back in town, Thomas decided to pick up some bread from Alan Dugdale's minimarket. And some cheese. It would make a nice dinner and would soak up some of the alcohol he was inevitably going to drink with Frank and the Colonel. Then, some more alcohol at home, no doubt.

"Afternoon, Thomas," chirped Mr Dugdale as Thomas walked into his shop. Alan Dugdale was a rakishly thin man who was in his fifties. He always wore an apron with "Alan's Mini-Market" printed proudly across the front. Thomas had once asked him if the name should be spelled with or without the hyphen. After Alan had stopped laughing, he'd replied that it was his shop, so he could spell it however he liked. Which seemed eminently reasonable to Thomas.

"How have you been?" asked Alan.

"Pretty good, thank you," answered Thomas. "I got myself in the paper, you know."

"I know," said Alan, scratching his chin. "But I don't pay much attention to the papers." He smiled at Thomas, and Thomas smiled back.

"Do you have any bread?" asked Thomas, scanning the rows of shelves surrounding the small shop.

"Loaves, rolls, and buns," he replied in well-rehearsed fashion. "Or, if you're feeling adventurous, baguettes."

Thomas opted for a baguette, as it made him think of France. "And cheese?"

"Too many to list," beamed Mr Dugdale proudly. "Would you like them alphabetically or in price order, lowest to highest?"

"I'm in a bit of a hurry, I'm afraid," admitted Thomas. "Can you recommend one?"

Alan considered it for a while. "Brie," he said at last. "Delicious. Do you want some prosciutto to go with it?"

"That's Italian, isn't it?" replied Thomas. "I don't want to be too cosmopolitan, Alan. I'll stick with the cheese."

Back outside, the clouds which had seemed about to engulf the town earlier were gone, and it had turned into a lovely afternoon. Thomas thought about taking a short detour through the park before heading to the Legion but he was worried about his new cheese in this heat. With hindsight, perhaps a hard cheese would have been better, he thought.

Walking along the narrow pavements, past WH Smith and a large tattoo parlour, he noticed several people looking at him. Not that he was bothered, it was just unusual. Most days, no one cast him a second glance. At the corner of Main Street, the man who played the panpipes hit a bum note, and that wasn't like him at all. Thomas had talked to the man in the past—his name was Benny—and Benny had told him that the panpipes were also known as the syrinx. But today he said nothing. He just looked at the ground.

By the Co-op, Mrs Halliwell waved to Thomas. A little further down the street, old man Jacobs made a point of asking him how he was. It was the first time Mr Jacobs had spoken to him for years. As he continued along the pavement, he shook his head and laughed. It was all very odd.

When he eventually got to the Legion, Thomas was very much regretting buying a soft cheese. The plastic bag he was holding was warm to the touch, and heaven only knew what was happening to the Brie.

Inside, it was quiet. Derek was behind the bar again, and he nodded to Thomas as he entered. It was the kind of nod you use when you're trying to get someone's attention, so Thomas went over to see what he wanted. There was no one else at the bar.

"Have a word with the Colonel, will you, Thomas," he said, waving a cloth in the direction of two men sitting in the far corner—the Colonel and Frank. The Colonel looked furious, his face as red as one of the tomatoes in Alan Dugdale's shop.

"I will," said Thomas. "On one condition."

"What's that?" asked Derek.

"Put this cheese in the fridge."

Chapter 18

Ian, Ellie, and Debbie

It was Ian's big day. When he came down to breakfast, a copy of the *Echo* was waiting for him on the kitchen table, next to a slice of toast and a cup of coffee. It was so flat and neatly folded that it looked as though someone had ironed it.

He hadn't slept well the previous night. Not for any particular reason, it was just one of those nights. Debbie had been irritated by his twisting and turning, and halfway through the night, she'd finally left to sleep in the spare room. After that, they'd both slept much better.

Ellie was in her pyjamas and was on her phone, sending messages as best she could with one hand. It seemed to Ian that this was the worst part of the whole ordeal for her—the inability to text her friends in comfort. Not the fact she'd almost died. We all have our priorities.

Debbie darted around the kitchen, opening cupboards as though she were looking for something and couldn't quite remember where she'd left it. Eventually, she laughed and held up her phone, then she too was tapping away at the screen. She was wearing a yellow skirt and a light blue cardigan. She looked radiant.

"Have you read it?" asked Ian, pulling up a chair to sit at the kitchen table. He pointed to the newspaper, and both women shook their heads, which was odd. Neither were known for their restraint, so he didn't quite believe them. Taking a sip of his coffee, he sat down to read, but he was soon feeling self-conscious, so he picked up the paper and took it outside. Debbie and Ellie said nothing. Which again seemed odd.

Outside, it was chilly, so he placed his coffee by the chair and went back inside to fetch a jumper. When he got back, he sat down and nervously opened the paper. Nothing on pages one to three, but he'd expected as much. Then, there it was—page five. Two stories, one headline: "The Heroes of Kingsley (?)". He had to stop himself from laughing. They were the oddest brackets he had ever seen.

First, he read the story about Ellie. He was pleased to see that it was just how he'd written it. Verbatim. He smiled to himself. It was good. Very good, in fact. Then, he read the story about Thomas Mirren, and he barely recognised it. Gone were the references to mental health and loneliness, replaced by an attack on an old man. An old man who was unable to defend himself and who had most likely thought he was doing nothing wrong. Thomas Mirren's name hadn't been mentioned, but it might as well have been. It was abundantly clear who the story was referring to.

His hand was shaking as he arrived back in the kitchen, collapsing into a chair. He placed the newspaper on the table, open at page five. Horrified, he sat with his head in his hands for a few minutes, unable to make eye contact with Debbie or Ellie. When, finally, he looked up, he saw sympathy in their expressions, and in a way, that made him feel worse. It also confirmed his suspicion that they'd read the articles too.

He really didn't know what to say.

Debbie walked over and hugged him, then Ellie put down her phone to join them.

"That story," said Debbie, pointing to the article about Ellie, "is fantastic. You should be very proud of yourself." She was beaming as she spoke.

"And that story," added Ellie, pointing to the second article, "is nothing to do with you. It reeks so much of Brian that it's practically his." And it was true, though Ian knew there would be no story if it weren't for him. And despite what she said, he could see that Ellie was disappointed. Probably not with him but she was disappointed, nonetheless.

"I'm going to speak to Brian about it," said Ian, and the two women nodded.

"You should," said Ellie. "It's not your story but it still has your name at the top."

It was nine-thirty by the time Ian pulled into the car park, and he sat for a few moments in his car. Throughout the journey in, he'd become increasingly annoyed, to the point where Brian had now taken on the form of a monster. Taking a few breaths to compose himself, he unfastened his seatbelt and got out of the car. It was chilly, so he buttoned up his jacket, and as he did so, he noticed that the metal poppy from Thomas Mirren was missing. He checked the other lapel, then went through his pockets, but it wasn't there either. So, he checked again, in that way people do even though they know they won't find anything. Then, he checked again. And for some reason, the loss saddened him more than it should.

Inside the office, it was busy. It was always busy on a Wednesday, what with the paper coming out and the associated calls. But today seemed busier than usual. Over by the photocopier, Anna and George, the trainees, were silently staring at their computer screens, while next to them, Jean, the office manager, was looking through some papers she'd just taken from the printer. As he watched them, he noticed Amanda strolling over to him, a broad grin on her face.

"The man of the moment," she declared, awkwardly attempting a bow. Her long, dark hair tumbled over her face, forcing her to blow several strands from her mouth before she could continue. "Well, that wasn't as cool as I thought it was going to be." She laughed. In her right hand, she held a copy of the *Echo*, already tatty and covered in blue pen. It was open at the page of Ian's stories. "Quite a scoop," said Amanda, and Ian wondered whether people actually used that term anymore.

"Well, one of them anyway," he said. "I'm seriously pissed off with Brian about the other one. It's nothing like the piece I wrote."

Amanda smiled softly, but he knew what she was thinking —he should have seen it coming. They'd known Brian for a long time, and he was always going to make the story into something tawdry, even if it destroyed Thomas Mirren. And Ian should have known that.

"Yeah, well," said Amanda with a shrug, "the other story's pretty damn good though. I'm jealous." She looked genuinely pleased for him. "Do you think you'll find the old man who disappeared?"

"Probably not," admitted Ian. "Though, you never know. Someone might have seen something."

Amanda agreed. "Are you going to say anything to Brian about the first article?"

Just as Ian was about to reply, Brian appeared and went straight into his office, closing the door loudly behind him.

"Good luck," said Amanda, giving Ian a supportive squeeze of his shoulder before disappearing in the direction of the kitchen. With a deep breath, Ian headed off to see Brian.

"I need to talk to you, Brian," he said as soon as he was through the door.

Brian pointed to the door and frowned. "For God's sake, Ian, shut the door, will you. Were you born in a barn or something?"

Ian had been born in a barn. Well, more like a farm. But it did have a barn attached. Though, of course, that wasn't relevant.

Shutting the door, he got straight to the point. "The story," he said. "The one with Thomas Mirren."

Brian held up a hand to silence him. "No need to thank me," he said without a hint of irony. "This is a big day for you, Ian. I don't want to take any of the credit."

If that was meant to put Ian off, it worked very well. All the things he'd been meaning to say disappeared. It took a monumental effort to refocus, and when he finally regained his composure, he noticed Brian staring at him as though he were an idiot.

"Well?" said Brian hurriedly, looking at his watch.

"The story," Ian repeated.

"Which one?"

"The one with Thomas Mirren in it." Ian paused and looked directly into Brian's eyes. "Well, it's pretty much all about Thomas Mirren, isn't it?"

Brian raised an eyebrow. "Yes. What's your point?"

Ian explained the situation to Brian; how the direction the story had taken was not what he wanted. It was his story, and it wasn't meant to be about a person. It was meant to be about something more significant. Something more important. But as he was saying it, he could see that Brian didn't care. He wasn't even listening. So, in the end, he gave up. As he always did.

"Anyway," he finished, "I don't want my name attributed to it."

"It already is," said Brian. "And unless you want to go around town taking back every copy of the paper, there's not much we can do about that, is there?"

And there wasn't—there was nothing Ian could do. His conscience had arrived too late.

As he was leaving the office, Brian delivered his parting shot.

"By the way, Jacqueline Chambers called from the *Chronicle*. Congratulations, they're running the Mirren story tomorrow."

Debbie got off the bus one stop early. It was a nice enough day, so she decided to walk the last part of the journey. She was warm in her blue cardigan but with roses in one hand and her handbag in the other, she couldn't be bothered with the struggle of taking it off and tying it around her waist. It would be cooler in the cemetery anyway. It was always cooler there.

The cold metal gate growled as she opened it, as though disturbed from a deep slumber. It moved slowly, creating tiny hills from the gravel of the path. Several pieces became stuck and were crushed, becoming white dust which rose into the air and floated away.

Peter Aldridge was there again. It was the only place she ever saw him nowadays, trimming the grass around his father's grave and tending to the flowers. She said hello to him as she passed, and he smiled, then went back to his work. He was such a dutiful son, and much more than his father deserved.

Towards the far end of the path, past the broken gravestones and the mossy benches, was the old man—the Butterfly Man. She'd nicknamed him that several years ago when she'd first started coming to the cemetery after her mother had died. He would sit there for hours, surrounded by lavender as the butterflies circled overhead. And it made her smile. The bench he sat on, the flowers, and the grave were always so well maintained, and she often wondered who he was. He had a kind face but there was also steel. She imagined he had many wonderful and outrageous stories to tell.

At her mother's grave, the old red roses had wilted. Though only a few days old and despite the special solution she'd added, they were still dying. Flowers never lasted long in this place, and she wondered how the old man's lavender grew so well. She'd thought of asking him once but had decided against it. People don't go to graveyards for a conversation.

Taking the old flowers from the vase, she laid them gently on the grass and replaced them with the fresh ones. Her mother had always liked red roses; they'd reminded her of her husband, whose school badge had had a red rose in the middle. It had been a long time since Debbie's father had died, so long that she wondered if she would even recognise him now were he alive and they were to pass in the street. Somehow, she doubted it. She couldn't even remember his voice anymore. Once, many years ago, she'd had a telephone with an answering machine. Her father had left her a message one day and it had been recorded on a cassette. Not long after, the machine had broken, and Debbie had thrown it away, forgetting all about the message on that tiny cassette. When she'd finally remembered, she'd realised that she'd thrown away one of the most important things she owned. And now her father was a ghost; a shapeless wraith whose voice she could no longer hear.

The slightest of sounds drew her back to the present. The Butterfly Man nodded to her and smiled as he walked past.

She smiled back. He seemed happy. Which was strange, given where they were.

It was time to go. The metal gate groaned once more as she pulled it closed behind her. But the sound was different this time. Like a purr, deep and resonant. It was the sound of contentment. The last person was leaving, and everyone could rest.

Walking down the lane, Debbie remembered the old flowers back at the grave, lying on the grass next to her mother. She should have taken them away, and she thought about going back. But this time, she didn't go back: there can never be too many roses.

The bus arrived, and before she knew it, she was back in town. It was three o'clock. Half an hour later, she was home. She had expected Ellie to be out when she got back, something about going into college to see her friends, so it was a surprise when she found the front door unlocked. Taking off her cardigan, she headed into the kitchen, where she found Ellie, sitting at the table with the newspaper open in front of her. She was crying.

Ellie couldn't decide what to wear. Her bed was covered in clothes, but none of them seemed right. She'd never cared about how she looked, just so long as she looked okay, but today felt different. She was going back to the college, at least for a while, and she wanted to look good. Not like someone who had been hit by a truck. In truth, she'd known what she was going to wear all along but it was fun going through the motions, emptying drawers and tutting in the mirror.

Finally, dressed in faded jeans and a dark hoody, she went downstairs to the kitchen. The idea had originally been to meet Lucy and the others at around noon, but for one reason or another, they were now meeting at half past three, just after the last lesson. Not that Ellie minded, she hadn't been feeling well most of the morning. Her arm had been playing up. She'd slept poorly the previous night.

In truth, she was feeling fragile. For the past few days, she'd treated her accident like most young people would, as though they were indestructible and could never get hurt. But it had finally caught up with her. She could have died. Probably would have died were it not for the stranger. And the realisation made her feel weak. All her life, she'd believed she was in charge, but now she knew she wasn't. Other people were in charge: faceless people in cars and trucks who didn't concentrate and who didn't even notice when they'd ran someone down. Those were the people in charge, not her.

And for the first time in a very long time, she felt like crying.

To keep her mind off things, she took off her hoody and ironed it. It looked no different. Then, she made lunch: toast and marmite. The toast fell onto her lap, and she had to change her jeans. Another pair, the same style—faded and torn. Like all her jeans. There was a comfort in familiarity.

And then she watched TV. Something nondescript and mundane.

When the doorbell rang, Ellie looked at her watch. It was three o'clock, and she needed to get going, or she'd be late. Looking through the frosted glass of the front door, she could see a figure, blurred and distorted. There was an orange jacket, and it looked like the person was carrying something. Mr Collins, the postman.

"You need to sign for this," said Mr Collins, holding out a large parcel. He'd always given Ellie the creeps, the way he looked at her like a predator. Albeit a very small one. In the animal kingdom, he would most likely have starved. She smiled at the thought as she signed for the parcel. The signature looked unrecognisable. Mr Collins handed over the parcel along with several letters, and then he left.

Back in the kitchen, Ellie placed the letters on the worktop by the kettle. They looked boring and were probably selling something. The package, on the other hand, with its NHS box and brightly coloured label, looked intriguing.

There was something very satisfying about opening the surprise parcel, the knife carefully slicing the sealing tape as the cardboard flaps popped and moved apart. Ellie took her time, making sure all the tape was removed before slowly opening the lid. Inside was a white plastic bag. It contained a pair of ripped jeans and a light grey hooded top, washed and folded. Ellie squeezed them before placing them on the table. The damage was beyond repair. By rights, they should be thrown out. But she would never throw them away. Folding the plastic bag, she placed it on top of the jeans.

Underneath the first bag was another of similar size, though perhaps a little heavier. Peeling the plastic tape and reaching inside, she wondered what it was. The material, coarse, almost rough, was unlike the other items. Removing the contents, she frowned. It was a jacket; a large blue jacket. No, not a jacket, a blazer.

Ellie placed the blazer on the side and considered telephoning the hospital to inform them of their mistake. But then came a memory—she was cold, and she was shaking. A gentle voice, a feeling of warmth and strong arms lifting her into the air.

She was shaking again now as she reached for the newspaper still lying on the table from earlier that morning. She turned to page five: *with his blue blazer and gentle manner.* Thomas Mirren.

Next to it was the story of the stranger. The hero. Her hero. The man who had saved her life, then disappeared before she could thank him.

She began to cry.

Chapter 19

Nicole and Michel

Nicole sighed sadly as she wandered around the house, looking for Michel. She wanted to go into town, and Michel had offered to take her on his bike. But she'd told him not to be stupid, so he'd gone off sulking, and now she couldn't find him. He was like a child at times. Nevertheless, she shouldn't have called him stupid.

Looking out of the kitchen window, she spotted him in the garden. "Ah, there you are," she said, stepping outside. "I'm sorry, Michel. You know I don't think before I speak sometimes."

Michel smiled as he tapped lightly on the end of his cigarette, ash dropping to the ground. He never could stay angry for long. His smile reminded Nicole so much of the young boy in the photograph on the mantlepiece, and that made her feel even worse. At heart, he was still young, even though his heart was old.

"Let's walk into town," said Michel. "I don't feel like going out on my bike today anyway."

Which was a lie, and they both knew it.

Nicole told Michel to finish his cigarette while she made a coffee. Afterwards, they could set off. As she made her way to the kitchen, she looked at the camel, still next to the photographs, and she decided that it would be nice to keep it there, at least for a while. There was no point boxing away memories.

The coffee was ready when Michel made his way back into the house. He smelled of smoke. Nicole used to hate the smell, but now she found it comforting, like the smell of an old blanket, though she would never say as much to Michel. He would always laugh when she chided him for smoking. The sound of her brother's laughter was the thing she cherished most in the world and the thing she was most afraid to lose.

"You can still ride into town," said Nicole. "If you like."

Michel looked at her and smiled. "I know I can," he replied. "But I would rather walk with you."

Which was the truth, and they both knew it.

Michel locked the door behind them as they left the house. It was completely unnecessary, of course, there was no crime in Saint Martin. Once, many years ago, somebody had daubed graffiti on the post office wall, but even then, the culprit had returned to clean it off. Michel knew the story well because it was him.

The camel was still next to the photographs. They'd decided it would be nice to keep it there for a while. There was no point boxing away memories.

It would take around thirty minutes to reach the edge of town, marked by the Morning Cafe. On a good day, it would take forty-five minutes to get home, such was the steepness of the hill.

"You know, going down the hill is harder on my knees than going up," observed Nicole, ten minutes into the walk.

"Not if you'd have come on my bike," replied Michel. Nicole knew he was smiling, even without looking.

"Perhaps I'm the stupid one after all," said Nicole, and Michel laughed. There was that beautiful sound again, filling Nicole's heart with joy.

It was busier than usual on the road that day. One car passed them by as they walked. Which was one car more than most days.

"Traffic's a nightmare today," grumbled Michel, and they looked at each other and giggled. It was Monsieur Dernier, rushing around as he always did in his old sports car.

"Late again," Nicole replied, laughing as Monsieur Dernier sped past, waving to them as he disappeared. Though quite what Monsieur Dernier had to be late for was anyone's guess. There was never a need to rush in Saint Martin.

They arrived at the Morning Cafe at half past eleven, too late for breakfast but a little early for lunch. Neither Nicole nor Michel had eaten that day, so they decided on cake. And coffee, of course.

Anne-Marie and Peter were both in the cafe, Peter behind the counter and Anne-Marie taking orders. Anne-Marie wore a blue dress, short at the knee and with a floral pattern on the arms. Nicole thought she looked very pretty, and she said as much to her when she came over to their table. Anne-Marie blushed. Peter, on the other hand, was wearing a grey cardigan and black trousers. Next to his wife, he looked unstylish and drab. Nicole mentioned this to Anne-Marie, who laughed so hard she almost dropped her notepad.

"If he's not in those cycling shorts, he can barely dress himself," said Anne-Marie, having regained her composure.

Remembering the cycling shorts, Michel shook his head. "Downright indecent."

Anne-Marie looked at him. "But sexy, no?" she replied, winking at Nicole.

The coffee and cake arrived five minutes later. For all his faults, Peter made excellent cakes. Today's was a bibingka, popular in the Philippines and made with coconut and rice flour. It was delicious. So good, in fact, that Michel ordered a second slice. Nicole shook her head as Michel tucked in, then ordered a second slice for herself too.

"I think I may have trouble walking up the hill," announced Michel a little later, rubbing his stomach contentedly.

"Well, you need to get some energy then," said Nicole. "We need to pick up some meat and wine from the market. Do you think perhaps we drink too much wine?"

"You can never drink too much wine," replied Michel, and they both laughed.

As they were leaving, Peter came over with a copy of the *Chronicle*. He'd bought it earlier that day, he said, but had finished it quickly, the paucity of news being greater than usual. Michel thanked him and stuffed the paper into his shopping bag, far enough down that no one would see it. Much to Nicole's amusement.

With the newspaper hidden, they left.

It was starting to get busy as they walked along the pavement to the market. Not Mercier's market, of course, a proper one. One that sold fresh meat and not pornographic magazines. Tuesday was market day, though in reality the market was open most days. But always on a Tuesday. Everything a person could want, within reason, was sold at the market, from cheeses and breads to kitchen items and clothes. There was really no reason for a supermarket in Saint Martin, and that was the reason Michel had opposed the plan to build one when he was mayor. The town's shopkeepers called him a hero, though the banks had less complimentary names for him.

"Three bottles of red wine, please," said Nicole to Madame Vindeur, the wine merchant. "And one white."

Michel looked at her, his confusion evident as he wrinkled his brow. "Who drinks white wine?"

"Marie," replied Nicole, thinking back to her daughter's recent visit.

"Only when there's no red," said Michel. It was Nicole's turn to look puzzled. Finally, she nodded.

"Sorry, four bottles of red, Madame Vindeur," she said, correcting herself, and the bottle of white wine was returned to its box.

On their way to Monsieur Viande, the butcher, they passed a stall selling clothes. Nicole noticed the dress Anne-

Marie had been wearing earlier. It looked much better on her than it did on the hanger. Anne-Marie could make even a sack look pretty. Next to the dress was a mannequin dressed in a stylish red shirt, though with no trousers, and for some reason she thought of Peter.

"Are you blushing, Nicole?" asked Michel, staring at his sister.

Nicole smiled and shook her head. "Don't you think Peter would look nice in that shirt?"

"An Englishman in French clothing? Have you started on the wine already?" He noticed the lower half of the dummy and started to laugh. "The trousers would be an improvement though."

Half an hour later and they were walking back up the hill to the house. Nicole carried one bag and Michel carried another. Michel was complaining that he'd been tricked, the heavy wine bottles clinking as they pulled on his arm. Nicole, who was trying hard not to laugh, carried a few sausages and little else.

"Who'd have thought sausages could be so heavy?" said Nicole as Michel began to sweat.

"Nobody, Nicole," replied Michel. "That's who."

At the top of the hill, Monsieur Dernier drove past again, this time in the opposite direction. He waved again, and Nicole waved back.

"He's going to be late home, I imagine," said Nicole.

Michel tutted. "Maniac."

That evening, they had sausages for dinner, very much average-sized in Michel's opinion. Later, he opened one of the bottles of wine, at which point all talk of sausages ended.

After they'd finished eating, Michel took the dishes to the kitchen and placed them carefully into the sink. He'd have a cigarette, then wash the dishes afterwards. On returning to the living room, he found Nicole reading the *Chronicle*. He smiled as she mouthed the words to herself. His English was good, but his sister's was much better. She was better at most things than him.

"I'm going outside for a cigarette," he said, but Nicole didn't look up. Deep in concentration, a look he was all too familiar with, he knew she hadn't heard him. So, he left her to her reading, and slipping on his shoes, he disappeared into the garden.

Outside, it was dark. And very quiet. Sat in his old wooden chair, he watched as smoke from his cigarette drifted lazily into the night, morphing from one shape to another— a ghost, a car, and finally a hand, claw-like and twisted. He looked at his own hands, wrinkled and old, no longer the smooth skin of his youth. Years of sunshine had taken its toll, and liver spots dotted his arms and back. But he had lived a full life, and those marks were his witness.

The outside light flickered on, and Michel looked back at the house. Nicole was shuffling around now, the newspaper consumed and the wine bottle emptied. She was singing to herself as she washed the dishes. She would be his one regret when he died. The thought of leaving her was almost too much to bear. But there was little doubt he would go first. She was far too stubborn to die.

He could smell the coffee before he heard Nicole arrive. She sat next to him and placed a small tray on the table between their two chairs. On it were two cups of coffee and two glasses of water.

"I won't be able to sleep," he said, pointing to the coffee.

Nicole grinned. "Since when were you unable to sleep?" she asked. "You're gone as soon as you turn out the light." Michel nodded. It was true. But Nicole hadn't finished. "Unlike me, who can hear your snoring through the walls. I can't remember the last time *I* got a good night's sleep."

"Now, I know you're lying, because I don't snore," teased Michel.

"Of course not," Nicole said. "It must be the ghosts."

They sat in silence for a while as Michel resumed his inspection of the smoke. Exhaling a huge cloud, he pointed to it and asked Nicole what it looked like to her.

"A wheel," she said confidently. And indeed, it did. It was perhaps the biggest smoke ring Michel had ever seen, and he was very impressed with himself. As the ring slowly moved, it elongated and stretched, causing Nicole to laugh. "Now, a map of Italy," she said, before pausing. "Without Sicily, of course." The shape hovered briefly, then disappeared. "And now your first bike."

Michel chuckled. His first bike had been stolen.

"Come," said Nicole when they'd finished their coffees. Michel picked up the tray and they went back to the house.

"What is it?" he asked as they sat at the table. Nicole was leafing through the newspaper again. The concentration was back, her lips moving silently as she flicked from one page to the next. Finally, she found what she was looking for, and her finger jabbed at the page.

"The dangers of excessive milk consumption," read Michel. He looked at Nicole. "Very interesting but we rarely drink milk."

Nicole shook her head. "No, here." She circled what looked like an internet address. "Some of the stories have a link to a website where there's more information. Did you know that?"

Michel had never noticed the addresses before. He made his way over to the computer and sat down. "What's the website address for the *Chronicle*?"

Nicole snorted. "Don't pretend you don't know it."

He typed in the address, and the story appeared.

"You're right," he announced. "There really is more information. Pictures too. I suppose there's only so much they can put in the newspaper. Limited space."

Nicole nodded, stifling a yawn. "Anyway," she said, "I'm tired. I'm going to bed."

Michel walked over and hugged her. "Thank you for washing the dishes."

"You can make breakfast tomorrow," replied Nicole with a grin.

It was a fair trade.

Chapter 20

Thomas

The story appeared in the *Chronicle* the next day. Though relatively small, there was an internet link at the bottom, where more information could be found—photographs and bits of information on the individuals involved. One such individual was Thomas Mirren.

Frank and the Colonel decided to intercept Thomas at his house. It was Frank who'd noticed the story first, and he'd telephoned the Colonel at once. The Colonel, for his part, immediately arranged for Captain Walters to do the poppies that day. Walters would be their distraction as Thomas was removed to a safe location. In this case, a car boot sale in the neighbouring town. It was like being in the war again.

On the way to Thomas's house, Frank decided he needed the toilet, so they were forced to go to the local petrol station, much to the Colonel's annoyance. Frank wouldn't have lasted long on the frontlines, what with his predilection for comfort breaks. He was eating a pastry when he returned to the Volkswagen.

"I hope you washed your hands," said the Colonel.

"Of course," said Frank, smiling as he held out the cinnamon Danish. "Would you like a bite?"

"No, thank you," replied the Colonel.

Ten minutes later, they pulled up at the bottom of Thomas's garden. He was yanking at the door handle, as usual. Noticing the Colonel and Frank, he smiled, and the Colonel felt his heart breaking.

"What have I done to deserve this?" asked Thomas as he squeezed into the back seat. "I feel like a general."

The Colonel passed Thomas the newspaper, and they set off.

"I didn't know you read the *Chronicle*," said Thomas as they turned out of the end of his road. Both men replied in unison that they didn't. "Well, that poses an interesting question then," continued Thomas. "If the two of you don't read it, and I certainly don't, why is there a copy in the Volkswagen?"

Frank and the Colonel looked at each other. It was the Colonel who finally spoke. "Page seven," he said, pointing to the paper in Thomas's hand.

Thomas leafed through the pages, stopping at page five to read a story about the dangers of milk. Part two. Noticing the Colonel's expression, he skipped the article and turned to page seven, as instructed. He didn't drink much milk anyway.

At first, he was unsure what he was supposed to be looking for, but as he scanned further down the page, he came across a piece entitled: "The Military Imposters". Not a large article but large enough. He knew at once what it meant.

The Volkswagen pulled into the farmer Kenton's field at a little after ten-thirty. Dozens of cars already littered the area, parked in neat rows and with small foldable tables at the back. On top of each table sat various assortments of rubbish, from used clothes to toiletries, old games to photographs. It was Thomas's idea of hell. Fortunately, several refreshment tents had also sprung up, and around each, a few small plastic tables waited invitingly. Thomas wasn't one to turn down an invitation, so that's where he headed, the Colonel and Frank in hot pursuit. He left the newspaper in the car.

"We need to talk," said the Colonel at last, so for the next five minutes, they sat in silence. Thomas had bought each of them a cup of tea and an overbaked scone, and as he waited for his drink to cool down, he watched in amusement as his friends fidgeted nervously. He wondered who would be the first to break, deciding that it would probably be Frank.

"Do you want to talk about it?" asked Frank finally, no longer able to keep quiet.

Thomas smiled and looked at him. "Nope," he replied, taking a drink from his tea.

"Perhaps we need to contact this rag and set the record straight," said the Colonel, his jaw clenched. "It's all lies."

"No, again," replied Thomas. "You know, Adam," he continued, "once a little bit comes out, all the rest will follow. And I've been no saint. You, of all people, know that."

"You only did what you were told to do, Thomas," complained the Colonel.

"But I did it anyway," said Thomas, and there was a finality to his tone that none of the other two were prepared to challenge.

The Colonel looked away defeated. He knew there was little point pursuing something once Thomas had made up his mind. Unless he ordered it, of course, and he would never order Thomas to do anything. "We should blow up the bloody lot of them," he said, smiling once again.

"I'd rather you didn't," Thomas insisted. "The only thing I've ever seen you blow up is yourself. And I'm not in the mood for carrying you around again."

The Colonel laughed, though Frank had no idea what they were talking about.

After finishing their drinks, the three men set off to look around the stalls despite Thomas's protestations. Thomas wanted another cup of tea, or perhaps something stronger if that was available, but the Colonel and Frank could see he was stalling.

And so, they found themselves rummaging through boxes filled to the brim with old books and magazines. Frank seemed particularly keen, and he reminded Thomas of an excited mole, burrowing deeper and deeper into one of the largest boxes Thomas had ever seen. Just as it looked like he was about to fall in, he suddenly surfaced with a battered book in his hand. It was *Winnie-the-Pooh*.

"I used to love the Pooh when I was a child," said Frank, waving the book around in front of the Colonel.

"Sounds disgusting," said the Colonel, taking the book and leafing through the pages. "Money for old rope," he said.

"What do you mean?" Frank asked.

"There's nothing to it," the Colonel explained. "Just a few short stories and several badly drawn cartoons."

"Badly drawn!" scoffed Frank. "A. A. Milne was a gifted artist."

"Not gifted enough to give the bear some trousers though," declared the Colonel. "Downright indecent."

The three of them burst out laughing.

Frank bought the book, the previous owner handing it to him in a brown paper bag.

Next stop was an elderly couple selling old postcards from the back of their camper van. There were hundreds of them, if not thousands, and every one had writing on it. Thomas thought it odd to sell postcards, as they were personal, and their messages would mean nothing to a stranger. He would never have sold a card from Ellen. It was apparently not a sentiment shared by others, as dozens of people crowded around, rooting through the boxes like pigs in search of truffles.

When numbers had thinned, the three of them moved over to the table. All the postcards were sorted by country, and in each box, there were perhaps a hundred cards, organised alphabetically. Thomas had never heard of many of the places.

"Saint Kitts and Nevis?" he asked.

"It's in the West Indies, Thomas," replied the Colonel, standing next to him with a fistful of postcards. "Part of the

Commonwealth."

Thomas shrugged. "Cozumel?"

"Same sort of area. Just off the coast of Mexico." Thomas was impressed. He decided to try one more.

"Battacruda?"

"That's not a country, Thomas."

A few minutes later, Frank came over carrying some postcards from Italy. Thomas recognised several places immediately. He took them from Frank and sorted through them, remembering the faded buildings and crumbling landmarks. Finally, he came to a card with a picture of a large church flanked on either side by statues of soldiers and saints. He knew it instantly.

He nudged the Colonel. "Recognise this, Adam?"

"I certainly do," replied the Colonel. "That postcard must be over seventy years old."

Frank leaned in to take a look. "How do you know that?" he asked.

Thomas laughed. "Because we blew it up."

Later, following two more cups of tea, the Colonel and Thomas were waiting for Frank, who was on another of his trips to the toilet. The Colonel was holding the brown paper bag containing Frank's book.

"You look like a right wrong 'un," said Thomas, chuckling. The Colonel tried to pass the bag to him, so he shoved his hands deep into his pockets and pressed his arms tightly to his sides. "Oh no, you don't," he said. "Frank gave it to you. He must know something I don't." It wasn't often that the Colonel looked uncomfortable. Frank trudged over, and a look of palpable relief spread across the Colonel's face. He wasted no time in handing the book back to Frank.

"The queues are a nightmare," declared Frank as the Colonel looked away in disgust. Frank grinned at Thomas, and the three of them set off across the field. Frank had seen a table earlier and wanted to visit it before they left despite the Colonel's aching back and Thomas's sore shoulders. They all agreed it would be the last stop before they headed home.

"Military paraphernalia," announced a red-headed man as they approached his table. He was chubby, with the posture of someone who had experienced much of his life from behind a desk. On the table in front of him were all manner of things, from knives and cap badges to ribbons and boots. Much of it looked fake to Thomas, and he picked up a bayonet which seemed to be made of tin.

"You couldn't even gut a melon with that," he whispered as the red-headed man looked for something in the boot of his car.

"It's a good job you don't need to gut a melon then, isn't it?" said the Colonel, tossing the bayonet up and down in his hand. "I reckon it could do an orange though."

The man returned with a wooden box, shallow and about the size of a chessboard. He moved the tin bayonet to one side and placed the box carefully onto the table. Two small clasps fixed down the lid, and he carefully opened them, then pushed the box forward so that the three men could see.

"Medals," he announced proudly. There were about forty in total of varying shapes and sizes, some without ribbons, though most of them intact. It was an impressive display.

Frank pointed to one. "I've got one of those," he said as he scanned the rest of the box. "But none of the others."

The Colonel smiled and patted him on the back. "You're a brave man then, Frank." Frank looked genuinely moved. Every soldier wants to be thought of as brave.

"I have that one there," added the Colonel, pointing to a copper-coloured medal in the shape of a six-pointed star with a red, green, and white ribbon. Frank smiled and nodded.

"Any of yours there, Thomas?" asked Frank, and the three men turned to look at him.

"No," replied Thomas. "I shouldn't think so."

The Colonel laughed. He walked over to Thomas and put his arm around his shoulder. "You won't see Thomas's medals being sold out the back of a Skoda," he said. "Not the important ones anyway."

Thomas stayed silent. He didn't like talking about medals.

Back at the Volkswagen, the Colonel retook his place in the back seat. Thomas was much happier that way. He preferred travelling in the front—the working men's seats. The three of them discussed what to do next. It was still early, and while Frank wanted to go straight to the Legion, the Colonel and Thomas decided to go home first, then meet up a little later. Outranked, Frank sighed and started the car.

The soil in the field was soft, and the Volkswagen's wheels spun several times before they made it to the road. The Colonel and Thomas twisted around in their seats and chuckled at the devastation, thick grooves criss-crossing the grass, clearly indicating their route to the gate.

"Kenton's going to be livid," the Colonel said, though he didn't seem concerned.

"When isn't he?" asked Frank. And it was true, Farmer Kenton was always angry. Even when he was happy.

They stopped at a small service station on the way back to Kingsley.

"Too much tea," said Frank, smiling as he got out of the car. The Colonel stared out of the window, not dignifying Frank with a response.

Ten minutes later, they were home. The Colonel got out first, his large house all manicured lawns and neatly trimmed hedges. Thomas was next. He noticed his garden gate needed painting.

For the next few hours, Thomas did what he often did during the afternoon—he made lunch, drank a cup of coffee on the garden bench, and chatted to Ellen. Then, he went to visit her in the cemetery. She smelled of lavender, and he breathed in so deeply that he thought his chest might explode. His eyes were watering when he left, and he blamed it on the hay fever even though it was the wrong time of year.

Then, he went to the Legion.

It was busy when he arrived, at least by the Legion's standards. Most of the people were regulars, give or take the odd unfamiliar face leaning against the bar. People smiled at him as he walked past, and Derek nodded, waving his bar towel in the direction of a table in the far corner where the Colonel and Frank could be seen huddled over a newspaper. The Colonel was scratching his head.

"Doctor who looks down in the mouth?" he said as Thomas sat down. They were doing a crossword, and as usual, they were stuck.

"Dentist," said Thomas, reaching for his pint.

"Ah, yes." The Colonel sighed. "That's what I was thinking." Which, of course, he wasn't.

With the crossword finished, they got down to the important business. Like talking rubbish and complaining about the beer.

At five o'clock, they left. At the end of Market Street, Frank said goodbye, slowly trudging off in the direction of his house. As Thomas and the Colonel reached the end of the Colonel's road, they continued walking, and soon they were back at Thomas's. Thomas had collected his Brie from the Legion and the Colonel had picked up some bread. The Colonel was in charge of sandwiches, while Thomas was in charge of drinks.

For the rest of the day, they ate sandwiches and drank beer. Then, they talked about the war. The encounter earlier that day had left the Colonel feeling nostalgic, and he reminisced about their time in France. He spoke in such a way that Thomas wondered if he'd been there at all. The Colonel talked of fields and flowers and magnificent buildings with beautiful gardens. But Thomas remembered mud. He remembered fire and gutted houses with burned trees. The Colonel's place seemed much nicer, and he would have liked to have gone there with Ellen.

It wasn't until later that the topic of the newspaper stories came up. The Colonel was still angry, but for the first time, he mentioned the other story—the one about the schoolgirl and her heroic rescuer.

"Funny that," said the Colonel, staring straight at Thomas. "Not many old men could carry someone that distance."

"I imagine not," replied Thomas, pretending to clean something from his hand.

"And all around the time you lost your blazer."

"It's torn," corrected Thomas, but he couldn't help smiling.

The Colonel shook his head. "You really don't care what people think, do you?"

Thomas shook his head. "Apart from my mother, there are only two opinions I've ever cared about—Ellen's and yours. And you both know the truth."

And they did know the truth. All of it.

As he was leaving, the Colonel turned to Thomas. "I'm sorry about what they wrote," he said, and Thomas could hear the sadness in his voice. "People don't really think that about you."

Thomas smiled. "In the end, they're just words, and they don't really matter." He shook the Colonel's hand. "But thanks for caring anyway."

Chapter 21

Ian

Ian left the house early that morning. The *Chronicle* was out, and he wanted to assess the damage, having worried about the *Chronicle*'s story ever since his conversation with Brian. As it turned out, it was worse than he'd imagined. Far worse. The printed story itself was relatively small, hidden somewhere between the lifestyle and business sections, but it was the website version that caused Ian the most concern, carrying as it did the bulk of the information. There was a link at the bottom of the newspaper story, and when Ian had checked it out on his laptop, he'd nearly fallen off his chair. At least the *Echo* hadn't mentioned Thomas Mirren by name; the *Chronicle* had included an old photograph. And though black and white and a little grainy, there was no mistaking who it was. Quite where they'd found such a photo, he couldn't begin to imagine, but in this day and age, anything was possible.

He'd decided to see Brian to discuss what had been written but Brian hadn't showed up that day. Something about a business lunch. As a result, he'd allowed his feelings to fester so that by the time he got home that evening, he was feeling quite down. Ellie's expression at dinner didn't help—she looked in a worse mood than him. According to Debbie, she'd been that way all day.

"Your mum says you were crying when she got home yesterday," he said. "Is everything okay?"

Ellie wanted to shout at him, to tell him that no, it wasn't okay. *She* wasn't okay. *Nothing* that was happening was okay. She wanted to tell her father that he was a fool who'd got things so wrong and had made such an awful mistake. But she couldn't. Not only because deep down she knew it wasn't his fault, but because Thomas Mirren wouldn't want her to. If he'd wanted people to know, he'd have hung around when he'd brought her into the college. Or at least given his name. But he hadn't, so she stayed quiet out of respect for him.

The movement of food around her plate stopped, and she looked up at her parents. "We need to apologise to him," she said. "Thomas Mirren."

"Erm, okay," said Debbie. "I understand it's not good for Thomas Mirren but I'm not sure what we need to apologise for."

"I never mentioned him by name, Ellie," protested Ian. "If anyone needs to apologise, it's Brian. Or that bloody Chambers woman from the *Chronicle*."

Ellie wanted to scream at them. They just didn't get it. You can't start something and then wash your hands of the consequences. Why couldn't they see that?

But because they loved their daughter, and because she had nearly died, they agreed. In the end, they almost always agreed with her. Because almost always she was right. So, it was decided—they would visit Thomas Mirren the next day.

The following morning, the three of them sat at the breakfast table. Ian had decided to take the morning off so he could apologise properly, not just some hurried sorry. Despite the protestations of the night before, he knew he was guilty. He knew Debbie and Ellie knew it too. And that was the hardest part.

Ellie, sitting in her usual jeans and hooded top, suddenly announced she was going upstairs to get changed, and Ian nearly toppled off his chair. Ellie never 'got changed'; hooded tops and ripped jeans just landed on her.

Fifteen minutes later, as Ian was emptying his coffee down the sink and Debbie tidied the plates, Ellie appeared. A transformation so profound that Ian stood for a moment and stared. No rips in the jeans, and no hooded top. She was wearing a long skirt and the blue jumper Debbie had bought her for Christmas. The smart one she had never worn. Her hair was tied back, and she looked so grown-up.

"Christ," said Ian with a smile. "What have you done with my daughter?" And as Ellie blushed, Debbie prodded him painfully in the ribs.

"You look beautiful," said Debbie, walking over to where Ellie stood and hugging her so tightly that she was unable to move, her damaged arm hanging limply in its sling, squashed and uncomfortable.

"I'm sorry," said Debbie, noticing Ellie wince. "Does it hurt?"

"It's fine," replied Ellie. Signalling to her clothes, she added, "Do you think they're okay? A bit over the top?"

"You look great," said Ian. "We'll be proud to be seen out with you."

Ian went out to the car while Ellie and Debbie put on their coats. From behind the steering wheel, he watched as they left the house and locked the door, before walking over to join him.

Despite the large amount of money they'd spent on the car, Ian had always found it small. Ellie wriggled in the back seat, vainly attempting to find legroom.

"Can you move your chair forward?" she asked him.

Ian shook his head. "Move behind your mother. There's more legroom there."

And there was, but barely.

It took ten minutes to get into town, the roads being empty. They parked at Ian's office, and as they were early, they decided to grab a coffee before going to see Thomas Mirren. Ian hadn't finished his coffee earlier, and he didn't really feel like one now, but for some reason he was feeling nervous. An extra few minutes before heading to the supermarket seemed like a good idea.

"Have you thought about what you want to say?" asked Debbie, as if noticing Ian's discomfort.

"Of course I have," he replied. Which was true. Though he wasn't entirely confident he could remember it.

Entering the coffee shop, they headed to a low wooden table by the window. The brown leather sofa was soft, too soft, and Ellie looked as though she were drowning in the cushions. Ian and Debbie sat on wooden chairs, and Ian laughed as she looked up at him from her position just off the floor.

"Nice furniture," he said as Ellie relocated to a more practical seat. "Though perhaps a bit soft."

Within moments of them sitting down, they were joined by the waiter. Or 'barista', according to his name badge.

"Hey, Ellie," he said, and he smiled at Ellie as if he knew her. He was tall and thin and had tattoos the length of his arms. Underneath his apron, he wore a black T-shirt with some sort of image that Ian couldn't make out, perhaps the top of a skull. Ian didn't like the way he looked at his daughter. Predatorial.

"Hi, Mark," replied Ellie, smiling back. A proper smile, not fake. Ellie was a good judge of character, so perhaps Mark wasn't so bad after all.

"You feeling better?" asked Mark, and Ellie nodded. "Great," he said. "We're looking forward to seeing you back at college." He smiled again and then left. Ian noticed that Ellie was blushing, but he decided not to say anything. He didn't want to embarrass her. It occurred to him then that he knew very little about Ellie's friends. In fact, he knew very little about her life at all. He'd have to work on that.

For the next few minutes, they chatted—well, Debbie and Ellie chatted, at least, while Ian mostly nodded along—and when they got up to leave, Ian realised he couldn't recall a single detail of their conversation. Debbie had often commented on his poor listening skills, and perhaps she had a point. He would have to work on that too.

Walking across the park, Ian smiled at the families out for the morning, their children playing on the swings. He had pushed Ellie on those swings many years ago, but to him, it seemed like yesterday. She'd laughed and shouted, much like the children now, and a part of him felt sad, for the good times now gone.

And then they were at the supermarket, walking through the doors and approaching a table. There were poppy boxes on the table but no poppy sellers, and Ian was ashamed to find that he was relieved. It's never comfortable to meet a person you've wronged, even unintentionally. He sighed and turned to Ellie, but as he did so, he heard a voice. It was soft but strong. And it cut through him like a knife.

"Hello," said Thomas Mirren. He wasn't wearing his blazer again. "Come to buy another poppy?"

When they'd walked through the door, Ellie had been chatty, but now she was silent. He turned to her and saw she was crying again. Not loud crying, where you sob and wail, but the other one, the dignified type, where your eyes become wet and a single tear rolls down your cheek. The worst type.

"Are you okay, Ellie?" he asked, and his daughter nodded silently. Debbie was looking in her bag for a tissue, and Ian searched through his pockets. While they were busy, Thomas Mirren looked at Ellie and raised a finger to his lips. In that moment, their agreement was sealed. When Ian looked up, Ellie was wiping the tear away and beaming.

"It's okay," she said, "I'm fine."

Straightening up, Ian took a deep breath, preparing to apologise. He exhaled and breathed again. He'd forgotten what he was going to say.

"This is my wife," he said. "Debbie." Debbie smiled and nodded to Thomas Mirren. "And this is my daughter, Ellie."

Thomas Mirren smiled at them both. If he was confused, he hid it very well.

"I've seen you at the cemetery," said Debbie. "With the butterflies."

"Ah, yes," replied Thomas Mirren. "They were my wife's favourites." He paused for a moment. "And I've seen you with the roses." Debbie smiled, and there was colour in her face.

"My daughter had an accident," blurted Ian, alarmed at the state of his apology. He pointed to her arm.

"Oh, so you're the one in the paper, are you, Ellie?" asked Thomas Mirren, his blue eyes sparkling like sapphires. "I'm so happy to see that you're okay."

Ellie lifted her broken arm and smiled. "Someone saved me," she said simply.

It was Thomas Mirren's turn to smile. "I'm sure anyone would have done the same."

Just then, Thomas Mirren's colleague appeared. He'd been shopping, and in each hand was a plastic bag. As he walked, a clinking sound emanated from the bags.

"I see lunch has arrived," Thomas Mirren said, laughing.

Moving to put the bags on the table, the friend was just about to say something when there was a commotion at the entrance, and in rushed three teenagers, laughing and shouting.

"Fraud," one yelled, throwing something at Thomas Mirren.

"Liar," another shouted.

"GET OUT!"

It was so loud that the three boys stopped in their tracks. Ellie was standing there, glaring at them, and as she moved towards them, they turned and fled. As they disappeared outside, Ian looked across at Thomas Mirren. He was grinning.

Thomas Mirren whistled, impressed. "That's a powerful set of lungs you have there. Nearly blew them away."

"I'm sorry about that," said Ellie. "Not the shouting, but what those boys were saying," she added.

"I'm sorry too," said Ian. "It's all my fault really."

Thomas Mirren's friend stood up from his chair, moving to stand next to them. "What do you mean?" the friend asked, sounding menacing. For an old man, at least.

Ian took a deep breath. "Both of the stories in the *Echo* were by me," he admitted. "The two on page five, I mean." He paused, attempting to gauge Thomas Mirren's expression. But he was unreadable, so Ian continued: "You weren't meant to be mentioned. It was never meant to be like that." He looked at the floor. "But it started with me."

Ian had no idea how Thomas Mirren would react. Anger? Disappointment? Perhaps even relief? But there was nothing.

"Did you want it to turn out like this?" he asked, looking directly at Ian.

Ian answered honestly: "No."

Thomas Mirren smiled at that. "So, everything's fine," he said. "A mistake, that's all, and we all make those." He looked across to Ellie, then back to Ian. "It's not your fault."

They were quiet in the car as they drove home, Ian unsure what had just taken place. Had he apologised enough? Did Thomas Mirren really not blame him? And what had Debbie and Ellie thought of it all? He got one answer straight away.

"I'm proud of you, Dad," said Ellie. "Dodgy start but you got there in the end." She leaned over and patted his shoulder.

He couldn't see it but Ian knew Debbie was smiling. "Yes, well done, love," she said.

Pulling into the driveway, Ian parked the car. The three of them sat in silence, relief descending over them like a warm blanket. For different reasons, the visit to Thomas Mirren had been tiring for them all. For Ian because he'd been afraid of how Thomas Mirren would react and what his own family might think of him; for Debbie because she loved Ian and she didn't want him to get hurt; and for Ellie because her father had done the right thing and had shown himself to be the man she'd always known him to be.

And because now she knew for sure it was Thomas Mirren who'd saved her. And whatever anyone else said, he *was* a hero.

Chapter 22

Nicole and Michel

It was raining outside. Not a downpour or even anything close. It was a constant drizzle; the kind you barely notice until you're soaking wet. Nicole stood at the kitchen sink, staring out of the window, wondering what to do with her day. She'd been up and down into town for the last few days, and her bones were aching. It was her body's way of reminding her to slow down despite what her mind wanted her to believe.

She'd thought about going on the internet to catch up with the news but, as often happened in their house, the internet was down. She had done what she always did—turn off the computer, then turn it back on—but for once, that hadn't worked, and now she was stumped.

The banging and crashing from upstairs signalled the imminent arrival of Michel. Every morning was the same, as though he were playing pétanque in his room. Then, there would be footsteps, measured and heavy on the old wooden stairs before...

"Good morning, Sister."

Nicole smiled. It was the perfect start to the day.

Michel's first job was to set the fire, which they kept all year round even during the hot summer months. It made the house feel homely. There was something comforting about the crackle of logs, even as the sun burned the fields outside.

Over recent years, with the elasticity disappearing from his joints, things had become increasingly difficult for Michel, to the point where Nicole had proposed leaving the fire unlit. Michel had scoffed at the idea, and he now carried the largest and heaviest logs he could find. His stupid male pride will be the death of him, thought Nicole. And then she was sad, so she thought of something else.

"The internet is broken again," she said as Michel looked up from the fire.

"Did you turn it off and on?" he asked.

"No, Michel," she said sarcastically, laughing.

Michel shook his head and apologised. But just to make sure, he turned the computer on again, then off, then on. It still didn't work, so it was time for Plan B.

"We'll just have to wait," said Michel. "Maybe it will sort itself out later." Work complete, he went to make a cup of coffee.

At breakfast, Michel asked Nicole if she was going into town that day, and when she replied that she'd be staying home, he asked if she'd be okay on her own. He wanted to go out on his bike. Nicole smiled. He would go anyway but it was nice to be asked.

Breakfast that morning was a simple affair: baguette, butter, and jam. There was some Brie in the fridge but breakfast was not the time for cheese—a rule Nicole strictly adhered to. Michel would eat cheese for every meal if she let him.

"Did you make this jam?" asked Michel, wiping a large dollop from the side of his mouth.

"That depends on whether you like it or not," replied Nicole.

"It's delicious."

"Then, yes," Nicole said, smiling. "I did make it."

"And if I hadn't liked it?"

"I would have bought it from town."

Nicole had picked the raspberries herself from the old bush at the bottom of their garden with fruit that was so succulent it was impossible to make bad jam. And Nicole knew how to make bad jam. In fact, she could make many types of food badly, though Michel had never once complained. He would eat an old shoe if she said she'd made it.

Michel spent a large part of breakfast explaining the setup of the new bike he was building—alloy frame and carbon seatpost. The rest of the setup was undecided, though given the number of hills nearby, a double chainring would probably be best. And should he install an electric hub? He'd been thinking about one ever since he'd turned eighty, but the shift to electric felt like an admission that he was getting old.

"You *are* getting old," observed Nicole.

"But I don't want my bike to know that," replied Michel.

In the end, Nicole advised that he should go with whatever made him happiest. On the proviso that he wore the correct shorts.

By eleven o'clock, it had stopped raining, so Michel set off. The loose gravel on the path crunched beneath his tyres, and Nicole waved to him as he disappeared. She then headed into the garden to feed the chickens. They needed their breakfast too.

Before Michel had come down that morning, Nicole had prepared the chicken feed for the day. It was always the same but they seemed to enjoy it. She smiled to herself; they had never complained either. It was mostly grain with leafy greens, berries, and bananas, all of which were grown in the garden, with the exception of bananas. For those, she would go into town, picking up a large bunch each week. The blackened ones that no one wanted because they thought they were off, when in reality, they were the sweetest.

Large metal bowl in hand, she carefully closed the kitchen door and headed into the garden. The chicken coop was near to the house, by the side of Michel's bike shed. The sound of clucking erupted at her approach. In the past, they'd kept nearly a dozen chickens, but now there were four—Pinky, Blinky, Inky, and Clyde, named after the four *Pac-Man* ghosts, though she couldn't recall why. There had also been a rooster until recently—Charles, named after Charles Aznavour, who Nicole had always liked. But Charles had died.

When Nicole arrived, the four hens rushed to the front of the coop. They pecked at the trough, gorging on the feed until, very soon, it was empty. Then, they disappeared back to their roosts where they would sleep, dreaming of bananas and the strange lady who brought them.

There were three eggs that morning, and Nicole wondered which hen had been lazy. She decided upon Blinky because she had that look. The world was full of lazy people, and they all shared a look.

Inside the kitchen, she washed the bowl and left it to dry by the sink. Then, she made a cup of coffee and went to sit in the back garden. She had no idea how long Michel would be gone, but today he had on his backpack, so she knew he would be a while.

It was beautiful outside, the water from the earlier rain glistening on the grass so that the fields shimmered. In the distance, the warm sun pushed against the clouds, engulfing Saint Martin in a thick haze. To Nicole, it seemed as though the town was on fire. As she looked away, she noticed a kestrel hovering above the trees like a shadow against the sun. It swooped, gliding over the field so fast it blurred. And then it was gone.

She had a lot to do that day, but she felt lazy, so she remained in her chair, enjoying the garden. But then she thought of Blinky, and she sighed before standing up and emptying the dregs from her cup onto the lawn. She was many things but she was not a hypocrite.

An hour or so later, she was finishing the dusting. Carefully inspecting the bookcase, she ran her fingers along the length of each shelf. Spotless. Next was the windowsill, then the coffee table, and finally the chest of drawers in the corner. All good. Finally, she turned to the mantlepiece: photographs and candlesticks. Passable.

But the camel? Now, that was a different story. On the base, next to the faded spot of blood from Thomas Haven's injured hand, there were various irregularities. On one part, it looked like a piece of butter, or perhaps honey. There was dust along its back, and around its feet were several specks of dirt, most likely ash from the fire. Nicole cursed to herself. She must have forgotten to clean it after the meal. Picking it up, she gently removed the dirt, then wetted her finger to clean off the butter, taking great care not to rub at the blood.

And soon it was clean. "That's why it should be stored away in its box," she said to no one in particular. She would never forgive herself if something happened to it. But it was fine. Disaster averted.

A little later, after finishing the washing, she ironed her clothes. Michel did his own ironing, but he never did it right, and his collars were always creased. He'd been out for nearly three hours by that stage, and she wondered where he was. No doubt in town gossiping, she thought to herself, or eating a sandwich.

Just then, she noticed a blue light blinking on the box next to the television—the internet router. It looked like it was working again. Walking over, she pressed the button to turn it on, and as she did so, there was a knock at the door.

Michel swore. It wasn't something he did often, but on this occasion, it was warranted. As the air whistled from his inner tube, he realised he was in for a long walk home. It had to be the furthest point, didn't it?

The first puncture occurred having ridden over some glass, though why there was glass on the road so far from town, he had no idea. Yet, punctures weren't a problem; he'd had thousands of them in the past, and now he always carried a spare inner tube. His tyres were made of soft rubber, better for comfort than the hard all-weather ones most people used. But as a result, they were weak. It had taken him fifteen minutes to repair, the tyre coming off quickly as he fitted the new tube. Unfortunately, it was the back wheel, so he'd messed with the chain, resulting in oil stains on his hands. And then he'd pumped up the tyre. And then it had burst. And then he had sworn.

And that was how he found himself now, a second puncture and no way to repair it.

The most annoying thing to Michel was not the puncture. Not even that it had taken place so far from home where no one could help. It was the fact that the second puncture had been avoidable. Very avoidable. It was a basic mistake— always check the seating of the tube before starting to pump. If not, it might pinch against the rim and burst. Even the most rookie cyclists knew that. And Michel was no rookie.

It was approximately eight miles to his house, and he was wearing cycling shoes, perhaps the most impractical shoes in the world to walk in, after a clown's. But what choice did he have? So, with his bike at his side and his rucksack over his shoulder, he sighed and set off.

Four miles from home and Michel's legs were tired. It was strange how he could cycle all day but after a little walking, he was almost always sore. He thought about resting. Then, he dismissed the thought.

At one point, Monsieur Dernier whizzed past. His long hair—though he was bald at the top—flowed out horizontally behind him as he waved. Michel waved back, but he would have preferred Dernier to stop.

Nearing home, Michel noticed a kestrel hovering high above the ground as it scanned the fields below. He watched it for several minutes, and it was still there when he crested the hill to begin the last leg of the journey down the long road to his house.

Before long, he caught sight of his house. It was such a relief that he felt like cheering. But there was someone walking up the hill, just past the house, so he didn't. Five minutes later, he bumped into Peter.

"Hello, Michel," said Peter. He was wearing the same grey cardigan and black trousers as the other day. Michel thought back to the semi-naked mannequin, and he smiled, though Peter didn't appear to notice. "I was just out for a walk, and I wondered if you'd like this?" he said, holding out that day's *Chronicle.*

Michel thanked him and tucked the newspaper under his arm, trying his best not to cover it in bike oil. The two of them talked for a while, and Peter explained that he was taking a break from cycling. He'd hurt his knee and needed to rest it. Michel told him about his punctures that day, and when he mentioned the part about the second puncture, the pinch puncture, they both laughed.

"Rookie mistake," said Peter, and Michel agreed.

As he was leaving, Peter pointed to Michel's clothes. He asked him why he preferred to wear baggy shorts rather than the tight ones most people wore.

"The tight ones hinder sexual performance," answered Michel. Peter looked nauseous. Michel said goodbye, leaving Peter to his thoughts.

Finally, back at the house, he leaned his bike against the wall and went to the door. He didn't want to get oil on the handle, so he knocked.

Nobody knocked at the door. Not even the postman. Nicole got up from the computer and walked over to answer it.

"I'm so sorry," Michel said as he made his way past her and into the kitchen. And while he washed his hands, he explained to Nicole all about the disasters of the day.

"I didn't know Mercier was bald," said Nicole after he'd finished washing himself.

"Well, either that or he's becoming a monk," replied Michel.

Back in the living room, they sat down, and Michel asked Nicole how her morning had been. She shrugged, mentioning the eggs and her suspicions about Blinky. Then, she told him about the internet potentially working again and the dirt she'd found on the camel.

"I could have sworn I'd cleaned it after the other day," she said.

"Did you find the butter on it?" Michel asked.

Nicole shrieked. "You put that there on purpose?"

Michel rocked back in his chair, shaking with laughter. "It's what Mother used to do with me to make sure I didn't miss anything. Why do you think I'm so diligent now?"

Nicole was just about to say something when she noticed the newspaper on the table. Michel explained that Peter had given it to them. Together, they took it over to the window, where they opened it and began looking for interesting articles to read. On page seven, they found one—people who pretended to be war heroes.

"There's no need, is there?" said Michel after they'd finished reading. "What good can come from shaming old men?"

Nicole shook her head. "Whatever these men, Thomas Mirren and the others, have done... they deserve better than this."

She was about to close the paper when Michel pointed to the internet address underneath the story.

"Let's try it," he said. "Maybe there's a happy ending."

Nicole smiled at her brother. He was always looking on the bright side. "There are rarely happy endings, Michel," she said sadly and closed the newspaper.

Michel laughed, turning on the computer anyway. "Just in case you get bored," he said as he made his way to the kitchen. "I'm going to make a sandwich. Do you want one?"

"Yes, please," Nicole replied.

He got a new loaf out of the cupboard. The old one was nearly finished, so he'd use that for his own sandwich. Nicole could have the fresher one. He retrieved a large slab of Brie from inside the fridge. Unable to resist, he cut a chunk from the corner and ate it quickly before Nicole had the chance to see. She would scold him for using his fingers and for not waiting until the food was ready but it was staring at him so seductively that he was unable to stop himself.

As he was slicing the bread, he heard a newspaper rustling, swiftly followed by several taps on the computer keyboard. Michel smiled to himself and hurried to finish the sandwiches. He was keen to read the rest of the story too. Despite what Nicole had said, he did believe in happy endings.

It was a few more minutes before the sandwiches were finished, during which time it had become increasingly quiet in the living room. He shouted to Nicole to tell her the food was ready and to see if she was all right. But there was no reply.

Walking back into the room, he found her at the computer, motionless, her hands at her sides.

"What's wrong?" he asked, but Nicole didn't move. In front of her, on the computer screen, was a picture of a man. A man Michel recognised at once. Handsome and with piercing eyes. There were tears streaming down Nicole's face.

At last, she turned to face him, and her eyes shone so brightly that he almost looked away.

"The Camel," she said softly. "He's alive."

Chapter 23

Thomas

Thomas had slept badly. Again. The Second Face had disturbed his sleep. As a rule, there were only two faces which Thomas dreamed about, the first being Ellen's, and at those times, he didn't want to wake up. But the Second Face was different. It was the face of a man in uniform, laughing as he peeled the skin from Thomas's back. On those nights, Thomas was more than happy to wake.

He'd first met the Second Face in France, the day Adam had been hurt. He'd beaten Thomas with a pistol, then scarred him with a whip. But for some reason, he'd decided not to kill Thomas that day—a decision he would later regret. Thomas had been dragged around for three days. Each evening, the Second Face had taken his fun, opening the wounds on Thomas's back as they attempted to heal. But what the Second Face hadn't understood was Thomas wasn't normal. As his body suffered, he'd become stronger, so in the end, the Second Face had had no chance. And one day, all trace of him had been erased.

The violence Thomas had shown that day was one of his few regrets. It was the only time he'd killed through choice rather than instruction. He was better than that. In the days following, he'd met up with his troops and was very soon fighting again. Friends are easy to find if you know where to look.

But he didn't see Adam again until after the war, and that was another of his regrets.

The Colonel had phoned twice that morning. He'd told Thomas that Frank had a hospital appointment, so wouldn't be going to the supermarket. He'd then asked Thomas if he was okay to go on his own until he could get there, as if he were somehow a child who needed looking after. Not a monster who erased people from existence. And that's what he was to some people—a monster. Not a hero, as others had claimed. Every coin has two sides.

He wanted to be at the supermarket by ten o'clock; it would take him a few minutes to get the boxes ready without Frank. It was just gone nine, so he had half an hour or so before he needed to leave. The postman had been, and at the foot of the front door was a small pile of letters, mostly brown envelopes, with a flyer for a new takeaway pizza place. As a rule, he didn't eat pizza, but he was feeling daring today, so perhaps he'd give it a try.

So that they knew how things were going, they always used Frank's pen for recording takings, sales, and so on. Frank had bought the pen especially for the job and he insisted on using it. It was long and fat and covered in gaudy gold plating which Frank insisted was solid gold. Thomas had commented that if it were made of gold, it would be too heavy and entirely impractical for writing. Which had made Frank laugh as he'd flexed his biceps, declaring it no problem for him even if it were made of osmium. That was the heaviest metal in the world, according to the quiz show Frank had watched recently. He was full of useful information like that.

The long and short of the situation was that Thomas now needed a pen. There were various disposable pens scattered about the house, but none of those would suffice. He would not be outdone by Frank and his gold-plated monstrosity.

At the back of a cupboard in his bedroom was a small wooden box. It contained his fountain pen, given to him by his mother when he'd first started school. Resembling a small, black torpedo, it wrote like a dream despite the bent nib. Or at least it had done when Thomas had last used it, which was over twenty years ago. He looked at it now, black ink crusting the nib like dried blood. Unscrewing the barrel, he shook the pen to check the cartridge for ink, and finding none, he threw the cartridge away. Also inside the box were two small cardboard packets, each containing new ink cartridges. Blue or blue-black, that was the choice, so he chose blue-black. A sombre colour, more fitting for the day.

As he was replacing the ink, he noticed another box, further back in the cupboard and half-covered by a piece of white cloth. Carefully lifting it, he moved over to the bed and sat down. The box was heavy, and on its wooden lid, crudely carved, were the initials *TM* and *EW*, set inside what was meant to be a heart, though to Thomas, it looked more like an apple. He clearly recalled the day he'd carved it, Ellen trying not to laugh as she'd hugged him and told him it was perfect. He smiled at the memory, but it was a sad kind of smile.

The first thing he saw when he lifted the lid was a piece of paper folded in two and placed carefully in the centre. He sighed as he opened it, gently running his fingers across the beautifully flowing script: 'Thomas Mirren, My Hero'. To Ellen, at least, he was a hero. And that was all that mattered.

Underneath the paper were the other things—the medals. So many, in fact, that he couldn't remember how many there were. On the right was a star-shaped medal, the colour of copper, with its faded red, green, and white ribbon. He'd received it with Adam when they were young and indestructible, a few weeks after the war had finished. But he'd never worn it.

Some of the medals had no ribbons, and he struggled to remember what many of them were for—some act of heroism, or barbarity, depending on how you looked at it.

And then there was the main one, right at the bottom, pristine and unblemished. He'd worn that one, though only because he'd had to. They'd wanted it for the photographs as people had shaken his hand and told him what a fine soldier he was. But afterwards, he'd taken it off, and he had never worn it again.

Carefully placing the box back where he'd found it, Thomas closed the cupboard door.

Then, he cleaned the pen.

The pile of letters by the front door stared up at him as he approached. With the pen cleaned, he needed to test the new cartridge, and what better than an envelope? Shuffling them, he decided upon one from the gas company—boiler cover, fifty per cent off for a limited time only. Very generous of them, thought Thomas as he scribbled on it. Memories of his schooldays came flooding back: Mr McCamley laughing and joking and generally doing very little teaching; the main hall full of boys as they struggled with their exams; and finally, Fatty Clark, who by today's standard was not fat at all, pointing to Thomas's pen and laughing.

"Why do you always carry it around in a box, Haven?" he'd sneered. "Think you're better than the rest of us, do you?" When Fatty Clark had grabbed at the pen, Thomas had hit him. Just hard enough that no one would ever touch his pen again. He'd earned two detentions that day and a scolding from his mother. But it had been worth it.

Thomas smiled at the memory, and when he looked down at the envelope, there was his signature: *Thomas Haven, class 1G.*

He was going to be late now. No time to look through the rest of the envelopes, so he placed them on the kitchen table.

"Something to look forward to later," he said, chuckling.

He did keep one though; a handwritten one with no address. Someone must have pushed it through the letterbox themselves. He put that one in his pocket.

Outside, it was a pleasant morning. One of those mornings that was too warm for a coat but too cool for shirt sleeves. His blazer would have been ideal.

It was precisely ten o'clock when he arrived at the supermarket, and by ten-fifteen he was sitting at his table, hot cup of coffee to his right, large slice of cake to his left. His pen was in front of him, next to a notebook and still in its box.

He had to wait half an hour before the first person came over. It was an old lady, and she smiled at him as she handed him a five pound note. She then took a small enamel poppy and told him to keep the change. Thanking her, he watched as she disappeared down the frozen food aisle, then took his pen from its box and placed a small tick in the book. Blue-black, definitely the right choice.

By twelve o'clock, the book was full of ticks, and Thomas was feeling very pleased with himself. Halfway through recalculating the total, he caught sight of the Colonel, his stride purposeful and with a big grin on his face.

"I just bumped into Harry Wiggins," said the Colonel, pulling up a chair. "Apparently, you've had a good morning." Harry Wiggins had bought a poppy earlier, one of the paper ones that comes with a pin. He'd stood chatting to Thomas and had asked what all the blue ticks were for. Thomas had explained that the *blue-black* ticks were sales and that today, he'd done rather well, at which point Harry had whistled, though it sounded more like a wheeze He'd then congratulated Thomas on his 'powers of boosterism', whatever that meant. He was last seen heading towards the meat counter.

"Yes," replied Thomas. "I've nearly sold out."

When the Colonel saw Thomas's book, he too whistled. And his whistle sounded exactly as it should—clear and melodic. A whistle of substance.

"You must have bought them yourself," he joked. "Trying to make the rest of us look bad."

"Not on my pension," countered Thomas, and the Colonel had no answer to that.

"Anyway," he said, "I'm sorry I'm so late. I had to post a letter to the florist to clarify the requirements for the parade. The queue stretched back to The Royal."

"Why don't you just email him?" asked Thomas. "Or better still, walk to his shop. He's only a mile or two past the Legion."

"To answer your questions in order," said the Colonel with a smile, "one, because I am over ninety years old. And two, because I am over ninety years old."

The Colonel's story reminded Thomas of the letter he'd put in his pocket earlier. Taking it out, he flattened it on the table with his book.

The Colonel eyed the letter suspiciously. "Handwritten and with no address," he said. "Could be poison."

"Exactly," replied Thomas. "That's why I waited for you to arrive. Your big lungs should soak it all up."

The Colonel was about to explain that lungs don't actually soak things up, but he decided against it. Instead, he went off in search of two cups of tea while Thomas opened the letter.

The handwriting on the envelope was untidy, almost childlike, and one 'r' was missing from his name. Inside, there was a note, again handwritten and in the same childlike script:

You're a disgrace to the memory of all the brave soldiers who died in the war. You should be ashamed of yourself!

At least, that was the gist of it. There were spelling mistakes and the grammar was appalling but the meaning was clear. Inside the envelope, along with the note, was a single white feather—the symbol of cowardice. The small feather felt soft between his fingers. It was the kind of feather you might find inside a pillow or a cushion. He sighed, placing the letter and feather back into the envelope. He was many things, but a coward was not one of them.

Then, he pictured the person who'd written the note plucking angrily at an old pillow, and he chuckled at the thought.

"You look happy," said the Colonel, returning to the table with tea and yet more cake. "Been buying the poppies again?"

When Thomas didn't respond, the Colonel looked at him. "What was in the letter?"

"Oh, not much," replied Thomas. "Just something and nothing."

"Hand it over, Thomas," said the Colonel, placing the tea and cake on the table and holding out his hand. "It's obviously not *nothing*. *Nothing* wouldn't stop you laughing at my jokes."

There was no point in refusing. From experience, Thomas knew the Colonel wouldn't give up. So, he handed him the letter. And for the next few minutes, the Colonel read and re-

read the note, opened and closed the envelope, and finally scrutinised the feather. Thomas started on the cake.

At last, the Colonel looked at him. "You know," he said, "I'd be angry if this wasn't so ridiculous. Not the grammar or the spelling, and not even the stupid feather." He broke off to look at the feather again. "It looks like it's come from a pillow," he said. "But the fact is, you're the bravest man I've ever known. And I've known quite a few."

Thomas took the envelope back. "Waste of paper, Adam," he said. "I should have left it at home." Putting the envelope back into his pocket, he finished off the cake.

The Colonel didn't stay much longer after that. Despite his denials, Thomas could see he was furious, and the last thing they needed was an angry face scaring away their customers. It was nearly time to pack up anyway. Thomas decided he'd stay a while longer, as he had some shopping to do. He was heading to the cemetery later, so would give the Legion a miss that day. He'd have to get his daily alcohol requirement at home. As the Colonel was leaving, he made Thomas promise to get rid of the letter, which wasn't necessary, as Thomas had already decided to do just that.

As he was packing up the boxes, Jenny came over.

"I'm glad I've caught you," she said. "I was afraid you might have left by now. Did Adam speak to you?"

It seemed strange when other people referred to the Colonel as Adam. But Jenny had known the Colonel for years through family, so Thomas didn't say anything.

"About what?" replied Thomas. "I sat next to him for over an hour, but we didn't speak about anything in particular."

He didn't want to mention the letter.

"I knew he wouldn't say anything," said Jenny, shaking her head. "He's very careful where you're concerned." Then, she laughed. "Like a bull in a china shop with everyone else, mind."

Jenny told Thomas about her conversation with the Colonel: it turned out someone had complained about Thomas selling poppies, in light of the recent newspaper articles. Jenny assured Thomas that she'd sorted it out, but she felt he should know anyway.

"Just to prepare yourself," she added. "In case you come across any idiots."

Thomas smiled and thanked her. "I've come across idiots all my life," he said, "but thank you for the warning."

Jenny shrugged, declaring once again that no right-minded people would believe a word of what had been written.

But not everyone was right-minded. Thomas knew that very well.

After Jenny left, muttering something about being late for a yoga class, Thomas finished packing up. He hadn't eaten much that day apart from cake, so he headed for the sandwich aisle. It was pizza for dinner from the new place but he needed something now. Scanning the several rows of sandwiches, he decided there were too many to choose from, so he grabbed the nearest one—prawn cocktail. You can never go wrong with prawns.

Then, he bought a bottle of whisky. You can never go wrong with whisky either.

Back at the table, he took out a tissue and dusted some cake crumbs into his hand. There was a cake wrapper too and bits of silver foil from a packet of mints. Collecting them, he placed them in his pocket and then straightened the chairs. As he was about to leave, he heard a voice from behind him.

"Phew. I was afraid you might have left."

Thomas turned around. Standing there was Ellie Rogers, U6A, smartly dressed and with her right arm in a bright blue sling.

"Everybody seems afraid I'm going to leave today," said Thomas with a smile. "New backpack, Ellie Rogers?"

Ellie laughed, bright and musical, and it reminded him of another person's laugh; a person he loved more than the world.

"The other one got damaged," said Ellie. "I really should be more careful."

"Yes," replied Thomas, "you should."

Ellie reached out her good arm. "This is for you, Thomas," she said. In her hand was his blazer.

Chapter 24

Ellie

Ellie had decided to go and see Thomas Mirren that day. She'd told herself it was to return the blazer, but in fact, she just wanted to see him.

Most of the morning was spent catching up on missed coursework. Unlike many of her friends, she actually enjoyed her studies. They were courses she'd chosen, after all— geography, business studies, and French. Who'd have thought that oxbow lakes and the works of Albert Camus could be so interesting? Business studies was dull, of course, but it made her dad happy, so she'd stick with it.

She'd originally planned to see Thomas Mirren at lunchtime, but she didn't know what time he had his own lunch, so she went for one o'clock instead, hoping she wouldn't miss him.

At twelve o'clock, she had just finished making a sandwich. Nothing adventurous, just ham and a packet of crisps. Prawn cocktail. Moving to the living room, she slumped onto the sofa and turned on the television. There wasn't much to watch, unless you wanted to buy antiques or upgrade your house, so she skipped to her station of last resort—the news. Once again, not much on, but then came a story about the upcoming Remembrance Day celebrations, and she was amazed to see how much work went into it. This year, it was seventy years since the Liberation of Paris, so a delegation from France was over. Standing next to their British counterparts, they looked scruffy and inelegant, like they had just woken up. They also looked bored, as though they would rather be somewhere else, and Ellie found herself getting annoyed.

Monsieur Fulminer, the French ambassador, was talking about something, but Ellie had stopped listening. All she could think about was how red his face was and how large. Like someone had overinflated a balloon, then added some eyes and a small mouth. It looked as though Monsieur Fulminer was about to burst, so she turned off the television and went back into the kitchen. She'd always been afraid of balloons.

Ellie watched houses and people pass by out of the car window on her way into town. She'd asked her mum if she could give her a lift, and her mum had said yes immediately. Since the accident, her parents had said yes to just about everything. But it was still a surprise; her dad rarely lent out 'his' car. She wasn't even sure why she'd asked, as she preferred walking.

Driving along Knox Road, she asked the radio to play some chart music, and when a song came on that she liked, she smiled to herself, her head bobbing in time to the expletives. Next to her, her mum shook her head and frowned disapprovingly.

They left the car at her dad's office, as it was near the supermarket. Her mum had a couple of things to do in town, so they agreed to meet in an hour. Taking her new rucksack, she checked herself in the wing mirror and said goodbye to her mother.

It was hot immediately inside the supermarket due to a heater by the doors, blowing hot air around the entranceway. For a moment, it felt like summer. Summer in Kingsley, anyway. She opened her bag and carefully removed what was inside. It was Thomas Mirren's blazer. Looking around the foyer, she couldn't immediately see him. She continued searching, nervously biting her lip, afraid he'd left for the day.

And then she caught sight of him on the other side of the entrance hall, straightening chairs at an old metal table. Taking a deep breath, she walked over.

"Phew," she said, arriving at the table as Thomas Mirren turned around. "I was afraid you might have left."

He smiled at that, then asked her if she had a new backpack, which made her laugh. And when she laughed, he looked so happy that she was glad she'd come. Ellie had so many things she wanted to say to him, and as they chatted together in the heat of the foyer, surrounded by strangers, she realised she'd forgotten them all. So, she handed him the blazer. And when he took it, he looked happy again. And that made Ellie happy.

"Have you had your lunch, Mr Mirren?" asked Ellie while he finished tidying the table.

"Please," he replied, "call me Thomas. Mr Mirren makes me sound old."

That made her laugh again, though it didn't sound like her laugh. It was somebody else's, clear and melodic, like small bells tinkling in the wind. He lifted his plastic bag, holding it out in front of him, and through the side, she could see a box of sandwiches. Prawn cocktail—a good choice. Next to the sandwiches was a bottle of whisky, not one of the small ones favoured by alcoholics, but a large one, like the one Dr Banner kept in his drawer at the college. The one he thought was a secret, though everyone knew about it. Seeing the bottle, Ellie looked away.

"This will do me." Thomas laughed, then noticed her discomfort. "Not the whisky, the sandwich." He lowered the bag, and as he was doing so, he told Ellie he was going to the cemetery that afternoon. He'd have his lunch there.

"So am I," replied Ellie, "Or at least I am now. I'll give you a lift, if you like. I'm going there with my mum." Which wasn't strictly the truth.

"Did you hurt your legs in the accident too?" asked Thomas. "It's only about a twenty-minute walk."

Ellie laughed. "My generation doesn't walk. Whatever next?"

"Probably why there are so many fat ones," declared Thomas, immediately apologising. "Not that you're one of them," he added quickly.

Ellie declared that she would only forgive him if he allowed her to give him a lift to the cemetery, and Thomas could see he was trapped. After putting on his blazer and giving the table one last check, he smiled to Ellie as they left together.

Kingsley's one-way system meant it would take almost as long to drive to the cemetery as it would take to walk. Nevertheless, Ellie took the opportunity to chat with Thomas as they went, and by the time they were at the car, she'd found he was excellent company. He was a fast walker, making it difficult for her to keep up, and she marvelled at his strength despite his age. She'd asked him how he managed to stay so healthy, and when he'd attributed it to prawn cocktail sandwiches and whisky, she'd laughed. Again. And she suddenly realised she'd laughed more in the last few minutes than she had done for weeks.

To her mum's credit, she didn't look surprised when Ellie walked up to the car with Thomas. Her mum's smile was so broad as she said hello that Ellie wanted to kiss her.

"I see my daughter has kidnapped you, Mr Mirren," she said.

"Thomas," corrected Ellie, as the three of them got into the car.

"Listen to this," said Ellie. They were driving along the main road out of town, Ellie in the front seat and Thomas in the back. She asked the radio for a song by Elton John—she didn't want one with bad language in it—and when the music started to play, Thomas nodded approvingly. He then asked for something by Benny Goodman, but the radio didn't know any songs by that name.

"Philistine," said Thomas to the radio before turning his attention to Ellie. "Your wireless needs updating."

"Who the heck is Lenny Goodman anyway?" she asked with a grin. But Thomas didn't answer, preferring instead to look out of the window.

They arrived at the cemetery just as another song was finishing. Ellie got out and walked around the car to help Thomas from his seat. But he was already out.

"You'll have to be quicker than that," he said.

Ellie's mum asked them if they wanted her to wait, and before Ellie had the chance to reply, Thomas said no. He thanked her before adding that it was a nice walk back to town. So, she left, leaving Thomas and Ellie to walk up the long gravel path to the church.

"It's miles back to town," grumbled Ellie as they walked. "She wouldn't have minded waiting, you know."

"Four to be precise," said Thomas. "How old are you, Ellie?"

"Nearly nineteen," she replied.

"Well, at your age, I was walking halfway across Europe. You should be able to walk forty miles, let alone four."

"That's why we have a car, Thomas," said Ellie, and Thomas could tell she was smiling.

By the time they reached the end of the path, Ellie was beginning to get warm. Thomas's walking pace was much faster than she was used to. She'd have to get into better shape, she decided, as it was a bit embarrassing being outsped by someone over four times her age.

The old gate was silent as Ellie pushed it open, swinging smoothly on its hinges before stopping gently by the side of the grass.

"That's odd," observed Thomas. "It always makes a right racket when I open it."

"You just have to be gentle," replied Ellie. "Not everything needs clobbering."

Thomas didn't say anything as they walked along the long path from the gate, the gravel crunching noisily beneath his feet. A gentle breeze brushed against his face. At that moment, he felt young again, or at least not the ninety years he was carrying. He wanted to tell Ellen he'd found his blazer and that a young girl who had a similar name to her had driven with him in an electric car with a music system so advanced it didn't know Benny Goodman.

"I'll leave you here," said Ellie. "I'm just going to visit my gran's grave over there." She pointed to the gravestone where Thomas had seen her mother just the other day. "Will you be long?"

Thomas shook his head. "No. Perhaps thirty minutes. Just long enough to eat my sandwich and update Ellen on what's been going on." And then he left, leaving Ellie with her gran who she'd always thought of as old, but if she were alive today, would be younger than Thomas Mirren.

In front of the gravestone was a small glass jug, inside which were several red roses. They looked tired, as though they needed water, so she reached into her backpack and took out the small bottle of water she always carried with her. Emptying it into the jug, she took a few moments to remember her gran, now long gone, the lines of her face beginning to blur. Ellie pictured her long grey hair, the thin mouth marked from years of smoking. Oh, how she could laugh. Such a powerful set of lungs, so it was ironic that those lungs would eventually kill her. Years of smoking had left a mark there too.

By the side of the jug were several other roses, drying in the sun and already beginning to fade. She thought about moving them but decided against it, not knowing what kind of creepy-crawlies lay in wait underneath.

After a few minutes, she glanced over to Thomas. He was sitting on a short bench, well-maintained and sturdy, and he seemed to be talking. In his left hand was his prawn sandwich. Every so often, he would stop talking to take a bite from it. The bench was surrounded by lavender, and a brightly coloured butterfly hovered above his head while another sat patiently on the gravestone in front of him. He looked like a statue, and she would have taken a photograph of him had it not seemed inappropriate.

At last, he got up, and as he walked along the path towards Ellie, she said goodbye to her gran and went to join him. He was whistling, though she didn't recognise the tune.

"Would you like to go to the park?" she asked when they reached the gate. It was a spur-of-the-moment question, and she was fully expecting him to say no.

"Sounds lovely," he replied. "We can take the bus from the end of the road."

"I thought you walked everywhere." Ellie laughed.

"Public transport is different," said Thomas, but they both knew it wasn't.

It was busy in the park, being a sunny day. Small groups of people dotted the grass, chatting and listening to music on their tinny phone speakers. Nobody was exercising in the bandstand as they walked past, just a small girl running around in circles as her mother watched on.

"I used to do that," said Ellie, pointing to the little girl.

"Was that before you stopped walking?" asked Thomas.

The walk up the hill was steep, but Thomas showed no signs of slowing, and as they reached the top, he asked her if she wanted something to eat or drink. They'd arrived at the Butterfly House. Ellie watched as Thomas headed inside and walked to the counter. He ordered her a coffee and got the same for himself. When he returned, he was also carrying two slices of cake.

"Nice people," he said as they headed over to the benches in front of the memorial.

"I know," said Ellie, trying not to spill her drink. It was filled far too full. "I went to school with the boy, and the girl is the sister of one of my friends. He's called Neil, but I can't remember her name."

When they arrived at the benches, they sat down. Thomas handed her a cake—a Victoria sponge with jam and double cream overflowing from its centre.

"Crickey," said Ellie. "How many calories are in this?"

"One," replied Thomas as he tucked into his slice. "But it's a very big one." She noticed him smile, and a small blob of cream stuck to his lip.

They must have sat there for half an hour, eating cake and drinking coffee. Thomas was easy to talk to. He listened to what she said and was full of interesting stories. She asked him about the Remembrance Day parade, and he told her he was looking forward to it. A little later, she asked him about his wife, and the smile on his face broadened as he recalled their times on this bench, eating cake and watching the world go by.

"It's a lovely name," she said at last. "Ellen. A bit like mine. Mine's short for Eleanor."

"You know," said Thomas, still looking into the distance as though not ready to stop thinking about his wife. "Eleanor is derived from Helen, via Ellen. I believe it means 'shining light', though I could be mistaken."

"'Shining light' sounds good," said Ellie.

It wasn't until they'd been at the park for around an hour, when they were getting ready to leave, that the topic of the newspaper articles came up. Ellie said again how sorry she was for what her father had written, or at the very least what he'd started, but Thomas waved it away.

"I don't care what people think about me, Ellie," he said.

"But *I* do," she replied, and Thomas looked at her, smiling.

"That's nice of you, Ellie," he said, "but at the end of my life, there will only be one person to judge me. And that's me." He wanted her to understand that, and she did. In the end, no one else mattered.

The ride back into town was uneventful. They had to wait at the bus stop for ten minutes, and when the bus arrived, it was half full. Two people, a man and a woman, said hello to Thomas and smiled at Ellie as though she were his granddaughter. It was a nice thought.

As they were getting off the bus, a third person spoke to Thomas. He was young and muscular, and he was wearing a faded T-shirt and camouflage trousers. On his arm, he had a tattoo—a crown above a rose, surrounded by a wreath. He nodded respectfully to Thomas and wished him a nice day.

"Who was that?" asked Ellie as they walked towards the town centre.

"Someone from the Duke of Lancaster's Regiment, judging from the tattoo," replied Thomas. "I think I've seen him down the Legion."

"Do you have any tattoos from your army days?" asked Ellie.

Thomas shook his head. He'd never seen the need. "The army is all in the past, as far as I'm concerned."

"Is that why you spend every afternoon at the Legion?" joked Ellie.

Thomas laughed. "Cheap booze," he replied, and this time it was Ellie who laughed.

Chapter 25

Michel

When Michel came downstairs the next morning, Nicole was gone. They'd stayed up until late the previous evening, and Nicole had finally revealed to Michel what she had seen all those years ago. Even now, after a long sleep, the thought made him shudder—the beatings, the whip, and the brave man who had not talked, remaining silent to protect a family he didn't know. If he was honest, Michel had never really understood Nicole's veneration of the Camel, but now he did. Of course, she'd mentioned what had happened, mentioned it every year, in fact, but she had spared her family the details. Until last night, at least. Then, it had come flooding out, and the thought was sickening. He couldn't begin to understand the burden she had carried all these years.

In the garden, the four hens were clucking behind the wire mesh of their cage. Michel looked into their food trays, finding it strange that they were empty. Not the kind of empty that followed a feed, but the empty of trays not yet filled. Further along the garden, out into the fields, there were birds and butterflies, the sound of a dog barking, and the soft rustle of leaves. But there was no Nicole.

As he came back into the house, Michel could hear his own heart beating. It wasn't unusual for Nicole to go out early but she had always told him or woken him or left a note. But today there was nothing, and coming so soon after the revelations of the day before, he was starting to worry. Climbing the stairs to her room, he gently knocked on her door, but she was not there. Nor was she in any of the other rooms. It was not strange anymore; it was alarming.

On the table in the living room, he noticed the newspaper, open at the page with the story of the Camel. The internet had called him Thomas Mirren, when his name was Thomas Haven.

"Who the hell is Thomas Mirren?" Michel muttered, looking at the story. Thomas Mirren lived in Kingsley, and he had been exposed by the *Kingsley Echo*. "And where the hell is Kingsley?"

A minute later and the computer was whirring into life. He logged onto the internet and searched for Kingsley. Then, he looked at a map.

"Lyon to Kingsley?" he whispered, his finger tracing a line from the centre of France to London. "About five or six hours, I would imagine." Then, he looked at the train timetable. And now he *was* worried. She wouldn't, would she? But Nicole had always been pig-headed, and Michel would put nothing past her.

As he was about to go looking for her, he noticed a note propped up against the photographs on the mantlepiece. He wondered how he hadn't seen it before. It was folded and placed alongside the picture of Nicole and him as children, and on the front, in Nicole's beautiful writing, was the word 'Michel'.

Dearest Michel, I have gone out for a while and don't know when I will be back. There's something I need to do. Nicole x

"Dear God, Nicole," he shouted. "You're eighty years old, not eighteen."

He ran to his room to put on his cycling gear. In next to no time, Michel was ready. He couldn't find his baggy cycling shorts, so for the first time in his life, he decided to go without. He would have to make do with the tight shorts he always wore underneath. The same type Peter wore. Glancing at himself in the mirror, he didn't like what he saw.

His sunglasses were by the door, next to his helmet. Even though he could be at the railway station within fifteen minutes, there was something he needed to do first. The computer was still on, so he walked over to it and sat down. He searched for the *Kingsley Echo*.

Then, he picked up the phone.

If anyone had been watching the road to Saint Martin that morning, they might have noticed a blur. Michel was travelling at speeds he hadn't reached for years, and the reason was twofold: firstly, of course, because he was worried about Nicole; but secondly, he didn't want to be seen half-naked. The faster he travelled, the less time he would be out in the open. He shot past Monsieur Paysan's farm, its old slate roof still cracked and in need of repair. Past Madame Modiste's house, gardens trim and bushes clipped. Then, past the Morning Café, with its smell of coffee and freshly cleaned tables. There was no time to look inside, but he knew it would be full.

On the corner of Rue du Moulin, Madame Bisset was busy in conversation with Monsieur Lafayette. She stared at Michel as he passed, and he was sure she was smiling. Rue de la Fontaine was busy, so he took a left and went around the church. It was a longer route but there would be fewer people. Unfortunately, old Dernier was there, and he tooted his horn several times as Michel whizzed by, causing people to stare as Michel cursed under his breath. The last leg was straight and, to his relief, mostly deserted. Twelve minutes after leaving his house, Michel arrived at the railway station. A new record.

Immediately upon his arrival, Michel noticed something was wrong. All the platforms were empty, with several coaches waiting by the road. One of the coaches was full, and groups of children pointed at him from the windows and giggled. Hurrying past, he spotted a station guard by the entrance, so he got off his bike and went over to see him.

"Monsieur Lagare," he said, leaning his bicycle against a green metal bench, "have you seen my sister this morning? I think she may be heading for England."

"No, Monsieur le Maire," replied Monsieur Lagare, who was busy cleaning his spectacles on a piece of cloth hanging from his belt. Monsieur Lagare was an officious man but good-natured, especially when mixed with alcohol. Not a single detail escaped his attention, so when he said he hadn't seen Nicole, it meant she hadn't been there.

Michel nodded and thanked him. "What are all the coaches for?"

"Signal failure," answered Lagare. "There have been no trains all day. Which is another reason I know your sister didn't leave from here."

"One of the coaches, perhaps?" asked Michel, and the station guard laughed.

"When have you ever known your sister to take a coach?"

Michel shook his head. It was true. Nicole had an inherent distrust of coaches—and buses, for that matter—though she had never explained why.

"Perhaps you could call her on her mobile phone," said Monsieur Lagare, thinking out loud. And this time, it was Michel's turn to laugh. Nicole would never have a mobile phone—something to do with radiation. He mentioned it to a stunned Monsieur Lagare.

"How very odd. Mobile phones are real lifesavers."

Judging from the number of people who are run over while looking at their phones, Michel would never have classed them as 'lifesavers'. Ambulance drivers and nurses, on the other hand. But he had no time to argue, so he wished Lagare a good day and left.

Michel pushed his bike for a while. The stress of the situation made him unfit to cycle. With rapidly beating heart, he needed to calm down; it was time to look at things from an objective perspective. If she hadn't taken a train and she wasn't at home, where else could she be? She hadn't gone shopping, her bags were still by the door, and besides, she'd been complaining of tiredness. Michel was at a loss.

"The thing that keeps me going will be the thing to finish me off," he said, but there was no one around to hear.

Slowly making his way back through town, he didn't mind anymore if people found his semi-nakedness strange. He was beyond caring. All he cared about was finding his sister. He trudged along Rue Fontaine, winding from the market to the old booksellers, his feet aching in cycling shoes not designed to be walked in. At Rue du Moulin, Madame Bisset had disappeared, and her place had been taken by a man he didn't recognise, wearing a heavy coat and being dragged along by two dogs. One of the dogs looked old, and its tongue hung out of its mouth.

"I know how you feel," whispered Michel. "But at least you don't have to wear these bloody shoes."

The second dog was smaller than the first, which was almost the size of a wolf, and it yapped constantly, jumping up and down as though standing on hot coals. Michel found it annoying, and he was pleased when the three of them finally turned a corner and vanished from view. He imagined that the large dog would grow tired of its companion one day and would eat it.

By the time the Morning Cafe came into view, he had been out for well over an hour. His feet hurt, and he was abnormally tired—the stress of the morning, he assured himself, rather than his advancing years. Outside, there were three tables, a white tablecloth on each, and various jars containing sugars, jams, and all sorts of fancy napkins. He looked at his watch—it was ten o'clock, and he still hadn't had breakfast. A few minutes at the cafe, a piece of cake and a coffee, and then he'd head home to formulate a plan. Maybe Anne-Marie could help.

One good thing about the Morning Cafe, apart from the coffee and fantastic cakes, was that it had a bike stand around the back. Previously, there had been one at the side, but Anne-Marie had replaced it with a small herb garden. She didn't want cyclists yomping through her parsley and thyme, so she'd asked Peter to build a rack at the back. And it was to that place that Michel now headed, pushing his bike down the narrow passageway between the cafe and the house next door, fastening it securely with one of the available chains. Each chain had a padlock, and each padlock had a combination code. Michel knew them all because they were all the same—1944, the Liberation of Paris.

Before heading inside, he checked the chain several times to make sure it was secure.

"For God's sake, Michel, put on some clothes."

It was Anne-Marie, sitting at a table by the window, a broad grin on her face. Peter was with her, reading a newspaper. Next to them was Nicole, a spoonful of cake inches from her lips.

His sister watched him as he walked over, the cake still hovering in front of her mouth, and Anne-Marie pulled up a chair. Peter, looking up from his newspaper, nodded to Michel and said hello as though it were perfectly natural for an eighty-year-old man to be wearing skin-tight cycling shorts.

"I've been so worried," said Michel as soon as he sat down. Anne-Marie immediately went to fetch him a drink, Peter tagging along behind.

"What about?" asked Nicole once they were alone.

Taking a deep breath, Michel explained to her in great detail all that had happened that morning: he'd thought it strange she'd gone out without telling him, then when he'd found the note, his mind had raced, and he'd thought she was going to do something stupid, so he'd got on his bike, but he couldn't find his shorts, and the railway station was closed, and his feet hurt, and—

"Slow down, Michel," said Nicole gently. "It's okay. See, here I am." And then she hugged him, and he felt safe again.

A minute or two later, they were joined by Anne-Marie and Peter. Anne-Marie handed Michel a coffee while Peter provided some cake—basbousa, an Egyptian semolina cake soaked in syrup. As usual, it was delicious, and Michel wondered if it would be rude to ask for another slice. But before he had time to ask, Nicole began speaking, and the moment was lost.

"I didn't sleep well last night," she began. "I was thinking about Thomas Haven, you see." Michel wasn't surprised. "When I came downstairs this morning, you were still asleep, and by eight o'clock, there was still no sign of you. I read the newspaper again, but I could not understand why they would have a picture of him in an article about imposters. And the more I read, the angrier I became, so in the end, I needed to leave the house to clear my head." She looked across at Anne-Marie and Peter. "So, I thought I'd speak to

Peter to see if he could unravel it. He's an Englishman, after all, and we all know what a strange lot they can be." She smiled at Peter. "No offence meant."

"Plenty taken," he said, laughing.

"Anyway," continued Nicole, "we had a good chat about it, and Peter has agreed to do some digging around."

Peter nodded, though it was a forced kind of nod, like he'd not had much input in the discussion. "I've got plenty of time on my hands now that I've hurt my knee." His eyes flitted between Michel and Nicole. "It's possible this Thomas Mirren is somehow not your Thomas Haven, you know. They could perhaps have used Thomas Haven's photograph by mistake." No one looked convinced; not even Peter. "Though, that's highly unlikely," he admitted. "Even for the *Chronicle*." He looked out of the window in thought. "His name was definitely Haven, right?"

"Yes," replied Michel and Nicole together.

"And that's definitely his picture?"

"Yes."

"Then, either they have the name wrong or there's something we haven't thought about."

And so it was agreed—Peter would help them find out what had happened. Nicole thanked him, and he headed back to the kitchen. Michel ordered another piece of cake.

Back at the house, Nicole and Michel ate lunch. Michel wasn't hungry after his two pieces of cake but Nicole had insisted he eat something else. Something healthy.

"I'm sorry I worried you, Michel," she said as they were tidying the dishes.

Michel shook his head, walking over to his sister and hugging her. "It is me who should be sorry for thinking you so irrational that you would rush off to England over this damned story."

"The thought had crossed my mind, I must admit," replied Nicole, but Michel could see she was joking. Or at least he thought she was. "Either way, we'll understand it soon. I cannot say how happy I am to find out he's alive. And whatever that newspaper says"—she pointed to the *Chronicle*, still open on the table— "I know that man is Thomas Haven."

As they sat in the garden that afternoon, cups of coffee in hand, they listened to the sounds of the countryside—the gentle autumnal breeze, the barking of dogs, and the contented clucking of four well-fed hens. They had come outside to decide upon a strategy, a way to find out what the story in the newspaper was all about, but they'd got no further than wondering what Peter was doing. He seemed confident of success, at least.

"I think we should telephone them," Nicole announced.

"Telephone who?" replied Michel, though he was well aware of who *they* were.

"The *Kingsley Echo*," answered Nicole. "Or whatever that rag calls itself."

"Yes," said Michel with a smile. "About that." His face felt very warm all of a sudden. "I already have."

Chapter 26

Ian and Ellie

Ian was running late. He'd wanted to get to work for eight-thirty to get started on a new story, but as often happened, time had drifted, and it wasn't until just gone nine o'clock that he found himself walking through the glass doors and into the office. He hadn't had the chance to get a coffee that morning, so after putting down his bag, his first port of call was the kitchen.

As he was making his way over, he noticed Jean waving to him from her desk—a 'get over here' type of wave, rather than a greeting. With the phone pressed against her ear, her spare hand flapped frantically, and Ian couldn't tell if she looked confused or amused.

"Someone wants to speak to you," she said, pointing at the phone before covering the mouthpiece. "Sounds foreign," she whispered.

Ian wanted a cup of coffee; he didn't want to talk to the person on the phone. Waving his hand dismissively, he attempted a detour, but Jean was having none of it, and a chair rolled into his path.

"I'll take it at my desk." He groaned as Jean smiled triumphantly. She pressed a button on her phone, and the phone on Ian's desk immediately began to ring. Slumping despondently into his chair, he picked up the receiver.

"Hello," he said slowly, unsure of the caller's standard of English. "How can I help?"

"Are you the person who wrote the story about Thomas?" It was a man's voice, and his English sounded fine. "Thomas Mirren," the voice added. There was something odd about the way he said Mirren, as though it didn't fit with the first name.

"I am," replied Ian. He couldn't be bothered to explain that the story wasn't specifically about Thomas Mirren. He'd done enough of that already.

"Then, why did you call him Mirren when that is not his name?" said the voice.

Ian shook his head, sighing to himself. It was going to be a long morning. "I can assure you, sir, that the person's name *is* Thomas Mirren. I checked it myself."

There was an intake of breath, then a moment's silence. It seemed to Ian that the person was angry.

"Then, I would suggest you research things a little more thoroughly in future," he said, causing Ian to sit up in his chair. "I saw his picture in that *Chronicle* rag, and I would know his face as easily as if it were my own." Again, there was a pause. "I don't know why he's called that now but he is Thomas Haven. H-A-V-E-N. And in 1943, he saved my life."

Ian was bolt upright now, fumbling around his desk for a pen and paper. He asked for more information, but none was forthcoming.

"I could tell you more," announced the man, "but you should look for it yourself. Undo some of the wrongs. Your boss has my details." Ian assumed he meant Jean.

"Now, I have to go. I'm in a hurry, you see. My sister is missing. He saved her too, by the way. And she's very angry." The man let out a small laugh. "In fact, I think she may be coming to England to kill you."

Before Ian could say anything more, the man hung up. It's not every day a stranger wants to kill you, and Ian wasn't quite sure what to make of it.

Jean wandered over and asked him what the call was about. It was quite unusual to get a phone call from anywhere outside of Kingsley, let alone abroad. Ian recounted everything that had been said, omitting the part about the sister, before asking Jean what she thought of it all.

"Well, he wouldn't be the first person to have changed his name," said Jean. "Or the last, I dare say. And there are lots of reasons why he might've done it."

"What sort of reasons?" Ian asked.

"Maybe to hide something from the past, not liking the person he got the name off, to honour someone, to start a new life, or just for the hell of it," Jean said, counting each reason on her fingers as she went. "And those are only a few of the potential reasons."

Ian wondered what Thomas Mirren's reason had been, if indeed that was the case.

But before looking into it, there were other things to take care of. Like his cup of coffee.

Later that morning, Ian made his way up the carpeted stairs of the town library. Chris Boddington, a friend from school, was the librarian, and if anyone knew how to find out about someone's past, it was him.

"Yeah, I know him," said Chris once Ian had explained the situation. "And I imagine most of the people in town do too. At least now." Ian shuddered at the thought. It had all got so horribly out of hand. Part of him wanted the telephone man's story to be true, but the other part didn't. In a way, he wanted Thomas Mirren to be an imposter, and not just because he'd started it, but because he couldn't bear the thought that he may have wronged an innocent man.

Seeing his discomfort, Chris smiled reassuringly. "Give me half an hour, Ian. I'll work my magic."

Ian thanked him and walked off to look around the endless shelves of books. As he disappeared, he could hear Chris tapping away at the computer on his desk.

The library in Kingsley had been underfunded for years, to such an extent that, were it not for a small army of volunteers, the town would have no library at all. Many of the books were donated, and in each aisle, thin metal shelves sagged alarmingly. Ian reached out and picked up a book, its yellowed pages rough against his skin. It was a copy of *Scoop* by Evelyn Waugh, and he recalled reading it as part of his English studies at school. Someone had done a drawing inside the cover, but he had no idea what it was. It seemed a popular book, he thought, with date stamps going back over twenty years. Flicking through the pages, he smiled to himself, remembering his schooldays, then carefully put it back on the shelf.

He browsed the bookshelves for another few minutes, then went back to see how Chris was getting on. As it turned out, he really could work magic.

"Thomas Haven, born on the twenty-second of December 1924," he announced triumphantly. "A little tricky to find but it's all there. It's a rare name."

When Ian asked him where he'd found it, Chris tapped the side of his nose and smiled. "Trade secret, I'm afraid."

"Any record of him being in the army, specifically during the war?" asked Ian.

"I didn't look," admitted Chris. "But that should be easy for you to find out. You must have looked it up when you searched for Thomas Mirren at your office." Ian nodded, but before he could add anything, Chris continued. "Oh, and they're the same person. Name changed just after the war. Mother's maiden name."

"Bloody hell," cursed Ian.

"You're in a library, you know," said Chris, shaking his head. Ian apologised, then thanked him for his help.

The remainder of his investigation could be done at the office. But first he was meeting Debbie and Ellie for lunch, so it would have to wait until the afternoon.

"So, how has your morning been?" asked Debbie as the three of them sat in a cafe. Ian and Debbie had ordered a sandwich, and Ellie was eating cake. Apparently, she'd eaten earlier.

"Well," he replied, "I think I've made a bit of a mistake." Debbie stared at him, though Ellie didn't seem to have heard him, her eyes not moving from her phone.

"About what?" asked Debbie, her brow furrowed with concern.

"About Thomas Mirren," replied Ian, and then Ellie stared at him too.

Ian proceeded to tell them about his morning, from getting into the office and his phone call with the man, to his visit to the library and the discovery Chris had made about Thomas Mirren. All the while, Debbie and Ellie listened, which was an unusual experience in itself, especially for Ellie. Most of the time, she found talk of his work quite dull.

"I don't know why he didn't just tell us all this in the first place," said Ian.

Ellie snorted. "Perhaps because it's none of our business."

"So, let me get this right," said Debbie, looking from Ellie to Ian. "Thomas Mirren was originally called Thomas Haven, but for reasons unknown, he changed his name. He may or may not have served in the war—he probably did, as Haven's not a common name—where he saved a Frenchman. And probably saved his family too, if not the whole town. So, he *is* a hero. He now lives in Kingsley, where he sells poppies and people think he's a fraud." She paused, as if checking her story. "Is that about right?"

Ian nodded. Said back to him like that, it seemed absurd, but there was no escaping the facts. The three of them looked at each other, as if by staring hard enough, they might understand what was going on. But they didn't understand. A few searches on the internet would hopefully reveal the truth.

When they finished their lunch, Ian headed back to the office. Debbie and Ellie had things to get in town, so they went off together. All things Thomas Mirren were forgotten, at least for the time being.

Inside the shopping arcade, Debbie picked up some printer paper which they didn't really need, but apparently it was better to have too much. Ellie carried it in her new backpack, and for her part, she bought some stationery—mainly pens and notebooks but also a new calculator. Her old one had been squashed by a truck. It wasn't long before they returned home.

Back at the house, Debbie went out into the garden while Ellie made coffee and turned on the computer. She had research to do. Leaving her coffee on an old notepad by the desk, she headed upstairs to get changed, the whirring of the computer hard drive fading into silence as she closed her bedroom door. Though it was by no means warm, it was muggy, in large part due to her thick cotton sling. It rubbed at her skin, and as a result, she'd taken to wearing collared shirts, the only ones she owned being heavy and uncomfortable. Searching her drawers, she found nothing more suitable, so she cursed, realising she needed to go shopping again. She obviously didn't have enough clothes. But at least she had five hundred sheets of printer paper.

Downstairs, the computer was finally ready. It was an ancient thing with outdated software and ponderous innards. It was fine for what Ellie needed—word processing and internet searches—but something a little more modern would have been good. She smiled to herself: they had a car that could talk, but a computer that was barely alive.

She could use her father's laptop, of course, but you should always be careful when using a parent's computer. You never know what you might find.

Now that the computer was on, she wasn't too sure where to start, so she opened the search engine: *How do you know if someone has been in the British army?*

It didn't take long for an answer. Listed from the top of the page to the bottom were numerous websites, all offering to supply the information she needed. Some charged a fee, but most of them were free. She clicked on a free one, and two boxes appeared. In the first box, she typed, 'Thomas'. In the second box, she typed, 'Mirren'. Then, she shook her head. There would be nothing. It was a silly mistake. Changing the second box to 'Haven', she clicked the search button again. And there it was: Thomas Haven, 1943 to 1947.

"Yes!" she cheered, looking around to see if her mother was watching. But Debbie was still in the garden.

Back to the search engine: *How do I know which medals a soldier has?*

Once again, there was a list. However, to get the information this time, she needed to register. But it was still free.

Finally registered, she filled in Thomas Mirren's details, and the computer hummed. When the results finally came, it was a complete mess: pages of numbers and long lists of dates; names, from Abraham Madden to Theodore

Murdoch, and a whole load of regiments. But then she found him. She sat there, her mouth half-open, staring at the screen.

"Bloody hell." She gasped. And then she started to laugh.

Ian didn't go straight back to the office. He decided to take a detour to the supermarket instead. Not that he especially wanted to see Thomas Mirren, or even that he had anything to say to him. Rather, he was intrigued. A part of him wanted Thomas Mirren to be a fraud, to validate what he'd written, and to show that he'd done the right thing. But another part, a larger part, wanted a hero. He'd never met a hero before. Sure, he'd read about them but they had always been elsewhere, intangible, and somehow unreal. Not living in Kingsley. It would be good if Thomas Mirren were one. Brian would be terrified, of course, and that was a bonus. He would try to blame someone else. Probably Ian. But it wouldn't work. He'd have to apologise, and Ian had never seen Brian apologise before. And what about Jacqueline Chambers? She would be in real trouble. The *Chronicle* had even printed a photograph.

It was very busy in the supermarket as shoppers moved frantically from aisle to aisle. But Thomas Mirren wasn't there, and neither was his table. It was like he'd never been there at all.

When he got into the office, Ian headed straight for his desk. He knew exactly what he was looking for. He turned on his computer and started his search. On the first website, he typed, 'Thomas Haven'. The search began, and as he waited for the results, he could hear Brian in his office, shouting at someone down the phone.

The program finished: one result.

"Yes!" he celebrated quietly before looking up to see if anyone was nearby. He was alone.

Next, he searched the website for military awards. Again, he typed in Thomas Haven's details. Brian was bellowing now, and people had stopped working in an attempt to hear what was going on. Ian closed his eyes, afraid of what they were about to see. He so wanted to hear Brian apologise. And then the results appeared.

As he sat there, fingers crossed and eyes staring at the screen, he started to smile.

"Bloody hell," he said. And then he started to laugh.

Chapter 27

Thomas

Thomas was with Frank again that morning. Frank had watched another of his quiz programmes and was bombarding Thomas with endless pieces of useless information.

"You're crazy." Thomas laughed as Frank imparted another pearl of wisdom.

"We're all crazy, Thomas." Frank smiled. "We're just too crazy to realise it."

"Thank you, Einstein," replied Thomas, shaking his head.

"Don't you mean Freud?" joked Frank.

"I don't know. You tell me, Einstein."

The poppy selling had gone well that morning, something Frank attributed to his presence rather than it being unusually busy in the store. It was a warm day, for October at least, and it seemed the whole town had decided to go shopping. As the queues grew at the tills, Jenny rushed back and forth, trying to keep a lid on the growing complaints. By the look on her face—her red cheeks and the perspiration on her forehead—she was feeling the pressure.

"Jenny's going to have a heart attack if she doesn't slow down," observed Frank, biting into his third chocolate bar of the day. Apparently, it was brain food.

"She'd be less rushed if she weren't constantly bringing you drinks," said Thomas, placing his coffee mug back onto the table. Frank looked at the mug and smiled.

At half past twelve, they called it a day. Thomas had skipped breakfast that morning and was starting to feel hungry, so they decided to get sandwiches and to eat in the park.

Having tidied up the poppies and stored the money boxes, they moved the table over to a nearby cupboard, imagining that Jenny would need the space, given how busy it was. Things had calmed down a little from earlier but it was still busier than normal.

"Bustling, rather than hectic," said Frank, flexing his impressive vocabulary before setting off in search of sustenance.

The sandwich aisle had changed since the previous day, with small cardboard flags now decorating the shelves. Thomas pointed to one of the flags; one he didn't recognise.

"Do you know that flag?" he asked, and Frank stared at it as though the answer was on the tip of his tongue. Then, he shook his head, and Thomas smiled. "It's Battacruda."

"Never heard of it," replied Frank.

"Just off the coast of Mexico," Thomas said, grinning.

Frank nodded. "Ah, yes, I remember it now."

As they were scanning the shelves, desperately trying to find a sandwich filling they recognised, Jenny walked over. She was composed again, like the Jenny of old.

"We're trying out a new range," she announced, pointing to several of the flags. "Head Office's idea, but we'll see how it goes." She was silent for a moment as she scanned the shelves like a parent admiring the artwork of their child.

"That's all well and good," said Thomas, "but what are they?" He picked up a box. "Chatpata pav?"

"Spiced vegetables inside a fresh pav bun," said Jenny. Seeing the look on Thomas and Frank's faces, she added, "It's very tasty."

"Any prawns in it?" asked Thomas.

"No," answered Jenny. "No prawns, Thomas."

The box quickly made its way back onto the shelf, and Frank held up another. "Schezwan paneer?"

"Indo-Chinese style," said Jenny. "Tomato, sour cream, and paneer." She looked at Thomas. "No prawns."

"Do you have *any* prawn sandwiches?" asked Thomas with a smile.

"I don't think so," answered Jenny. "But we have crayfish."

"Is that like prawn?"

"A very big prawn, I suppose."

"I'll have one of those then," said Thomas, and Jenny passed him a box from the bottom shelf, next to the Italian tramezzini.

Jenny left to check on the queues, leaving Thomas and Frank to contemplate what else to buy in addition to the sandwiches. As Thomas was looking at the crisps, Frank stared towards the entrance.

"Your mate's back," said Frank, nodding his head in the direction of the foyer. Ian Rogers had just entered, and he seemed to be looking for somebody.

"Christ," moaned Thomas. "It'll be the wife next." He pulled Frank's arm so that the two of them disappeared behind the sandwich display. He then grabbed Frank's sandwich and held it out in front of him alongside his own.

"What are you doing?"

"Camouflage," replied Thomas, and the two of them giggled like children. Snatching some flags off a nearby shelf, Frank covered his face with Germany and Japan, and there they stood, motionless like statues. And it worked, because the next time they looked, Ian Rogers was gone.

"Traitor," said Thomas, pointing to Frank's flags. "Well, that accounts for the Volkswagen."

"We're all one happy family now," said Frank. "At least for the time being."

In the park, it was surprisingly quiet. The two men sat on a bench next to a wooden statue of an elephant on which someone had drawn a pair of spectacles. There was a climbing frame nearby, and next to it were some plastic steps which made noises when you stood on them. They watched as a small boy leapt from step to step, and the tune he produced was wholly without melody.

"That would drive me crazy if I lived nearby," said Frank, pointing to the steps. There were flats on the other side of the park, and Thomas noted how all the windows were closed—not surprising, given the racket.

"We're all crazy anyway," said Thomas.

Frank looked at him and chuckled. "Some more than most."

Frank had polished off his sandwich and was already on his crisps by the time Thomas took a bite of his own. He rolled the filling around in his mouth, searching for the taste of prawn but finding none.

"Tastes nothing like prawn," he announced as Frank looked up from his crisps.

"What does it taste of then?" he asked.

"Chicken."

They stayed in the park for around half an hour. Frank produced a chocolate bar from his pocket, his fourth of the day, and he offered half of it to Thomas. It was a brand that had been popular since before the war, and they both commented on how much smaller it looked compared to the colossal slab of their youth. Frank decided it was probably the same size and that everything looked bigger when you were a child, but Thomas just thought it was smaller. Whatever the dimensions, it still tasted good.

They left the park when the racket from the steps became unbearable.

"Quick pint to keep us going until we get to the Legion?" suggested Frank as they walked past The Royal. Thomas nodded, and the two of them turned into the pub, its heavy oak door squeaking as it opened.

"Could do with a bit of oil there," noted Thomas, walking over to the bar. Frank went to get a table, all of which were free, and Thomas joined him a minute later with two pints of beer and some more crisps. Frank said something about cholesterol and saturated fats, but Thomas paid no attention. There'd been enough trivia for one day.

The discussion moved on to the upcoming parade. Frank seemed excited about carrying the wreath, and he asked Thomas about its weight. It had been many years since he had carried it. Thomas had been wreath bearer several times in the past, and for weight, he suggested around a tenth of the Colonel.

"When have you ever lifted the Colonel?" Frank laughed.

"I've carried that man halfway across Europe in my time," replied Thomas, barely exaggerating.

The three of them were to be at the front of the parade, Frank in the middle with the wreath, the Colonel and Thomas on either side. Thomas and the Colonel hadn't missed a parade in over fifty years. It was a highlight of the calendar. It would be a proud day for Frank, and Thomas was happy for him.

Everything was due to start at nine o'clock on the Sunday morning, with everyone meeting at the Legion. They would then set off at ten o'clock sharp—the Colonel was very strict about that—and would arrive at the memorial for ten-thirty. After a few speeches, mainly from local councillors and the mayor, Frank would get to do his bit. Frank and the Colonel had been busy arranging things for days, and once again, Thomas wondered why so much work was involved. It reminded him of the rule he'd been taught at school, something about work expanding to fill the time available for its completion. He couldn't remember the name of it but it seemed relevant, all the same.

He let Frank chunter on for a while, enjoying his friend's enthusiasm as he listed off the number of people they'd spoken to and the shops they'd visited. Again, Thomas wondered when they'd done all that. They'd been with him most of the time. Though, it didn't really matter, he supposed. We all embellish our achievements once in a while.

Another person entered the pub—a thin man in his seventies with long brown hair and handsome features. The barman looked up and sighed, as if he were working himself into an early grave. The 'quick pint' had transformed into two and was in danger of increasing further, so they decided it was time to leave. Pint number three was set for the Legion.

"You know who that was, don't you?" asked Frank as they walked along the street towards the main road. "The guy who came into The Royal."

Thomas shook his head. "No," he replied. "He looked a bit like Mick Jagger. Do you think it was him?"

Frank laughed. "Maybe. I hear he likes to drop into The Royal when he's not touring." He smiled at Thomas. "No, it was Mark Adamson. Of Adamson and Son."

Mark Adamson had one son and one daughter, and the name of his firm had always annoyed Thomas. His daughter had left home as soon as she'd turned eighteen, so perhaps she felt the same. The last thing Thomas had heard, she was a lawyer and the son was a layabout.

"Prat," said Thomas.

"I believe he speaks highly of you too." Frank chuckled as they approached the Legion.

Parked alongside the whitewashed walls of their second home was the absurdly stretched car of the town's mayor. Two small flags fluttered at the end of the bonnet, above the headlights, and there was a thin scratch running along one of the doors, the result of a keying several weeks earlier. In the driver's seat was Alan Thomson, formerly of Thomson's Butchers, and he waved to Thomas as he approached. He had been a good cricketer in his youth, but an accident with a meat cleaver had left him unable to bowl, so now he did nothing. He drank a lot, which made him unsuited to driving, but that didn't seem to bother the mayor. So, as a result, everyone was happy, except perhaps the person who'd keyed the car door.

"How are you, Alan?" asked Thomas through the car window.

"Pretty good thanks, Thomas," replied Alan. "Knocking off in half an hour."

They chatted for a while and then Thomas said goodbye. Alan wound up the window, and as his car seat reclined, he closed his eyes and fell asleep.

"Hard life," said Frank.

Inside the Legion, several men stood by the bar. They smiled at Thomas and Frank as they entered, and they asked how the poppy selling had gone. As Frank eulogised about his sales prowess, Thomas looked across the bar at Derek, who was drying glasses on a white towel hanging unhygienically from his belt. Derek looked back, then nodded in the direction of a table at the far side of the room. The Colonel was there with the mayor and old Bob Wallace, the leader of the council.

Derek shook his head. "I'd give it a while, if I were you," he whispered, loud enough for everyone to hear. He would have made a terrible spy. "Bit of a ding-dong."

Twenty minutes later, the mayor and Bob Wallace stormed out of the Legion. Neither of them said anything as they left, the mayor reserving a hard stare for Thomas. Thomas, who held no great love for the mayor, smiled and raised his glass. As the door slammed behind them, Derek leaned over and presented Thomas with a tray of drinks—three pints and three whiskies.

"On the house," he said, and Thomas thanked him, quickly taking the tray before Derek had the chance to change his mind.

Thomas realised he hadn't seen Frank for a while, not since he'd finished fabricating his sales numbers a few minutes earlier. Looking around, he noticed him at the slot machine, pumping pound coins into the slot one after another.

"Feeling lucky?" he asked as he walked over with the drinks.

"Yes," replied Frank, staring accusingly at the machine.

"How much have you lost?"

"About twenty quid so far," replied Frank, which was an impressive feat in such a short space of time. Just then, the machine started to flash, and five pound coins appeared.

"Lucky sod," said Thomas with a laugh. A smiling Frank pocketed his winnings, and the two of them went over to join the Colonel.

"Idiots," hissed the Colonel as they sat down.

"That's not very nice," observed Thomas.

"Not you," said the Colonel. "Obviously."

"Obviously," replied Thomas.

The three of them helped themselves to the drinks—a pint and a whisky each. They raised their glasses towards Derek, who waved his dirty towel in reply. Thomas and Frank then looked at the Colonel, the signal for him to begin.

As it turned out, there had been some grumblings at the recent council meeting. One or two members were concerned about the recent newspaper reports, the result of which was that the mayor had been asked to speak to the Colonel. The leader of the council had decided to come too, as it made him look important. It was perhaps not appropriate for Thomas Mirren to participate in the parade this year. Next year maybe, when this untidy mess had blown over. But not this year. They'd been quite categorical about that.

But the Colonel could be categorical too—no Thomas Mirren, no Colonel. And in fact, no Frank, no Derek, and no one else either. So, no parade. And that had upset the mayor. It was unthinkable that there would be no parade. Certainly not while he was in charge.

And so, there was an impasse.

When the Colonel had finished, Thomas glanced across at a crestfallen Frank.

"Don't worry, Frank," he said. "I was thinking I might give it a miss this year anyway. My shoulders have been playing up, and I can't risk having to carry Adam."

Frank snorted. "You really are an idiot if you think I'd go without you." It appeared that Frank could be categorical too.

There was no point arguing, as neither Frank nor the Colonel would countenance the idea of a parade without Thomas.

"If only they knew," said the Colonel. "They'd be thoroughly ashamed of themselves." Which Thomas doubted very much, the members of the council not being known for their sense of shame. To them, everything was opposites—good and bad, black and white—when in reality there were so many shades of grey.

That evening, sitting in his front room with the curtains closed, Thomas watched as the light from the fire danced around the photograph of Ellen. He put down his glass of whisky and fell asleep. It had been a long day. For the first time in a long time, he felt sad.

Chapter 28

Nicole and Michel

Nicole didn't quite know what to make of Michel's admission. He'd been impulsive. He was many things— strong, loving, honest—but impulsive was not one of them. And by his own admission, he had also been rude. Again, not like him at all. So, when he'd told her about the telephone call, she really didn't know what to make of it.

But it was a start. At least they knew where the story had come from. All they had to do now was find Thomas Haven. Where to begin?

It was early morning, and Michel was making some breakfast. Nicole had fed the chickens and was about to turn on the computer.

"I've got no idea where to start," she said to Michel as he came into the room with bread and jam and two cups of coffee. His hair was dishevelled and his eyes looked puffy, as though he'd slept poorly the previous night. Placing the breakfast on the computer table, he scratched at his chin.

"To be honest," he replied, "I've not thought much further than turning the computer on." Chin satisfactorily scratched, he leaned over and peered at the screen. "There must be something like a census website or army records. He was Thomas Haven in 1943, so that's a good place to start."

They decided to have breakfast first and so made their way to the kitchen. Wanting the truth and fearing what you might find are powerful companions, so a few minutes more wouldn't hurt.

"What do you think we'll find?" asked Nicole as they sat at the kitchen table.

"Probably nothing at the rate we're going." Michel could see Nicole was worried, but he was absolutely sure they would find nothing bad. Thomas Haven was a good man. Of that, there was no doubt.

"I hope he's had a good life," said Nicole quietly. "With happiness and love. He deserves that much."

"I'm sure he will have," said Michel reassuringly. "If he could find a way out of the situation he was in all those years ago, I've no doubt he could find a little happiness."

Nicole laughed as Michel tried to steal a piece of her bread. It split in two, leaving him with the smallest piece. "Come on," she said, standing up. "Let's get going."

And two hours later, they were no further forward than they had been at the start.

Peter's leg was hurting. It had been painful all night, resulting in far less sleep than he would have liked. Unable to straighten it without it aching, he'd tossed and turned so much that Anne-Marie had ordered him into the spare room, with its uncomfortable bed and rattling windows. Which hadn't helped.

Downstairs in the kitchen, he yawned and got ready to start on the food preparation. He was planning a new cake, one he'd found on the internet—an Indian mawa cake, milk-based and flavoured with cardamom and pistachios. The cardamom had proved especially difficult to find.

"Didn't you promise to look into that soldier thing for Nicole?" said a voice from behind him as he lay the ingredients neatly into rows. It was Anne-Marie, fully refreshed by the look of it after her night in their comfy bed, with the double-glazed windows and the warm duvet.

"I can do that later," said Peter. "I've got a mawa cake to get ready." Anne-Marie walked over and hugged him, and he smiled, knowing the mawa cake would have to wait.

"Okay," he said, unwrapping himself from her little finger, "I'll look at it now." He washed his hands, drying them on the old towel by the door, then kissed Anne-Marie. As he disappeared into the living room, he shouted back, "I'll need to make a phone call first."

"Who are you calling?" she asked, following him into the living room.

"Just an old friend," he said. "Works in a library in England. If anyone knows how to find this soldier, it'll be him."

It was nearly an hour before Anne-Marie saw Peter again. She'd listened to him for a while talking on the phone, but when he spoke to his friends, he spoke so quickly that it frustrated her. Her English was excellent but once he got going, it became another language.

There was plenty to do anyway. The cafe was getting busier, almost by the day, and they were now at the stage where they were no longer losing money. She smiled to herself as she chopped fresh onions, and very soon, she found she was singing. It was a song she'd first heard in England on the evening she'd met Peter, the man she had come to love. He had asked her to dance and she'd said yes. And they'd been dancing ever since.

"Are you crying?" asked Peter, returning to the kitchen following his phone call.

"Crying from happiness," replied Anne-Marie with a smile, her eyes stinging from the onions. "Did you find anything?"

"You're not going to believe it," he said, taking her by the hand and leading her into the living room. And as they sat together, Anne-Marie still crying and Peter shocked, he told her everything.

"It's no good," moaned Nicole as they ate their lunch. "He's a ghost."

Michel smiled but his confidence was waning too. "We're just looking in the wrong places."

"So, what are the right places?" asked Nicole grumpily.

"If I knew that, we wouldn't be looking in the wrong ones."

It was hard to argue with that. Two hours of searching had left them irritable, so they'd decided to take a break. The break had expanded, and now it was lunchtime. Things were not going to plan.

The internet was a disappointment. It was supposed to contain everything, but when they really wanted something, it wasn't there. Or at least it was so well hidden that it might as well not have been there. What was the point of it if they couldn't find anything?

In the end, Michel took the dishes to the kitchen. Neither of them had eaten much. He was about to leave them in the sink for later but Nicole came in, so he turned on the taps. Nicole giggled, and it was the giggle of a young girl, catching her brother for the thousandth time.

"Very efficient, Michel," said Nicole.

"You know me, Sister," he replied, keeping his back to her. "Why put something off that can be easily done now? That's always been my motto."

"Always," confirmed Nicole with a smile so bright she illuminated the room. "Well, while you do that, I'll go out and feed the chickens."

Out in the garden, Nicole had an uneasy feeling. Something felt odd; it was much quieter than it should have been at that time of day. At the sound of her arrival, the chickens would always make a fuss, but today they were silent. Very strange indeed, thought Nicole. Arriving at the coop, she immediately saw why—Pinky, Blinky, and Inky were all present but she couldn't see Clyde. The three remaining hens strutted around as though looking for their friend, but Clyde had disappeared. Straight away, Nicole's mind rushed back to the day Charles had passed. Much like today, Nicole had found the coop with one chicken missing. Soon afterwards, she'd found Charles lying on his back, clawed feet pointing to the sky. Charles had been killed by a fox—there were numerous in the nearby woods. The fox hadn't been hungry, so he'd killed Charles for the fun of it. Dragged him from his home and slaughtered him without mercy. It was what foxes did. Later, she'd found a hole in the coop, just big enough for a fox's head.

The first thing Nicole did was stick her head into the coop, and as she did so, Blinky pecked at her ear.

"Not helping, Blinky," snapped Nicole, causing Blinky to scuttle away, clucking indignantly. She was not used to being talked to like that.

But there was no hole; at least none Nicole could see. She wondered if perhaps the door was loose. Again, all was as it should be. Nicole scratched her head. There was no means of escape, so where could Clyde be?

Just to be sure, she walked to the bottom of the garden to where she had found Charles, and she searched along the fence for signs of intrusion. There were none, of course. Michel had secured it so thoroughly following Charles's misfortune that even Houdini would have had trouble getting in. Clyde had simply vanished.

Back in the house, she asked Michel if he'd seen anything. Michel shook his head. He was due in town later that morning to discuss the upcoming Armistice Day parade, but he asked Nicole if she would prefer him to stay at home so that they could search for Clyde together. Nicole liked the idea very much but she said no. The parade was important to

Michel, and it wouldn't be the same without his input. As a recent mayor, he would sometimes carry the wreath.

Just as Michel was about to argue, there was a knock at the door.

"Christ, this hill seems to get steeper every time I walk up it," groaned Anne-Marie. They had left the cafe around ten minutes earlier, and she was already regretting her choice of both footwear and coat. The shoes had heels, albeit low, and she'd realised early on that training shoes would have been better. Much like the ones Peter was wearing, smugly.

"You should have worn trainers," said Peter with a laugh, and she stuck out her tongue.

Her coat was the one she'd bought in England when she was a student. It was thick and heavy and utterly unsuited to autumn in Saint Martin. Peter, in his thin breathable jacket, had warned her it would be too hot, but she had ignored his advice. Now, she couldn't take it off without admitting she'd been wrong.

Better to boil alive than to admit defeat, she thought to herself.

"You should take off that coat," advised Peter as the gradient of the hill once again increased. "It's uncomfortable watching you."

"It's fine," replied Anne-Marie, a drop of sweat making its way slowly down her back. But they both knew it wasn't fine.

They reached the top of the hill fifteen minutes later. Anne-Marie was feeling much better now she'd taken off her coat. To her surprise, Peter had said nothing—no gloating, no

'I told you so'. Nothing. And in a way, that made her feel worse. Peter was carrying her coat, so all she had in her hand was a cloth bag. Which was another thing she needn't have brought.

As they approached the front gate to Michel and Nicole's house, they saw a chicken.

The chicken was standing between the two wooden gateposts, and if that wasn't strange enough, it was pacing back and forth like a sentry on guard. As Peter waved his hands, attempting to move it, it cocked its head and looked at him as though he were an idiot.

"That looks like Pinky," Anne-Marie said. "Or Blinky or Inky or Clyde."

"I think it's Clyde," replied Peter.

"How do you know?"

"Because she always gives me the evil eye."

"You should pick her up and take her inside," said Anne-Marie, and Peter looked at her as though she'd just asked him to cut off his manhood.

"My hands are full," he replied, a little too quickly. It was clear he was afraid of the hen. But, sure enough, his hands *were* full, what with Anne-Marie's coat and the various printouts regarding Thomas Haven. So, it was up to Anne-Marie to do the catching.

Clyde didn't move as Anne-Marie approached, nor did she complain as she was scooped up and placed into the cloth bag. In fact, she looked rather happy. It had been worth bringing the bag, after all.

The long gravel path to the house was always immaculate. Nicole, more so than Michel, was very house-proud. Michel was more of a security man, preferring to mend fences as his sister battled with the weeds. But to visitors, and the occasional passers-by, the house was beautiful, with whitewashed walls and neatly cut grass. The only blemish was Michel's bike shed, set aside from the house, its door unpainted and with an old wheel leaning against the wall. The wheel was buckled, like a contorted hula hoop, and had been there for as long as Anne-Marie could remember. The story, according to Michel, was that it had been damaged in a crash. He kept it there as a reminder to be careful on his bike, especially regarding stray trees. But according to Nicole, he was just too lazy to move it. The truth, no doubt, lay somewhere between.

On the front door was a door knocker in the shape of a lion's head, copper-coloured and polished. It was old and worn, and it reminded Peter of his home in England. His parents had bought a similar one when Peter was a child, and it guarded their house to this day.

Anne-Marie knocked four times, Peter standing behind her as Clyde eyed him suspiciously. At first, there was no answer, but then came the sound of footsteps, heavy and measured, crashing along the hallway. A moment later, a key rattled and the door opened, revealing Michel, squinting in the bright daylight. His face was creased.

"Hi, Michel," said Peter. "Everything okay?"

"Fine," replied Michel. "I've just been drinking lemonade. Very bitter."

Anne-Marie held up her cloth bag.

"I see you've found Clyde," said Michel. Peter smiled proudly. "Please, come in."

Anne-Marie entered first, the cloth bag held out in front of her, Clyde squirming inside, trying to see what Peter was up to. And as Peter came in, Michel looked at the coat he was carrying.

"Anne-Marie's," said Peter matter-of-factly. Michel nodded, then looked at the coat Peter was wearing.

"Gore-Tex?" he asked, and it was Peter's turn to nod. "Breathable?"

"Very."

Michel smiled. "Nice. Perhaps Anne-Marie should get one."

By the time the two men reached the living room, Nicole and Anne-Marie had gone outside, where they reunited Clyde with the other three ghosts. They were still wondering how Clyde could have escaped when they returned to the house. Neither of them had an answer, so they decided to blame Michel. Michel, for his part, said nothing. It's best not to second-guess a chicken.

The four of them chatted for a while over glasses of lemonade, homemade from the day before. Michel chuckled to himself as Peter took a sip, noting with amusement how the muscles on his face contorted as he drank.

"Delicious," said Peter, but it looked like he was crying.

"Anyway," said Anne-Marie, "Peter has been doing some research." She held out her hand, and Peter passed her the papers he was carrying. His hands free, he took a handkerchief from his pocket and began dabbing at his eyes.

Anne-Marie handed over the papers, and Nicole took them to the table, where she was joined by Michel. Setting them down, the two of them started to read. It was some time before they looked up.

"Bloody hell," said Nicole, breaking the silence. And then she started to laugh.

Chapter 29

Ian and Ellie

Ian sent a text message to Brian. He would have preferred to tell him about his discovery face-to-face but Brian hadn't returned that afternoon. He'd then intended to wait until the next morning but having discussed it with Debbie, they'd decided it best to let him know straight away. Which was a shame.

It took Brian two minutes to reply. Most of the message was filled with profanity and spelling mistakes, and when Ian had shown it to Debbie and Ellie, Debbie had opened a bottle of wine. They'd then discussed Thomas Mirren, and before long, they were a little drunk. Not Ellie, of course, but she did have a glass, and she was more animated than Ian had seen her in a long time. Which was nice.

The next morning, he got into the office early. Brian immediately called him into his room.

"Thank God I decided not to mention him by name," said Brian from behind his desk, his face pasty and drawn. Ian could tell he hadn't slept well. "I told Jacqueline Chambers, and she screamed." He shook his head slowly. "Actually screamed. She's for the chop, that's for sure. Especially given the current climate. It's her fault, of course." Ian suspected Jacqueline Chambers's future was not why Brian had slept poorly. "But what about me?" And therein lay the source of his insomnia.

"I'm sure you'll be fine," said Ian, privately hoping he was wrong.

"You should have researched it more thoroughly, Ian," continued Brian. "It was all there."

Ian took a deep breath. He had prepared for this. "I sent you several emails on the subject, Brian, giving you plenty of warnings. I told you we couldn't be sure. It's all there in black and white." Even Brian could see it was going nowhere, so he slumped back in his chair, defeated. Anyway, he had a new job for Ian; a new story.

"I want you to write a piece on Mirren," he said. "Something heroic. Like the other one you did. Something to stop him suing us."

Ian smiled to himself as he left Brian's office. He'd never seen the man so uncomfortable.

He telephoned Debbie as soon as he got back to his desk, and they arranged to meet up for lunch. It was a warm day, so they decided to eat in the park. When Ian offered to pick up some sandwiches, Debbie told him not to, as she and Ellie would make some. Ellie was keen to go to town anyway, said Debbie, so now she had her excuse.

Putting down the phone, Ian noticed Brian leaving the office. He looked ill, his face pale and sweaty, and as he scuttled out the doors, it was clear he was done for the day. A full uninterrupted day lay ahead; enough time to make a solid start on his new story. Now he knew more about Thomas Mirren, it wouldn't be hard for Ian to put something together. But this time he wanted to do things right, and that meant getting Thomas Mirren's consent.

Ellie came downstairs just before ten o'clock. She had slept extremely well, and as a result, she was still feeling tired. The better she slept, the more tired she often found herself. But it was a pleasant kind of tired; the comfortable type where you feel as though you're wrapped in warm blankets. Rather than the other one where there are no blankets and all you want is a dark place to crawl into.

When she arrived at the kitchen, her mother was making sandwiches. Ham and cheese mainly but also some roast beef and mustard. She was cutting the crusts off Ellie's sandwiches. Ellie didn't mind the crusts anymore but she didn't have the heart to say so. Now, it just made her sandwiches look small. Ellie reached into a cupboard, pulling out some crisps and a couple of chocolate bars.

"Might as well go the whole hog," she said as she placed the chocolate and crisps on the table. "What are the sandwiches for anyway?"

Her mother looked up from the crust cutting. "Fancy an impromptu picnic?"

Ellie raised her eyebrows. Her family didn't do impromptu. And they didn't really do picnics either. "Erm, sure," she replied. "Are we celebrating?"

Her mother laughed. "Yes, I suppose so. Your dad's made Brian ill."

Grinning, Ellie reached back into the cupboard and pulled out a packet of biscuits. "Then, we'll need these too," she announced. "Dad's not in trouble then?"

"No. Brian probably is though." As a rule, Ellie wasn't the type to be happy at other people's misfortunes; for Brian, she would make an exception.

Her mother explained about the phone call and how they'd decided to meet for lunch in the park. Ellie decided she needed to get changed into something smart to celebrate the occasion.

Ten minutes later, she was standing by her bed, a blue jumper and black jeans laid out neatly in front of her like someone squashed flat; so flat that even the creases had been destroyed. Like she could have been, she thought, and she sighed. She hadn't thought about her accident for a day or two, yet here it was again, popping up to remind her.

But today was a good day. She was alive and she was having a picnic, and it would take more than an accident to ruin that.

She was becoming an expert at getting changed using only one arm, and in no time at all, she was dressed and ready. The mirror on the wall reflected the image of a young woman, pretty but with lines on her face. Lines of worry about things so unimportant she could no longer remember what they were. Maybe something someone had said, or a glance she had misinterpreted the way she had always done. Until recently. Now, it didn't matter.

"You look lovely," said her mother as Ellie came down the stairs. "Are those new jeans?"

"No." Ellie smiled. "I've just never worn them before."

"That's because they're not ripped," observed her mother.

"Probably." But that was the old Ellie.

She had taken just enough time so as not to be needed for the sandwiches. They both knew it but neither of them said anything. On the table were three bags, each one containing sandwiches, crisps, and chocolate bars. The packet of biscuits was there too.

"Feeding the five thousand?" Ellie laughed.

Her mother nodded. "Looks that way, doesn't it?"

And then it was time to go.

"Do you mind if we walk?" asked Ellie, placing the sandwiches into her rucksack.

"No, of course not," replied her mother, "that would be lovely."

Despite her mother's protestations, Ellie carried the rucksack herself. It made her feel useful.

At the end of Harbour Street, they turned onto Swan Lane. Mr Collins was there, out in his garden, trimming a hedge that was already flawless. His thick glasses made his eyes appear huge, something which Ellie had always found unnerving, as though he could see the slightest of imperfections. And when he smiled, his teeth glistened in the sunlight. They were perfect, like his hedge, and it was as though another man's jaw had been grafted onto his head.

"Hello, you two," he said cheerfully, the words cascading smoothly over his immaculate teeth. Ellie looked at her blushing mother. Then, she looked at Mr Collins. He reminded her of a predator, preying on her mother, so she grabbed her mother's arm, smiled, and hurried them both past.

"He gives me the creeps," she said once they were out of earshot. Her mother didn't respond.

A little later and they were nearly at the town centre, having taken a long detour to avoid the old industrial estate. They would go that way again in the future, but for now it held too many memories. A reminder of what might have been; a thought so unbearable they now took the underpass, with its lewd graffiti and mild stench of urine.

They exhaled as they exited the passageway, gulping down vast lungfuls of fresh air.

"What does choda mean?" asked Debbie.

"I don't know," replied Ellie, even though she did.

On the outskirts of the town centre, it was already getting busy. It was a warm day, and people had surged from their homes, congregating in groups as they twittered like birds and blocked the pavements. On the corner by the bookmakers, a large group of pensioners holding walking sticks and wearing training shoes grumbled about the weather.

"It's too hot," moaned Mrs Goodwin in her buttoned-up overcoat and thick woollen scarf. "Feels like I'm going to melt," added her husband, wafting his face with gloved hands.

The park was busy too, though not as busy as Ellie had expected. Her father was already there, perched on a bench about twenty metres from the old plinth. The plinth had held a memorial at one stage, but the memorial had been broken, so it now sat empty, save for the occasional beer can or bag of dog poo. At first, her father appeared not to notice them, and Ellie had the urge to creep up on him like she did as a child, scaring him so that he laughed and wheezed as if he were fainting from fear. He didn't laugh enough nowadays. But before she had the opportunity, he noticed them and waved, and her chance was gone.

"That's a lot of food," said her father as she unloaded the three bags from her rucksack. When the biscuits followed, he laughed, rich and melodic, and she beamed. And for a moment, it was just the three of them, laughing in an empty park on a bright autumn day.

Her father told them about his conversation that morning —how Brian had squirmed, and how he had enjoyed every moment of it. He told them about the story he'd been tasked to write, why he'd been asked to write it, and what he planned to say. And all the while, Ellie listened and her mother smiled. And as he talked, no one remembered the sandwiches, the crisps, or the chocolates slowly melting in the sun.

"So, when we've eaten, I'd like to find Thomas Mirren because this time I want to do right by him," said her father. "I'll only write the story if he's happy for me to do so."

Ellie hugged him with her one good arm. It was good to see her father so excited. But she already knew Thomas Mirren would say no.

After they'd finished the food, her parents held their stomachs and competed for who was the fullest. Ellie guessed it was her father. He'd polished off half of the sandwiches and a lot of the crisps despite his assertion that he wasn't hungry. Her mother had eaten most of the rest and Ellie had taken the chocolates. And some of the biscuits.

Over by the far wall, two men who had been drinking beer and eating nothing had fallen asleep. One of them was snoring loudly. While her parents tidied up the remnants of the food, Ellie helped herself to another biscuit. They were the ones made of oats and honey, full of calories but claiming to be healthy. So, an extra one was fine. More than fine, in fact. Beneficial.

Just as they were leaving, Ellie noticed a man walking down the path and into the park. He was wearing a blue blazer and carrying a plastic bag. Pointing him out to her parents, they watched as he strode over to the empty plinth and sat on a bench. He seemed to say something, though there was no one else around. Then, he opened his plastic bag.

They followed him over to the plinth, and the man in the blue blazer looked up. He was holding a sandwich, and he held it out for them to see.

"At last," he said, smiling broadly. "They're doing prawn sandwiches again." Her parents glanced at one another, eyebrows raised, and Ellie held in a laugh.

"I beg your pardon?" asked her father.

"It's a long story, Mr Rogers," said Thomas Mirren. "And not easy to explain without sounding unhinged." He looked at them, one by one, and when his eyes met Ellie's, he smiled again. "What can I do for you all?"

Ellie's father explained to Thomas Mirren all about what he'd found out at the library and through his research at home. He apologised, once again, for the story that had been written, and Thomas Mirren told him, once again, that it was fine. He then outlined Brian's request for a further story and the reasons behind it. It would focus on Thomas Mirren and would shed him in a much more positive light.

"So," he said, "what do you think, Mr Mirren?" He hesitated before adding, "Or would you prefer Haven?"

"Mirren is best," said Thomas. "And to answer your first question: no."

Ellie's father looked at her, then at her mother, and finally back to Thomas Mirren. "Does that mean you'll be suing the newspaper?"

Thomas Mirren laughed at that, and it was a laugh of genuine amusement. "It's a no to that too."

Ellie's father nodded and thanked him. He assured Thomas Mirren that he wouldn't be writing the story, irrespective of what Brian had to say on the matter, and the two men shook hands.

"And you can tell your boss," added Thomas Mirren, "who sounds like an idiot by the way, that if he takes it out on you, I *will* sue your newspaper." And that was the end of it as far as Thomas Mirren was concerned.

And indeed, that was the end of it for Ian too, for Ian Rogers never did write the story. He was a man of his word, after all. But that's not to say that no one wrote the story, because there was someone else who was in much more trouble than Ian and Brian. And she was already looking into Thomas Mirren's past.

As Ellie and her parents were turning to leave, Thomas Mirren suddenly stood. He looked uncertainly at Ian.

"How did you find it all out, by the way?" he asked.

Ian shrugged as if it had been easy, when in reality it had been quite the opposite. "Well, it's actually quite a funny story."

As he recounted to Thomas Mirren the tale of the telephone call from France and the strange conversation he'd had with the man, Thomas Mirren was silent, his expression impassive. But Ellie could see the emotion. It was in his eyes. She saw sadness and regret, pain and hope. But most of all, she saw happiness. A happiness that for these people at least, things had turned out well. People he'd feared dead despite his best efforts. They were fine, and they remembered him. There is something joyous in being remembered.

"So, they survived," Thomas Mirren said quietly, shaking his head slowly. "Adam told me they were okay when he left them, but I've always feared the worst. I told them I would try to go back one day; say hello. But I never did." He was no longer really speaking to Ellie and her family. He thanked Ian and then sat on his bench by the empty stone plinth, head in his hands in disbelief.

The three of them left the park, heading past the sleeping men. As they were turning the corner, Ellie looked back at Thomas Mirren and smiled. He was eating his prawn sandwich.

Chapter 30

Thomas

Over the next few days, Thomas thought a lot about what he'd been told. He wondered whether to tell the Colonel, but in the end, he decided not to. It was a subject they hadn't discussed in a long time, as he knew it was a painful memory for his friend. The fact Thomas had endured so much was a hard thing for the Colonel to bear. He blamed himself entirely for Thomas's injuries and what he'd gone through. It was a guilt that had haunted him ever since. Thomas would tell him about Michel and Nicole Moreau when the time was right.

It was the day before the parade, and apparently there was a great deal to do. At least that's what the Colonel and Frank were saying. Thomas wasn't selling poppies that day; he was needed at the Legion, which was fine by him. He enjoyed watching grown men fussing over preparations that were already complete.

The morning had started off cold, forcing Thomas out of bed early. For the first time in many, many years, he'd dreamed about France. In the dream, he was walking up a hill, long grass tugging at his boots, with Adam over his shoulder, swearing at him and insisting he was fine. Which, of course, he wasn't. Earlier in the day, Thomas had blown up a bridge near an old railway station, and Adam had wandered too close to the blast. He liked explosions, so he always stood too close. The result was another injury and another journey over Thomas's shoulder. It happened so often that it had become something of a joke. But Thomas didn't mind.

1943:

Thomas and Adam had finished eating lunch and were looking to blow something up.

Adam shielded his eyes and pointed off into the distance. "Look at that bridge. How perfect is that? Loads of Germans. Like ants on a turd."

Thomas nodded his agreement, and they made their way closer.

The bridge had blown up easily enough. And so had Adam, straying too close to the bridge despite Thomas's warnings.

"Bloody hell, Adam," Thomas said. "Not again."

Adam was looking down, watching with interest as a red stain spread across his stomach. "Can you use a little less explosive next time, Thomas?"

"It's a bloody great bridge, Adam," Thomas replied, scrambling over to his friend. "Or at least it was."

"I'm fine to walk," protested a pale Adam as Thomas slung him over his shoulder.

"Of course you are," said Thomas, setting off towards a hill in the distance.

The hill led directly out of town. Behind them, there was screaming followed by gunshots in the distance. There was fire, lots of fire, a crimson hue soaking the sky. The killing had started. Not because of the bridge, but because that's what soldiers did when they were angry: they burned things, and they killed people. People who had nothing to do with why they were angry. The way foxes kill chickens even when they're not hungry.

As Thomas walked up the hill, he didn't bother to look back or try to remain hidden. He wanted to get Adam to safety, at least for a while, so he took the most direct route. They'd be seen, of course, and the enemy would come for them, but that was a problem for later. At the top of the hill was a house, silhouetted against the evening sky, dark and unwelcoming. But to Thomas, it was wonderous. It was safety, it was refuge, and it was where he most needed to be.

The heat on Thomas's back was intense, sweat soaking his shirt. Adam had stopped swearing, and that was a bad sign. Then, just as he was about to stop, a man came rushing from the house. He held a knife in his hand, small like a fruit knife, and his face was masked with fear. Thomas had no desire to kill him, so he held up his hand and asked the man to stop. And as he looked at him, Thomas saw something he had seen many times over the past year—courage. Here was someone so incapable of harming him that it was almost funny, yet he was prepared to try, and Thomas respected him for that.

"English," said Thomas simply, and then he saw relief. The man seemed to sag under his own weight, as if melting in the heat. He signalled to Thomas, and together they walked back to the house.

And that was when he first met Nicole and Michel Moreau, Nicole in a blue dress and Michel in black shorts, with a white shirt and brown braces. They were holding hands, and when Nicole saw him, she smiled, and the whole room became bright.

Hearing a knock at the door, Thomas put down his coffee. He had been sitting in his armchair for a long time, thinking, and as he got up, the thick cushions slowly expanded as though inflating. Then, the chair filled out, and before long, it was like new.

Money well spent, he thought, and he remembered the day they had bought it. Thomas had wanted it as soon as he'd set eyes on it, but it was expensive, and they'd needed much more than just one chair. He'd told Ellen they should get as much as they could within their budget, but she'd smiled, replying that they should buy less but of quality. Things would last longer that way, she'd said, and they could add to it later. She'd been right, of course, so they'd spent the next few months with the one chair. They'd taken turns to sit in it while the other person lay on the old sofa that had come with the house. The same sofa that was still there now. The one Ellen had secretly loved. The one she had lain on in her final days as she'd become weak and Thomas had slowly died inside.

The Colonel was at the door, a big smile across his face. A folded newspaper lay across his arm. He reminded Thomas of a mobster in one of the old films, hiding a machine gun or a knife. But Thomas couldn't imagine the Colonel as a mobster in his grey chino trousers and smart tweed jacket. He seemed more of a salesman.

"Recognition at last," said the Colonel as he entered the house, thrusting the newspaper into Thomas's hand with well-rehearsed precision. It was a copy of the *Chronicle*.

"Congratulations, Adam," replied Thomas, not looking at the paper. "For what though?"

"Not me, stupid." The Colonel laughed. "You." He pointed to the newspaper. "Page four."

They walked over to the table, where Thomas put down the paper.

"Would you like a coffee?" he asked, and the Colonel nodded.

"We'd better hurry though," he said. "Lots to do."

A couple of minutes later, sitting at the table with their coffee, the Colonel unfolded the newspaper and turned it to page four. Thomas put down his cup and looked at the headline: 'The Hero of Kingsley. Our Apology.'

And there it was, half a page of it, with a big picture of Thomas in the middle in his army uniform. The journalist, Jacqueline Chambers, had certainly done her research. This time around, at least. In the article, she'd written about Thomas's time in the army, where he'd served, and with which regiment. Then, his years at the bank and his marriage to Ellen, before finally finishing with Kingsley. His medals were listed—all of them, more or less. Apparently, he was a national treasure.

"I wish they'd make up their minds," said Thomas as he closed the paper. It was all a bit much, and he actually preferred her earlier piece. At least that one hadn't felt quite so intrusive. If he'd wanted people to know about his past, he would have told them. He wasn't a hero. Far from it.

"Come on, Adam," he said, putting on his blazer and opening the door. He left the *Chronicle* on the table. He'd throw it away later. "We've got a lot to do, you know."

Alan Thomson was leaning against the mayoral limousine and yawning as they approached the Legion. He was puffing away on a cigarette. When he saw Thomas, he waved, the cigarette flying from his hand and rolling under the car. Thomas pictured the car exploding, covering the area with small pieces of Alan Thomson. When nothing happened, he felt strangely let down.

"Bloody hell," cursed Thomas as Alan continued waving. "I could do without this."

The Colonel laughed. "Hard work being the town's hero," he said. "I'll deal with the mayor, don't worry. Make yourself scarce for a few minutes if you don't want to see him."

Thomas nodded, said hello to Alan Thomson, then went for a walk around the block. One circuit took precisely five minutes. He knew because he'd timed it. After his third lap, the mayor's car had disappeared, but Thomas did one more lap anyway, as he didn't like odd numbers.

Last lap finished, he finally made his way into the Legion. The door creaked as he entered, but it was nothing a bit of oil wouldn't fix, thought Thomas. He was immediately greeted by a full room and a huge round of applause, which was Thomas's idea of hell. The Colonel was waiting at the bar, next to Frank, holding a tray full of drinks. Three pints of beer and three whiskies. And a packet of prawn cocktail crisps.

Behind the bar, Derek saluted him. Thomas smiled, hurrying awkwardly to his table in the corner, where he was joined by the Colonel and Frank. They were loving every minute of his discomfort.

"Has this got anything to do with you two?" asked Thomas, downing his whisky. His friends took turns denying their involvement, which meant they were both guilty. Thomas shook his head. "It'll all be forgotten about in a day or so," he declared, more out of hope than belief.

"Of course," said Frank as the Colonel raised his glass.

"To the hero of Kingsley!"

Thomas laughed. "Bugger off," he said, then opened the crisps.

As it turned out, the mayor had been quite adamant that Thomas should lead the parade and even carry the wreath. It had all been a terrible mistake, he'd insisted, and he would like to apologise to Thomas personally. Perhaps they could talk at the parade. The Colonel had promised to pass on the information.

"Frank carries the wreath," said Thomas, and it wasn't a suggestion.

The Colonel agreed.

"Given what's happened, I'm more than happy for you to carry it," Frank said. But Thomas had made his decision, and it was Frank's turn to carry it.

The rest of the morning, and much of the afternoon, revolved around final preparations. Thomas had heard it all before, and he soon found his mind wandering. Eventually, he stopped listening altogether. It wasn't until the Colonel asked him a question that he was forced to pay attention. His heart wasn't in it, they all saw that, so he excused himself and headed out to get some lunch even though sandwiches had been brought in.

"We'll be here if you need us," the Colonel said.

The small park was empty. He didn't go to the supermarket, and he didn't buy anything to eat. He went to the empty plinth. He'd been there many times in the past with Ellen, and she had always joked that his name would be on the plinth one day. He'd laughed, horrified at the thought. He wished Ellen was there now, as he was unsure what to do, and that scared him. Ellen would have known; she always knew. But this time, he was on his own. He'd muddle through in the end, of course, because that's what he did without Ellen: he muddled through. He just needed a little time to get there.

He didn't go back to the Legion that afternoon; he stayed in the park, on one of the benches. At around three o'clock, it became busy, and the racket from the musical steps began to irritate him. The grumbling sounds from his stomach reminded him that he was hungry, so he got up. He'd make something to eat at home.

It was an odd experience walking back through the town centre. People stared at him and waved. The same people who'd pointed and shook their heads a few days earlier. Every so often, a complete stranger would say hello. Dennis Tooley, who disliked Thomas, even came over to ask him how he was. Thomas replied that he was fine, and Tooley patted him on the back. He didn't like being touched on the back.

At the end of Winden Street, Thomas took a detour through the old industrial estate. It would be peaceful there, providing space and time to think. The decaying buildings conjured images of France during the war. Looking back, he realised they were good times for him. Horrific but good. He had friends, excitement and, most importantly, other people told him what to do. Not much thinking involved, and that made life easy. Shoot this, blow that up, carry Adam. Simple. Now, he was seen as some kind of saint. The Second Face had seen him for what he was though—brutal and monstrous.

But those were the days before Ellen, and the thought of her made him smile. And for the rest of his walk home, the sky seemed just a little bit brighter.

The lock clicked as the door closed behind him. Soon after, it was bolted too. He took off his blazer and hung it on his peg, second from the end. The end peg had always been Ellen's, but now it was empty. He'd given her coat to a charity shop long ago, but he wished he hadn't. Some things are too precious to give away.

On the small table beneath the coat rack was a photograph. It showed a couple standing side by side. The woman was smiling. The man was tall, with blue eyes and a bright yellow tie. It looked like he'd been laughing.

Thomas picked up the newspaper and took it into the kitchen, where he dropped it into the bin.

"Best place for it," he said as the newspaper disappeared silently into the darkness.

He made himself a corned beef sandwich and took it with him to his armchair. He didn't really like corned beef but it stayed fresh. If you covered it with mustard, you could barely taste it anyway.

There was an old film on the television—*The War of the Worlds*, with Gene Barry and Ann Robinson, and he settled down to watch it. He'd seen it when it came out, and he remembered enjoying it. He'd watched the remake too over fifty years later, but that one wasn't so good. Too many special effects.

When the film finished, there was another one—*Rear Window*, with James Stewart and Grace Kelly, so he watched that too.

It was early evening when the telephone rang. At first, he wasn't going to answer it, presuming it was just Frank. But it kept ringing. In the end, he was forced to get up. He imagined it would stop just as he was about to pick it up, but it didn't. And as he held the receiver to his ear, he heard a voice. A woman's voice.

Chapter 31

Nicole and Michel

Michel didn't like wearing a tie—his neck felt constricted. And it was hot.

"Stop squirming." Nicole laughed as she straightened the knot. "It's not going to kill you to look smart for once."

"Well," replied Michel, "I don't see you wearing one."

"No. I wouldn't like it. I imagine it feels like being strangled."

They were going to a council meeting. It was the day before the Armistice parade, and final preparations were to be discussed. Nicole didn't really need to be there but she wanted to make sure Michel didn't agree to anything he shouldn't. He was easily led at times. It was lunchtime, and the meeting was scheduled to start at three o'clock, so they had plenty of time.

"Remember the time they wanted to reroute the march away from the church and past Maison Mercier?" asked Nicole as she put on her cardigan. "You agreed to it, and it nearly destroyed his shop."

Michel chuckled at the memory. He'd walked around with a massive grin for weeks afterwards. "Shame that."

They left the house at a little before two o'clock, but not before Nicole had checked, and double-checked, the chicken coop. It didn't pay to take chances.

It was overcast outside, making the day feel warm, much to Michel's annoyance. Nicole giggled as Michel tugged theatrically at his collar. For her part, she'd made a point of wearing a light summer dress, open at the neck, and it hadn't gone unnoticed.

"You're wearing that on purpose, aren't you?" moaned Michel.

"I am. One of the few advantages of being an elderly woman. I do not bow to convention." She smiled at Michel. "You, on the other hand, would cause quite a stir if you turned up without a tie." Michel set off, staring stubbornly into the distance.

It had rained earlier that day, and the road into town sparkled as they walked. It was like strolling on tiny diamonds in a movie or in one of the picture books Nicole had enjoyed so much as a child. She linked arms with her brother, and he smiled at her.

"It's going to be a good day today, Michel," Nicole declared.

"It already is," he replied.

At the bottom of the hill, they met up with Anne-Marie and Peter. Seeing Peter, Nicole started to laugh. Dressed in a grey suit and green necktie, he fumbled with his collar as though a thousand ants were crawling inside. Like her,

Anne-Marie was wearing something more suitable for the weather, and she looked radiant in her cream blouse and long yellow skirt.

"She made you wear a tie too?" asked Michel, walking up to Peter.

"And a bloody suit," he groaned. "The tie doesn't even go with it."

"Then, why not wear another one?"

"Because the only other one I own has piano keys on it," explained Peter. "Bought as a joke," he added quickly, by way of clarification, in case Michel thought him the kind of man who would wear such a thing.

"Would you like a coffee before we head off?" asked Anne-Marie, but Michel shook his head. He was keen to get going. Peter then announced he'd made a special cake that morning to celebrate the occasion, a Victoria sponge, and it was decided they would all return for a slice after the meeting. The thought of the cake, as well as the opportunity to take off his tie, was almost too much for Michel.

They arrived at the meeting with ten minutes to spare. While Michel had a cigarette, the other three went inside to look around and find their seats. Michel would be at the large meeting table, along with a dozen or so councillors. He always had the same seat.

Once the attendees were inside, Madame Bavarde, the current mayor, stood and welcomed everyone to the meeting. There were about fifty people in total—a miraculous number for such a meeting. Four or five was the norm, the inhabitants of Saint Martin caring little about the running of the town so long as it was run well.

An hour later, that number had dwindled to around ten. But by that stage, much of the business had been completed —the timing of the parade, the route, who was doing what, and so on. Michel had spoken briefly but the tie seemed to have done its job, and by and large, he'd kept quiet. Nicole was feeling very pleased with herself.

By four-thirty, it was over, and a minute later, Michel and Peter were chatting to each other in front of the town hall, cigarettes in hand and neckties in pockets. They were looking much happier now. Nicole and Anne-Marie smiled to each other as they went over to join them. During the meeting, there had been several announcements, one of which concerned a display in the mayor's parlour—a small exhibition of photographs depicting life in the town during the war. A celebration but also a way of remembering just how important those times had been. All four of them were keen to take a look.

Michel and Nicole had been to the mayor's parlour often in the past, especially Michel, but it was the first time for Peter and Anne-Marie. Peter whistled as he entered the room —a voluminous cavern with huge oak tables and thick velvet curtains. Opulent chandeliers hung from the ceiling, and around the walls were paintings of mayors past and present, with one in particular catching Peter's attention.

"Who's this attractive beast?" he asked with a smile, and Michel appeared to blush.

"A bit more hair there," said Michel.

"Dark hair too" observed Peter as Anne-Marie came over to stand next to him.

"You were very handsome, Michel," she said.

"*Are*," corrected Michel.

Portable display stands had been erected along the far wall where the mayor's desk had once been, and on each stand were dozens of photographs. Beneath each photograph, written in thick black text, was a short description. The parlour was nearly empty, so they went over to take a look. Many of the images were instantly familiar—the church, the main road, the town hall, and the market square. They laughed as they pointed out each place they recognised, commenting on how little the town had changed despite the passage of time. In one photograph, depicting the local rugby team, Michel thought he spotted his father, but the picture was blurry, and it was difficult to be certain. It made him wonder if he'd recognise his father today if he walked past him in the street. He was adamant he would—it was his father, after all—but a part of him was not sure. And that was a terrible thing to realise.

On the furthest board were pictures from 1943, a year before the Liberation of Paris, with several of the photographs showing nothing but silhouettes and flames. There was the church, black and defiant before a dark, thunderous sky. Further along was the old school, windows broken and the roof half-destroyed. Then, there was the railway station, untouched and with German troops in front, no older than boys, staring at the camera and holding up their rifles. Anne-Marie gasped as she pointed to another picture: a building at the end of a road, with sandbags around the doorway and a small boy hiding in the shadows. On either side of the doorway were two bay windows with curtains closed.

"The Morning Cafe," she said. Peter leaned in to take a look. Sure enough, it was, though it had been a house at the time.

"Monsieur Lelache lived there then," said Michel, remembering the small man who was always laughing and who had been the town's postman. "People said he was a coward, but he was no more a coward than the rest of us. He was just afraid."

The furthest photograph showed a house. It was small and alone and sat on top of a hill, with fields all around. There were tall trees with thick hedges, and in the sky, there was nothing except the sun so bright that even the shadows had fled.

"Maison Moreau," said Nicole, reading the words written underneath. "August 1943." She turned to Michel. "Just a short time before it all happened."

That afternoon, everyone was sitting at a small table by the window of the Morning Cafe. Everyone except Peter, that is, who had taken it upon himself to be proprietor, cook, and waiter all rolled into one. This was a time for the others to reminisce, to laugh, and to gossip about the past. He knew that, and so he kept himself busy while his beautiful wife and her two friends ate cake and drank coffee.

Michel didn't talk much, preferring to shovel huge amounts of Victoria sponge into his mouth, a large blob of jam tumbling onto his chin. The two women laughed as Michel looked questioningly from one to the other until, finally, the jam dropped onto his plate. Then, he laughed too. It was nice, thought Peter, to be a part of something good.

Late afternoon, Anne-Marie closed the cafe. There had been something of an influx half an hour earlier, and she and Peter had been busy with customers. Now, with the door closed, they rejoined Nicole and Michel.

"Glass of wine, anyone?" asked Peter. The others nodded.

In truth, Peter wasn't a great fan of wine, but in Saint Martin, that was tantamount to sacrilege. As a result, he poured out four glasses of red, set them on a tray, and then he poured himself a gin.

Placing the glasses on the table, he picked up his drink. "You three can fight over the extra wine," he said, raising the gin to his lips. "This one's for me. Gin. London. Perfect."

Nicole and Michel stared at him as though he'd just slaughtered a child, but Anne-Marie beamed, and there was so much love in her look that he felt like his chest might explode.

"I'm the luckiest woman in the world," she exclaimed, kissing him hard on the lips as Michel reached for the spare wine. He was beaming too as he sat there with two glasses of red wine.

"And I'm the luckiest man in the world," joked Michel.

One drink turned into two and then Nicole and Michel said their goodbyes. As Anne-Marie shut the door, Nicole saw a look in her eyes that made her blush.

"Early night for someone." said Michel, chuckling as they set off up the hill, the whispered sounds of the town gently fading into the distance.

Nicole and Michel linked arms, and with each step, they moved closer to the setting sun, its final moments staining the sky crimson. On top of the hill, their small house stood proud, a perfect silhouette that reminded Nicole of the pictures they'd seen earlier in the day.

"It was nice to see the old photographs," she said to Michel.

"Nice pictures," he agreed, "though sad at the same time." The glimpses of a year so wonderful and yet so utterly horrific had stirred up unwelcome memories; memories he had no wish to revisit. Of course, it had been nice to see the old faces and the old places where he and Nicole used to play but behind it all, lurking in the background, was a horror no person should remember. It devoured, it ruined, and the past was the only place for it.

"I would like to look at the newspaper again when we get home," said Nicole softly.

"I know," replied Michel, placing his arm around her shoulder.

By the time they reached the house, it was dark.

In the garden, the sun had disappeared, and all that remained was darkness. But it was the good kind of darkness, peaceful and quiet. The kind which envelops you and makes you feel safe. Nicole held a glass of wine while Michel sat next to her, puffing on a cigarette. She'd wanted to check on the chickens when they got back to the house, more out of habit than concern, but she'd opted for wine instead. Wine is often the best choice. She could hear them anyway, chattering away as they prepared for the night. It was Pinky talking now—she recognised her sound. She was always the loud one but the first to fall asleep and the last to rise. Not too dissimilar to Michel.

"It was funny seeing Lelache," announced Michel, appearing from an immense plume of smoke. "I haven't thought of him for years. Decades even."

"Yes," agreed Nicole. "Didn't he die on the toilet?"

Michel started to laugh. "I think that was Elvis Presley. And anyway, it was just a rumour. How could anyone know such a thing?"

Nicole shrugged in the darkness. "The cafe hasn't changed. That photograph could have been taken yesterday. Without the sandbags, of course." She paused. "I wonder what happened to them. What happens to thousands of sandbags when they're no longer needed?"

"No idea," replied Michel. It wasn't something he had ever thought about.

Later in the evening, they watched some television. Most of the programmes had already started, so they ended up watching a documentary about train journeys. The one they watched seemed to be heading through Russia, and it looked cold. Whenever Nicole thought about Russia, which wasn't often, the word 'cold' usually sprang to mind. Not only the weather, but the people too, although she'd once met a very charming Russian man. His name was Vladimir, and he had not been cold at all.

"Bit too cold for me, that one," observed Michel when the programme had finished, and they were once more in the garden. It was completely silent now, with even the four hens sleeping. "The people, too. Cold climate, cold race."

"Yes," said Nicole. "But I'm sure they're not all like that."

Nicole went inside to look at the newspaper while Michel stayed in the garden to finish his cigarette. When he eventually went in to see her, she was closing the newspaper and folding it for storage. This was the one time they would not be throwing away the *Chronicle*.

"You know," said Nicole, "I was thinking I might make a phone call."

Michel smiled and walked over to her, carrying the papers Peter had brought earlier. "I thought you would." He placed the documents on the table next to the folded newspaper. "Everything you need is in here. It's fair to say Peter has been quite thorough."

Nicole didn't say anything as her brother left the room, the sound of his footsteps softly disappearing up the stairs.

She picked up the phone.

Chapter 32

Ian and Ellie

Ellie was ready early that morning. It was the day of the parade.

"Beautiful," exclaimed her mother as she walked down the stairs and into the kitchen. Ellie had never been comfortable with compliments, so she blushed, making her mother laugh. She had on a new pair of trousers and a blue top with a motif spread across the chest. She'd never worked out what the motif was, but she liked it, all the same.

Her mother wore a white jumper and her yellow skirt— the one she wore to the cemetery. The one Ellie's grandmother had bought her that made her look carefree even when she was solemn. Ellie had always loved her in that skirt.

Next came her father, trudging down the stairs in dark jeans and leather sandals. He was sent straight back upstairs to change into something less bohemian. Ian Rogers was not a bohemian man.

They left the house at nine, deciding to walk into town. It was a warm day, with a blue sky. A blueness so vast and so perfect that to Ellie it looked unreal. As though someone had spent so much time drawing the ground that they'd become bored and had filled in the sky as an afterthought. No clouds, no birds, nothing. Just blue.

They stopped at a cafe for something to eat, even though none of them were hungry. It was a rule—do not pass a coffee shop without buying a coffee and a sandwich.

At just gone ten o'clock, they arrived at the memorial. There were plenty of bad things about Kingsley, but a reluctance to celebrate was not one of them. Along much of the road leading to the memorial, large numbers of people had turned out, smiling and chatting and generally enjoying themselves. In some places, the pavements were so full that Ellie and her parents had to walk along the road, but in the end, they found a space. It was a good space too, twenty or so metres from the memorial, with a clear view of the dignitaries and their bored-looking partners. Ellie's father nudged her.

"Look at them." He laughed, pointing towards the mayor and the leader of the council. They looked like marionettes in their freshly dry-cleaned suits, the mayor clearly uncomfortable under the weight of his thick cloak and heavy golden chain. He was smiling and waving but it was not the smile of a happy man. "All turned out to greet Thomas Mirren," observed her father, "when only a few days ago, they didn't want him here at all."

Next to the mayor was his wife, and standing next to her was a face Ellie recognised at once. Her father was shaking his head.

"What's Brian doing up there?" she asked.

"Same as the others," he replied. "Covering his arse now that the real Thomas Mirren has been revealed." But the real Thomas Mirren had been there all along, thought Ellie.

Suddenly, the crowd stirred. Emerging from Alma Street was the procession. Uniforms poured onto the main road: men and women, young and old, their heads high in the bright morning sunshine. These were the people of Kingsley; people who had given so much. Every last one of them was a hero. At the head of the column were two old men, the grins on their faces so mischievous that Ellie started to laugh.

Through the applause, Thomas's friends, the Colonel and Frank, waved to the mayor. The mayor waved back but it was more a raising of the hand.

"Where's Thomas Mirren?" her father asked.

"Sending a message, I would imagine," her mother replied. A message to the mayor and to the council.

Ellie didn't recall too much more of that morning: boring speeches and lots of cheers. Her mind was elsewhere. But as they were walking home, they all agreed it had been fun. There was something about a parade that brought out the best in people. Even the mayor seemed to be happy in the end. Only Brian had looked miserable throughout.

By the post office, they bumped into Daniel Aveneo, the reception manager from the college, still wearing his black hooded top. He was smoking a cigarette. When he saw Ellie, he smiled.

"Hello, Ellie," he said. "You're looking much better than the last time I saw you." Ellie laughed and thanked him once again for his help. He looked embarrassed and quickly turned to her father. "Nice to see you again, Mr Rogers."

The two men shook hands, and the four of them chatted for a while about the parade and the college and things in general. As they were leaving, Daniel asked if they'd ever found the man with the blue blazer, and Ellie's father looked at him, a puzzled frown betraying his confusion. Daniel explained how the man who'd saved Ellie had covered her in his blue blazer, and Ellie grinned.

"Yes, Daniel," she said. "We did find him."

Her father looked at her, and then he smiled.

"Ah," he said.

And he was no longer confused.

Chapter 33

Nicole and Michel

Michel had finished setting the table. All that remained were the finishing touches. As Nicole fussed around, straightening spoons and rerolling napkins, Michel watched on, amazed at her industry. In truth, each adjustment made little difference but they made her happy, and that was the important thing.

"It's perfect," he said as Nicole shifted a fork. "Everything is perfect." Michel was in a good mood. The parade had been a success, and everyone had left happy. All except old Mercier, who'd fallen over and twisted his ankle. "It went well this morning," he said, "and it will go well this afternoon."

Nicole smiled at him, that shy smile he loved so much, and he felt as though his heart was breaking. He wanted so much for the day to go well for her.

A few more adjustments and they were ready to go. Michel stood at the door, his white shirt ironed and his black trousers neatly pressed. He held out Nicole's coat, and she smiled at him as though he were the finest gentleman in the world.

"Thank you, Michel, but it's warm outside, so I'll go as I am." She checked her reflection in the mirror. "Do you think I look okay?"

"Every inch the wonderful woman you are," he said, ushering her out the door before she could find anything else to distract herself with.

On the road into town, Michel was pleased to be without his tie. He'd worn it all morning, and that was enough. With a cool breeze blowing into his open collar, he felt comfortable. Comfortable that he wasn't being strangled, and comfortable that this was going to be a good day. Nicole seemed to sense it too, and they laughed as they walked down the hill, a bright sky above them, cloudless and clear. Blue.

At the foot of the hill, they stopped off to see Anne-Marie. She was cleaning the tables and straightening the menus. Nicole asked her where Peter was, and she shrugged.

"His knee's feeling better, so he's gone out on his bike." She looked at Michel and winked. "Baggy shorts too."

"Hallelujah." Michel laughed.

Anne-Marie invited them in for a coffee and some cake. Peter had been up early that morning, working on his latest creation—Japanese mochi cakes filled with red bean jam. Tempting as it was, they politely declined. They had somewhere to be. The last they saw of Anne-Marie, she was waving from the door, radiant in the sunshine in her blue dress and new breathable jacket.

As the Morning Cafe disappeared from view, they turned down Rue de la Fontaine and headed towards the church. The area around the church itself was deserted; a stark contrast to a few hours earlier. Then, it had been a sea of bodies, jostling for a view of the parade. But now the bodies were gone, and it felt like the parade had never happened. Attached to the side of the church was an old storage building, faded and crumbling and grafted to the main building like a boil. In the past, it had been used to store furniture, but now it was a ruin. Nicole pointed to it, and Michel laughed, remembering how they would hide there as children, pretending to be pirates, while their parents communed with God next door.

At last, they reached the station. Monsieur Lagare was there, cleaning his spectacles and leaning against the entrance as though it would collapse if he moved.

"I see you found each other," he chirped as Nicole and Michel walked by.

"Long story," said Michel, and Lagare nodded as if too busy to hear it. He then went back to cleaning his spectacles.

"What was that all about?" asked Nicole as they entered the platform.

"Still a long story!" grinned Michel.

Sitting next to each other on the warm platform bench, Michel and Nicole looked every inch the old married couple. Strangers to Saint Martin had often mistaken them for a pair. At first, it had bothered Michel, but not now. Now, it was fine. There was no one in the world he would rather be next to.

"Would you like a chocolate bar?" he asked, opening the bag he was carrying.

"No, thank you."

"How about a mint?" enquired Michel.

Nicole smiled. "Yes, I'll have one of those, please. Do you have a rabbit in there as well?"

Michel shook his head. "No rabbit, I'm afraid, but I do have some crisps and an apple."

"How long are we planning on being here?" Nicole chuckled.

Michel looked at his watch. "Not long now."

Nicole fell silent.

At first, the sound was faint; so faint it could hardly be heard. Like needles falling onto the track. Then, there was a hum; a thousand bees racing along the rails. And finally, there was a train. It was a train Nicole had waited for her whole life. It was the past and the future, and it was every day between.

Nicole stood as the train slowly rolled into the station, and Michel smiled. Together, they held hands as the carriage doors opened.

Just one person got off the train that day, but it was the only person that mattered. He was tall, and he was handsome.

He had the most amazing blue eyes.

Chapter 34

Thomas

Thomas was not an impetuous man. He had been impetuous many years ago, but then Ellen had died. Now, he just waited.

"Christ almighty," he said, locking his front door and buttoning up his woollen coat. It was cold and it was early. Too early. But he had a long way to go.

The Volkswagen was waiting at the end of his path.

"Are you prepared?" asked the Colonel as Thomas got into the front seat. As usual, the Colonel was in the back.

Apart from the clothes on his back, all Thomas had with him was a small case. "You know me," he said. "I'm not one for preparations." The Colonel shook his head but he was smiling. "How about you?" asked Thomas. "Ready for the parade?"

The Colonel laughed. "We've been ready for weeks."

As if on cue, Frank started the engine and the Volkswagen glided down the road. The streets were empty, save for the occasional jogger. Ten minutes later, they were at the station, its giant silhouette punctuated by the bright fluorescent lights of the ticket office.

"Do you know when you'll be back?" asked Frank as Thomas closed the car door behind him.

"Not really," he replied. "Maybe tomorrow." He looked at Frank and smiled. "Can't have the old-timers upstaging your big day, my friend. Enjoy yourself and have a great time." But Frank didn't mind being upstaged. He wanted Thomas next to him at the parade, and his downcast expression made Thomas feel guilty. Thomas didn't know what to say, so he said the first thing that came into his head: "I'm sorry."

"Don't be," said the Colonel from the back. "Now, hurry up or you'll miss your train."

But Thomas didn't miss trains. Punctuality, like preparation, was not his strong point, but he never missed a train.

The train arrived on time, quietly appearing from out of the darkness. At first, he heard the whisper, like pins dancing on the track, and then it was bees, the gentle hum as the engine drew near. And then it was the train, curving into the station like a huge metallic snake, its windows revealing row upon row of empty seats.

"At least I won't have to stand."

He arrived in London at a little after seven, and by eight, he was on another train. This one was busier but not by much. Which suited Thomas just fine.

"Can I get you something to eat, sir?" asked the train guard half an hour into the journey.

"What do you have?" replied Thomas. He'd been trying to get some sleep but his seat was too hard, like sitting on concrete.

"Mainly crisps and sandwiches," replied the guard. "And various drinks, alcoholic and non-alcoholic." He opened the small metal door at the side of his trolley and began listing off the foods. Unfortunately for Thomas, there were no prawn sandwiches, so he opted for cheese. The only crisps available were Hula Hoops, which Thomas didn't consider to be proper crisps, but he took them anyway. At least there was beer.

"That will be six pounds, please." The guard smiled, and Thomas coughed. He thought about saying something unpleasant but he kept his mouth shut for once. It wasn't the guard's fault, after all.

By the time he arrived at his next changeover, he'd managed half of the sandwich—nearly all bread—and most of the Hula Hoops. The beer can was empty. Carefully disposing of his litter, he got off the train and headed along the platform. His connection was due in five minutes, and another hour after that, he would be there.

The last part of the journey was by far the most pleasant, rolling through countryside and small, picturesque villages. He found himself wishing the train would slow down. It had been years since he'd been in this part of the world, and it was exactly as he remembered. Every few minutes, the train would stop and a few passengers would disappear. Occasionally, someone would get on, but it was rare, and Thomas soon had the carriage to himself.

It wasn't long before he started thinking of Ellen. She was never far from his thoughts. He'd always planned to return to this part of the world one day with Ellen by his side but things had come up. Insignificant things, looking back, but things that had seemed so important at the time. And then time had run out, and it was too late. He had few regrets, but this was one.

The carriage door opened, interrupting his thoughts, and a young man entered. Dressed in a blue uniform, he had short dark hair and a thin, close-cropped beard. He pointed to the door.

"Your stop is next, sir," he said. "Have you been to Saint Martin before?"

"A very long time ago," replied Thomas. "I'd always planned on returning."

"Well, you are here now," said the man. As he was leaving, he turned back to Thomas. "I'm from around here," he announced with pride. "The town was saved by the English during the war. Without them, it would have been destroyed." Thomas smiled, remembering the Colonel aimlessly blowing things up, including several parts of himself.

"Is that so?" said Thomas, and the young man nodded before leaving to continue along the train.

It was mid-afternoon by this stage, and as the train slowed, Thomas noticed a church in the distance. The last time he'd seen it, it had been on fire. He was glad it had survived.

And then the train stopped. Picking up his case, he walked to the door. As he stepped off the train, bright sunshine washed over him, warming his back and making him smile. At the far end of the platform were two children, a girl and a boy. They were holding hands, and when they saw him, they waved. The girl seemed to be crying.

Beneath the perfect blue sky, Thomas walked down the platform. He recalled the Moreau family all those years ago, so afraid yet so wonderfully brave. He pictured Adam laughing and joking, too stubborn to die, as blood soaked through his clothes. And he thought of Ellen. He'd finally fulfilled his promise to return, and she would be proud of him.

A hero is a person who is admired for their courage; a person of noble qualities who achieves great things. But a hero is also just a name. To the people who mattered, Thomas was neither hero nor monster. He was Thomas Mirren. And that was enough.